RUINATION

HELLFIRE AND HALOS, BOOK 1

J.N. BAKER

This is a work of fiction. Names, characters, places, and incidents are either the products of the author's imagination or used fictitiously. Any resemblance to actual persons, living or dead, businesses, companies, events, or locales is entirely coincidental.

Cover Design by Covers by Combs
Edited by Tina Winograd and Shannon Page

For my husband and daughter.
Thanks for putting up with my constant shit, not to mention the endless hours spent cursing at a computer screen.
I love you both with all of my twisted heart.

27 YEARS PRIOR

Blood coursed through my veins as I sprinted down the dark alleyway, a Cheshire grin plastered on my face. I couldn't lie, I loved the chase. It gave me such a rush—even if I was the one being pursued. Pumping my arms, I pushed myself to move faster, putting more distance between my attacker and me.

We'd done this dance before so many times. Centuries worth, really. It was a cat and mouse game I could play in my sleep. And while I could admit he usually won, I had a shit ton of fun in the process. Wreaking havoc was in my blood. Literally. Chaos was the name of the game, and again, I fucking *loved* it—almost as much as the uptight bastard hated it.

A beating of air against my back told me my winged foe was close. I risked a glance over my shoulder.

Shit.

He was closer than I'd thought. I was hoping to make this round last at least another couple of years. The asshole was getting better. Good for him; it only took him a few centuries.

"Give up!" I heard him yell at my retreating backside. I knew there was a reason I'd wanted to wear my cheeky cutoff shorts this morning. Shorts that were now riding up that much higher.

Enjoy the view, holy boy. I reached back and gave my half-exposed ass a slap, earning me an extra growl from Mr. Self-Righteous.

I took a sharp right, heading down the main street, dodging the many passersby that shrieked as we shoved through them. Likely all they would see was a man chasing a woman. Most would think it was a cop in hot pursuit of a perp. Humans were stupid creatures. They tended to turn a blind eye to the supernatural. Especially in a big city like this where most of them had their eyes glued to their devices.

Fine by me. It only made my job that much easier.

Somewhere in the distance, I heard the distinct sound of metal on metal as two cars collided. I smirked. Damn, I was good. Just another day in the life of an extraordinary demon. Even in the middle of the chase, I could ruffle a few of the world's feathers. And a certain angel's.

"Stop!" said angel shouted. Dammit, he was right behind me. A few more feet and he'd have me in striking distance. I really needed to start carrying weapons. Not that they'd do me much good. Bastard couldn't die.

But I could. Even if only temporarily.

My eyes darted to the busy street and immediately one of the hundreds of taxis veered off course, careening onto the sidewalk directly behind me, cutting off my attacker's path and damn near hitting him in the process. Too bad it hadn't. That had been my intention. Still, it gave me just enough time to pull ahead of him, but not much.

Behind me, I heard him stomping across the hood of the taxi, the irate driver screaming at him. Without a second thought, I ducked into one of the many high-rises. I might not be able to outrun him, but I could definitely outmaneuver him.

The moment I stepped into the multi-business building, the power shut off and I groaned. Sometimes my own chaos bit me in the ass. Okay, maybe more than sometimes.

Squinting through the darkness, my eyes quickly adjusted. I made a beeline for the stairwell, swinging open the heavy metal door and taking the steps two at a time until my legs were throbbing and I thought they might give out.

"Demon tits! How tall is this blasted building?" I huffed, rounding yet another corner only to find more stairs.

My attacker charged up the stairs below me. Based on the sound of his heavy footfalls, he was rapidly eating away at the distance I'd put between us.

Growling, I forced my legs to keep going. No way was I going to let a damn charley horse lead to my demise. Hell was great and all, but I wasn't ready to go back yet. I was having way too much fun this time around. At least, until stairmageddon. I should have taken my chances on the damn street.

"Fuck this," I hissed under my breath.

I slipped through a door on the next landing, finding myself in some sort of a nine-to-five office. Being Sunday, the space was empty, everyone off for the "Lord's day." It was meant to be a day of worship but most used it as an excuse to sit around on their asses and watch television while they worked off Saturday's hangover.

But not me—it was my favorite day to work. It had a poetic sort of irony to it. Plus, it only further pissed off Mr. Holy Man. Someone got his tighty whities in a bunch when he didn't get his day of rest. Not my fault he refused to take a day off from chasing me and trying to remove my head from my shoulders.

I closed the door silently behind me and sprinted across the vacant space to find somewhere to lie low until he left. He'd give up eventually if he couldn't find me; he usually did. No fun for the cat if the mouse disappears.

As the door from the stairwell flew open and slammed into the wall, I dove under the nearest desk, swallowing the curse that dangled from my lips.

"I know you're in here," he growled, his voice as deep as it was smooth. Angels weren't supposed to have voices like his—the kind that had my damn toes curling. Maybe the big man upstairs did have a sense of humor after all. "I can hear your blackened heart racing—smell your fear."

Fear? I nearly snorted. The arrogant fuck gave himself way too much credit if he thought I was afraid of him.

Living on the edge like this was my drug of choice, hence my racing heart. Besides, it was hard to be afraid when I knew I'd get to come right back out to play if he killed me. As much as he tried, he was never getting rid of me. Not for long, at least.

The only downside to him killing me was that I had to relive childhood all over again before really getting to wreak havoc on the Earth once more. But still, even kids knew how to raise a little hell.

Getting on all fours, I inched away from the sound of his approaching footsteps as quietly as I could until I was on the opposite side of the office. A glance out the floor-to-ceiling windows told me we weren't far from the nearest subway station. I hadn't realized when we were on the street just how close we were to it. I knew this city's subway tunnels like the back of my hand. If I could get down there, I was home free.

I just had to somehow get past Mr. Death to All Demons and his bloodthirsty blade, and then make it back down the thousands of stairs that seemed to also have it out for me.

Sure. Easy. No big deal.

"Come," he ordered, and heat immediately pooled low in my stomach at that one word. I couldn't help it; my Hellion mother was a succubus. Surely it was that affecting me and not Mr. Holy Pants himself. "Face your fate," he continued.

"Maybe it's you who should try *coming*," I shot back, unable to help myself. I flattened my spine against the closest desk, slowly pulling one of the drawers open. I reached inside, fishing around until I found what I wanted.

"You'd probably be a lot less uptight if you did," I continued, holding the letter opener like a dagger at my chest. "Or maybe that's exactly why you're such a grumpy asshole; you don't have the necessary equipment. Probably built like a Ken doll below the belt, huh? Such a shame. Hell, I've already come twice this morning. You don't know what you're missing."

The responding growl was much closer now. I held my breath as his muscular legs came into view, stepping next to the desk I was hiding behind.

Before he had a chance to spot me, I threw myself toward him, driving the letter opener deep into his thigh. The fact that it was designed to look like a miniature sword was fitting.

Too bad it hardly fazed him.

Note to self: never bring office supplies to a sword fight.

He snarled and I ducked as his much larger blade came sailing toward me, slicing the air where my neck had just been. Even as he stalked after me, I couldn't fight the smile tugging at my lips. He was so fun to mess with. Did the other demons have this much fun with their holier-than-thou counterparts too?

I continued to retreat, taking two steps back for every one he took forward. Each wastebasket I passed burst into beautiful flames, sending tendrils of smoke up to the ceiling. It wasn't long until the sprinklers overhead kicked on and a blaring alarm sounded. It was perfect chaos and I savored it.

Almost immediately, my clothes were soaked through and sticking to my flesh like a second skin. And mine weren't the only ones. My eyes trailed down the length of my enemy's massive body. Satan's left nut, why did anyone need that many muscles anyway? As they flexed beneath his white T-shirt, I started to think of many, *many* reasons why.

The real sin here was that chiseled body was wasted on *him*.

When I finally shook this asshat, I was going to find a good, hard lay. Clearly, I needed it.

"It must be so hard for you," I said as I moved away from him, inching toward the exit. My fingers slipped up the flat plane of my exposed stomach and his eyes tracked the movement. "Seeing all the amazing, *delicious* things this world has to offer and not being able to take part. Maybe *hard* isn't the right word, though."

I grabbed hold of the zipper of my sports bra and gave it a small tug, and he quickly averted his eyes. I threw my head back and laughed. His stormy gray eyes snapped back to me, full of anger and something else. Getting away just got a hell of a lot easier.

"Eat your heart out, *Ken*," I purred before yanking the zipper all the way down until my sports bra popped completely open.

Mr. Sexy Angel whipped his head away from me so fast, I thought it might break clean off. I took my opening and bolted for the exit. My true mother always said a woman's breasts were the ultimate weapon. Ha. Apparently, she was right about that. I'd have to remember that for future use.

Maybe I needed to try life as a nudist next time around.

I growled as I sprinted down the first flight of stairs, knowing exactly how many more were awaiting me. If only naked breasts could deflect stairs as easily as they did angels. I struggled to tug my bra back together and zip it up. Pounding footfalls echoed somewhere above me and I picked up the pace until I was bursting back onto the bustling city street.

"Help!" I screamed, and a few of the thousands of passersby looked up from their precious phones to spare me a glance. "There's a man chasing me!" I continued, jabbing a thumb over my shoulder. "He attacked me!"

With perfect timing, said attacker stormed out of the building and all eyes landed on him. Based on the looks on their faces, no one seemed to notice the sword now strapped to his broad back, let alone the two giant *wings*. Ignorance was bliss.

"Please, help me!" I cried out again, letting a tremor into my voice.

The men around me leaped into action, a few of them stepping forward to defend me, blocking my evil attacker's path. The grumpy Ken doll's eyes narrowed on me and I blew him a kiss before turning and hightailing it for the subway station.

With all due respect, not today, Satan. This pretty little demon was going to live to see another sunrise.

Pausing momentarily at the subway entrance, I grumbled as I stared down yet another set of stairs. At least these were far shorter, and they would likely lead to my freedom. I took them three at a time, descending below the earth's surface. I needed to get into the tunnels before my nemesis managed to catch up to me yet again.

But a shriek at the top of the stairs said he already had.

He was being an extra persistent fucker today.

Make one little comment about a man's junk—or lack thereof—and he lost his ever-loving mind.

If that had him this bent out of shape, he was really going to lose his shit when he realized I slipped out of his fingers yet again. Because I was going to. If I could get to the other side of the tracks, I knew I could get away from him. He didn't know these tunnels like I did. I was one with the darkness, born from it. The bowels of this city weren't much different than the bowels of Hell.

The blaring horn of the approaching train had me moving.

Getting a running start, I shoved through the thick crowd of people, knocking them out of my way as I sprinted toward the tracks. My foot hit the edge of the platform and I shoved off, leaping through the air. In a blink, I touched down on the other side and couldn't help the grin stretching across my face.

I could taste the freedom already.

The small scream, followed by a woman's wail, put a halt to my celebration, making my normally hot blood run cold.

I spun around to see a child lying on the tracks,

unmoving. And then the train horn sounded again, one bright light illuminating the tunnel as it rushed forward.

I had one rule—yes, occasionally even demons had a moral compass—and mine was simple: no innocents. Specifically, children.

"Stop the train!" someone shrieked.

My feet were moving me back toward the tracks before my brain had a chance to catch up. I leaped down to the small figure, a boy who had to be no more than five or six. He let out a whimper, blood leaking from a cut on his forehead as he blinked up at me, his entire body trembling. Or perhaps it was the tracks themselves that were vibrating as the train raced straight toward us.

Wasting no more time, I scooped the child into my arms and tossed him up to a pair of outstretched hands that quickly pulled him onto the safety of the platform.

And then the horn sounded a third time. Three strikes and I was out.

The world around me moved in slow motion as I whipped around to face the fast-moving metal beast, a flash of white light from the headlight taking over my vision.

Was this what people saw when they died and took the elevator ride up instead of down?

Scrunching my eyes shut, I threw my hands up, bracing for impact. At least I'd go knowing that Holy Fuck didn't get the honor of sending me back to Hell this time. For once, I'd get to die for something noble.

What a strange concept.

As I prepared to reenter the fiery depths of Hell, a pair

of hands grabbed hold of me, hoisting me into the air with a beat of strong wings.

Next thing I knew, my back was slammed into something hard, the air rushing out of my lungs as my enemy's muscular body pressed flush against mine, pinning me to the brick wall.

"The boy?" I asked, trying to catch my breath. A hard feat with him pressed up against me like he was.

"He lives" was all he said, and dammit all to Hell and back if the deep rumble of his voice didn't send shivers down my spine in a way that had me arching into him, making his eyes widen momentarily.

Looked like he did have the necessary equipment after all. Interesting. I'd have to remember that little tidbit for our next round of cat and mouse. Anything to get under his skin.

He quickly schooled his features, stepping away from me, but keeping one hand firmly locked around my throat. Those intense gray eyes bored into me, conflict written into his angelic features. Fucker really was something to look at, even in the dark shadows of the subway tunnel. I'd never been this close to him before without a sword against my throat. Not to say that wasn't still coming. In fact, I was sure it was. I knew how this dance worked.

I shook away my lustful thoughts. Barking up the wrong tree with this one. Hell, the wrong species. Mortal enemies. Good versus evil.

"Good," I said with as much of a nod as I could manage

with his massive hand around my neck. And then it hit me. "You…saved me."

It wasn't a question and he damn well knew it. His handsome face twisted into a scowl, nostrils flaring. I knew the fingers of his other hand were flexing on the hilt of his sword without even seeing them.

My archnemesis, tasked with killing me, *saved* my ass. I almost snorted. I was pretty sure he just wanted to make sure he was the one to do the deed. Extra brownie points with the big man upstairs if he was the one to send me back to the blissful bowels of Hell.

And here I'd thought greed was a deadly sin.

He brought his face close to mine, our noses nearly touching. "Why did you save the child?" he asked, his hot breath fanning across my skin.

My brow furrowed. "He's just an innocent kid."

A low growl left his lips and I bit my own lip in response, noticing how his eyes dropped to my mouth, his grip on my neck loosening.

His eyes found mine once more. "When has that ever stopped you before?"

Now it was my turn to growl, eyes narrowing on him. "In the hundreds of years that you've chased my ass, when have you ever known me to cause direct and purposeful harm to a child?"

He scoffed. "You leave harm everywhere you go, *demon*." He spat the word like it was intended as an insult. But that's what I was. I wasn't ashamed of my origins.

A smirk tugged at my lips. "The demon you just saved,"

I pointed out. "Maybe you don't hate me so much after all."

Before he could respond, I lunged forward, my mouth crashing into his. I was surprised to find his lips weren't nearly as carved from granite as the rest of his hard body. In fact—and maybe it was the rush of adrenaline messing with my head—they almost seemed to soften against mine.

A shockwave of electricity crashed into me before he shoved me away from him, slamming me hard against the wall. Almost immediately, I felt the cold kiss of his sword before he shoved it through my chest.

"This time, why don't you stay in Hell where you belong?" he whispered against my ear, a slight tremor in his voice.

He yanked the bloody blade free and the world around me faded to black. The last thing I saw was the flash of white of my angel's wings as he turned and walked away from me, leaving me to die alone as was par for the course with us.

PRESENT DAY

I'd always had bad luck.

"Giselle," one of my many foster fathers once said, "if not for bad luck, you'd have none at all."

Bad might have been too light a word for it.

My parents died in a car accident when I was a baby. Since I had no other family that would claim me, I jumped from foster home to foster home because no one wanted to keep me longer than a few months.

Apparently, I was unlucky for those around me too.

Which meant I was typically a party of one. Just me, myself, and I against the world. And that was fine by me. Not many friends wanted to stick around when they realized you were the reason their life was falling to shit. People could only handle so much. And my life was definitely a bit *much*.

I'd been present in three bank robberies—yes, I said

three. And that's not including how many liquor-store holdups I'd witnessed. I always took the stairs on account of being trapped in more elevators than I cared to admit, usually with people of questionable morals. Oh, and I had crashed so many cars that no insurance companies would take me.

Call me crazy, but I had no plans of stepping foot on an airplane in this lifetime. Not after the ten-car pileup I was pretty sure my presence had caused. I mean, the bus tires had been working perfectly fine until five minutes after I sat down and then they just…fell off.

But, that was my life—chaos—and after twenty-seven years, I was used to it. Hell, I was even okay with it. I just rolled with the many punches. Who needed drugs when every day was a high?

So, when I realized I had a stalker, I wasn't really shocked. Sure, it sucked ass, but it was par for the course with me. One more crazy turn of events in my life to keep me on my toes.

I felt his eyes on me as I stepped onto the sunny Las Vegas strip from my afternoon shift as a blackjack dealer. It was about the only job I could keep. The casinos loved me because patrons never—*ever*—won against me. Which meant that I'd made some enemies along the way. At first, I'd wondered if my stalker was one of them. Though I had a hard time believing I'd forget a face as sinfully beautiful as his.

His eyes bored into my back, piercing me between the shoulder blades like the sharp tip of a knife. Part of me wanted to stop and check because that's exactly what it felt like. I would know, I'd been stabbed before…twice. But, I mean, did I die? Nope. And I fully planned on keeping it that way.

I walked a little faster, moving to where the crowd thickened, loud and rowdy tourists surrounding me. The strip was my home and I knew it like the back of my hand. I was fairly confident I could lose him. I'd done it once before.

The first time I'd seen him was when I was watching some kid stealing books in my favorite bookstore. Call it vain but I initially thought he was interested in me. I mean, I was pretty easy on the eyes, if my past experiences with men—both good and bad—told me anything. And dude was hot—with a capital H. I'm talking fanning-yourself-in-public-while-clamping-your-thighs-together kind of hot.

I wasn't sure I'd ever seen a finer looking male specimen before, and with the number of bachelor parties that rolled through my city, I saw plenty. This guy topped the charts. A girl could dream.

I'd caught sight of those stormy gray eyes from the top of the *Mystery* section and my lady bits flared to life. I was actually a pro at seduction. Some might say a little too good; it had bitten me in the ass more than a few times. But when his eyes met mine, I found I desperately wanted to be bit by this one.

I had thrown him my best flirty smile and continued on through the store, feet leading me in the direction of my favorite aisle: Lady Smut R'Us. Or as normal people would call it, the romance section. I had hoped that Mr.

Greek God, who was putting all the shirtless cover models to shame, would follow me. But much to my lady bits' utter dismay, he never approached me. In fact, he'd completely vanished.

My hotter-than-hell Prince Charming slipped out of my fingers just like that.

And then I'd spotted him a second time, looking at me from the other side of the liquor store when I was getting my weekly restock of wine. At first, I thought maybe it was fate, and then I remembered this was *my* life we were talking about. Not the life of some fictional character who fell into the arms of the man of her dreams who just so happened to have a six-pack and a dick the size of her forearm.

No, this was no fairy tale and he was no prince.

The way his intense eyes had tracked me as I moved to the checkout counter was one I unfortunately knew all too well. It was predatory, sending chills down my spine. And not in the good way. All the red flags had gone off, and I'd learned in my short life to listen to those warning signs if I wanted to stay alive. I'd gotten the hell out of there, a bottle of wine clutched firmly in each hand.

And now Mr. Sexy Stalker was watching me yet again, making my panties wet despite the warnings blaring in my stupid brain.

Probably best not to sleep with your mouthwateringly sexy stalker with his lightly sun-kissed skin, corded muscles, and hair that begged to have fingers buried in it. Yep. Not happening. My vagina was batshit if she thought she'd win this one. She would get a hot shower and a powerful pair of double-A batteries and be happy with it.

I liked my morally gray characters like I liked my ink —on paper.

The midday sun beat down on me and I did a quick check of my surroundings, rushing to formulate a plan. I knew I had to lose him before going home. I didn't need the crazy asshole knowing where I lived. It was bad enough he'd been able to find me so many times already, especially in a city this overpopulated.

I made a mental note to swing by the police station as soon as I was able. Normal people with regular luck did that, right—reported crimes? Though, with how the rest of my life usually went, the cops would likely laugh at me. And who would blame them? After all, the guy hadn't actually *done* anything to me…yet. He hadn't even spoken a single word to me.

Still, couldn't be too careful. I didn't want to end up on one of those crime podcasts or some shit like that.

Reaching into the tote at my side, my fingers slipped around my trusty stun gun, bringing me a small amount of comfort as I clutched it firmly in my concealed hand.

I ducked into the nearest casino, walking into a wall of cigarette smoke. The obnoxious dinging of slot machines surrounded me, making me feel oddly at home. "Sin City" always felt right to me, despite how vile it often was.

Being the weekend, the casinos were pretty crowded, even during the middle of the day. It was going to make it that much easier to lose him. At least, that's what I hoped.

If I could shake him, it would only be a ten-minute run from the casino to my apartment.

And by *apartment,* I meant the rundown hotel room on the far end of the strip that one of my past foster brothers let me use, likely out of guilt for his parents choosing not to adopt me. They were the only family to keep me for more than a few months while I was a teenager. And even though they didn't want to keep me—none ever did—I was still grateful for the roof over my head while I had it. It was more than most gave me in my youth.

I'd run into their son, Chad, a couple years after I'd turned eighteen. He'd taken over the decrepit hotel and offered me one of the rooms. He rented it out to me for next to nothing, which was good seeing as I wasn't exactly swimming in the Benjamins.

Fun fact, you didn't get fantastic tips when you were the dealer at the table where everyone lost their hard-earned cash.

Again, I couldn't help but wonder if my stalker was a disgruntled gambler who'd lost his life savings at one of my tables, leading to his divorce and his children being ripped away from him. It happened more times than I could count. A few times, I'd watched it play out right in front of me. Some people just didn't know when to quit.

Speaking of people not knowing when it was time to walk away, I moved past a table just as the dealer dragged away a substantial pile of chips from a player. Defeat flashed across the intoxicated man's face followed almost immediately by a dangerous look of determination. I gave it five minutes before he was either at the ATM or a local pawn shop telling himself he could win it back.

Keeping my hand on my stun gun, I risked a glance over my shoulder to see Mr. Tall, Dark, and Stalky stepping into the casino. Even through the haze of smoke, I could see his eyes scanning the room. He was so focused on finding me that he hadn't even noticed the entire group of half-dressed bachelorette partygoers who stopped what they were doing to turn and ogle him. One of them even went so far as to step in front of him, flipping her hair over her shoulder before placing a well-manicured hand on his chest.

Without sparing her a glance, he shoved past her.

Sorry, ladies, he apparently only has eyes for me.

The question was *why*? Did the little flirty smile at the bookstore trigger something in him? Did he think because I'd eye-fucked him that I now belonged to him? Did he want to eat my heart for dinner and make a blanket out of my skin like in all those twisted crime shows?

Yeah, I liked my heart and skin right where they were, thank you very much.

I crouched and moved deeper into the busy casino, slinking between the many slot machines as I headed in the direction of one of the high-end restaurants. None of the casino patrons spared me a passing glance. This city was full of interesting characters. A woman creeping around damn near on all fours was commonplace. Unless I was running past them on fire, no one cared about my existence. Even then, I still might go unnoticed.

"How many in your party?"

I nearly jumped out of my damn skin at the hostess's words. The beautiful brunette looked down at me from her podium, one perfectly shaped eyebrow raised. Yep, she thought I was crazy. I mean, I had just been practically crawling into a five-star restaurant.

"Look, I need your help," I rushed to say, going with honesty. Women were supposed to look out for one another, right? When they weren't tearing each other apart, that was.

Another glance over my shoulder told me my stalker was getting closer. He hadn't spotted me yet, but it was only a matter of time. "There's this guy and I think he's following me," I told her. "I need to get out of here without making a big scene. Please, help me."

As those three words left my lips, a strong sense of déjà vu slammed into me hard enough to have me stumbling back a step. I closed my eyes and shook my head, blinking away the image of a high-rise I'd never seen before.

What the...

"Through the kitchen," the hostess said, pulling my focus back to her face. She gave a small jerk of her head. "There's a door that leads to the parking lot. I'll call security."

I straightened slightly, ignoring the feeling of eyes landing on my back. "Thank you," I told her with a nod.

Wasting no time, I moved as quickly and calmly as I could through the restaurant, making a beeline straight for the double swinging doors. Without looking back, I pushed through, leaving the luxury restaurant behind for the chaos of the stark white kitchen. The second the doors swung closed behind me, I took off, shoving past the many cooks and servers as I headed for the glowing "exit" sign.

Bursting through the metal door and into the fading daylight, I didn't stop, sprinting through the parking lot and back onto the strip. A few people shouted obscenities at me as I pushed through the thick crowd, only slowing to make sure I wasn't being followed. I ran hard and fast until my building came into view. Even then, I didn't stop. Not until I was standing in front of my door, chest heaving and side splitting.

I blew out a shaky breath, resting my forehead against the paint-chipped door. I'd made it. For today, at least.

But why did I find myself hoping we'd get to do this dance again tomorrow? And why did the prospect of my sexy stalker appearing out of nowhere and slamming me against this door have heat pooling between my legs?

God, there was something seriously wrong with me. Maybe it was the adrenaline, or maybe I was just over-sexed. I'd always had a high drive and this had been my longest dry spell to date. I definitely needed to get laid soon—and *not* by the man who was stalking me. That was a hard pass.

"Giselle," I heard Chad, my foster brother of one twenty-seventh of my life, call as I slid the key card into the slot on my door. "You're late on the rent!"

You have got to be kidding me...

"No, I'm not," I shot back through clenched teeth,

adrenaline still coursing through my veins. "I put it in the box a week ago. You know I always make sure to stay current."

I yanked my room key free, cracking the door open for a quick getaway before turning to glare at the big man storming toward me.

He wasn't much to look at. Not bad but not great either. Maybe it was because, for a tiny fraction of both our lives, he'd been somewhat my brother. Or maybe I was just comparing him to the man following my ass. Chad was the typical jock who'd hit his peak in high school. He'd been a brick shithouse in school but he'd gone a little soft around the middle and his hair was prematurely thinning.

"Well, it's not there and the rent was due two days ago," he said, lifting those big shoulders in a shrug. "Figure it out. I expect my money by Wednesday."

Yeah, he wasn't the friendliest guy. But he was the longest stretch of good luck I'd ever had in my life, outside of maintaining my casino gig. Chad had given me a place to stay and he'd never taken advantage of me when I was his parents' foster kid, and that wasn't always the case with the houses I'd stayed at. So, he was all right in my books, even if there was a chance he was suddenly trying to swindle me for some extra cash.

Cash I most certainly didn't owe him because I'd put the rent in the damn box.

"I already paid," I said again to his retreating back.

He waved at me over his shoulder with a finger I wasn't a fan of. If you were going to tell someone to fuck

LUCAS

I stood outside of her hotel room, cloaked in the shadows of the falling night as I tried to decide what to do.

It didn't make sense. None of it. She wasn't reacting at all to my presence. At least, not in the way she should have been—the way she always had.

It was almost as if she didn't know who I was…

Which was impossible. Our lives had been interwoven far too long to ever forget.

I'd spent centuries spilling her vile blood. Never in all that time had I been able to sneak up on her like I'd done at the bookstore. I'd followed her for a full twenty minutes before she'd even noticed me. And when she saw me… There was no recognition at all on her face. And then she'd just gone off to buy a stack of filthy books like nothing had happened. What kind of game was she playing this time? And what on this unholy Earth was that smile about?

It didn't really matter. I'd figure it out one way or another. She'd never been able to outmaneuver me for long and this would be no different. If she thought she could escape fate by playing dumb, she had another think coming.

I never failed in my mission. Ever. And she knew that. It was what I was created to do. I was on this Earth to make sure she wasn't. In the end, I would send her straight back to Hell just like I'd always done.

Unless it wasn't actually her.

It was a thought that had crossed my mind at least a hundred times since I'd found her a month ago. Something was...*off* about her. About the entire situation. It was why I hadn't run her through with my blade when I first found her, and why even now, I couldn't seem to get myself to break down the door and end this here and now.

Outside of her lack of recognition when she saw me, it had taken me far longer than usual to find her this time around. Not that that in itself was altogether unheard of. But usually by the time she hit her early twenties, she'd already caused enough chaos and damage in whatever city she was living to draw in divine attention.

But not this time. It had been nearly twenty-seven years since her cursed rebirth and she'd stayed relatively quiet. I'd actually started to think that maybe she'd finally stayed in Hell where she belonged when one of my associates noticed the spike in gambling addiction in this horrid city. It took me another month of scouring these filthy streets to find her, dealing cards and ruining the lives of any who stepped near her table.

But that was all she was doing.

She woke up, went to work, went grocery shopping, ordered things online, and read on her breaks. For the first time in the hundreds of years I'd dealt with her, she was living an almost "normal" life. She wasn't actively chasing chaos like I'd watched her do in the past. If anything, chaos was after *her*. In the span of four weeks, I'd watched her go to the emergency room twice and nearly get crushed by a vehicle more times than I could count. One could say she was the one being dealt a bad hand.

But it was her, it had to be.

I'd chased her for centuries and she'd always been born to the same damned body. A body created for one purpose: to tempt the hearts of men.

A shiver trickled down my spine, remembering the way that body had felt pressed against mine in the dark depths of that subway tunnel. And that kiss. I growled, wiping my mouth with the back of my hand, trying to remove the fires of Hell that still lingered there after over a quarter century. Her taste had stayed with me long after she'd gone.

That was what she did—she messed with people's heads.

This had to be yet another of her tricks. She wanted to confuse me, to throw me off my game as she nearly had back then. Well, it wouldn't work. I would not be bested by a *demon*. She would fall to my blade again, just like she always had.

I took a small step back as a couple stumbled down the walkway, unable to keep their ring-less hands off one another. They fumbled to open the door to their room and I grimaced. Humans were foul creatures with their drunken ways and lustful thoughts. Not to mention their vile, violent tendencies. Though it wasn't entirely their fault. It was demons like *her* spreading sin throughout the land.

She had to be stopped. They all did.

When the couple disappeared into their room, I moved forward, watching as the lights in her room flickered off. Peering through the sliver of space between her curtains, I saw her sprawled out on her small bed, a towel draped over her body and her red hair fanned out around her like flames. She had a small black object clutched in one trembling hand.

Before I could determine what she was holding, a buzzing sound filled my ears. I reached into my pocket and pulled out the phone, my eyes never leaving the window.

"Did you take care of her?" a deep voice rumbled through the device the second it touched my ear.

I swiftly moved away from her hotel room. "Not yet," I ground out, keeping my voice low, eyes darting to the still-closed door.

"What is taking you so long, Lucas?" the man on the other end of the line asked. "It has never taken you this long to take care of a mark. Losing your touch?"

"I'm—" I paused, not wanting to admit I was having doubts as to if it was actually her or not. Especially not to someone like Zain. He was my brother in arms; I'd known him for as long as I could remember. But he was also after the archangel position—a title I'd been chasing for nearly two centuries—and he would do anything to be the one who got it. Including sabotage me.

"You're what?" he snapped when I didn't respond.

I swallowed the growl rising in my throat. "Watch your tone with me, Zain. We are equals, you and I."

He chuckled. "For now, brother."

"Don't you have a mark of your own to worry about, *brother*?" I asked, once again checking the window and door for movement.

"I took care of him last night," Zain said, sounding far more prideful than one of our kind ever should. "Fastest I've ever found him. I'm thinking of asking the Arches to assign me additional targets. It will look that much better when they go to pick the new archangel, don't you think?"

I did think. In fact, *I* was the one who'd told him my idea of multiple targets. We were each assigned one high-powered demon to keep in Hell. When we removed them from the Earth, we shifted our focus to the many smaller, low-level demons, keeping them in line until our marks returned. But the number of high-powered demons had gone up exponentially in the past few decades and we were slowly becoming outnumbered.

My fingers flexed around the hilt of my sword. He was taking my idea.

"What on God's green Earth do you want, Zain?" I bit out, wings twitching behind me as my agitation grew.

"I just wanted to see if you needed a hand with your mark." I could hear the smirk in his voice.

"I don't need your help," I bit out, pushing the *end* button hard enough to crack the screen.

Blowing out a breath, I shoved the phone back into my pocket and unsheathed my blade.

I would end this tonight. And then I would take my idea to the Arches. I wouldn't let Zain take what I'd worked so long for. They only gave a new archangel title once every five hundred years.

I was not going to miss my opportunity.

Stepping back to the window, I peered into the room and found her in the exact same spot on the bed. There was a fresh sheen of sweat coating her flushed skin, her face scrunched slightly as if she was in some sort of pain. Her whimpers traveled through the thin window pane and I furrowed my brows. Was she having a nightmare?

Could demons even dream?

I inched closer to the glass, my breath fogging it over. Without thinking, I reached up and wiped the haze away, the soft squeak not deterring her from whatever she was doing.

In one hand, she still clutched the black object to her chest—it looked like some sort of weapon. Her other hand was buried beneath the towel, fingers dancing between her legs. Her hips arched against her hand, the towel creeping higher up her bare thighs as a small moan slipped past her parted lips.

The air in my lungs left in a hiss and I nearly dropped my sword. Fire ignited deep within me, the heat of it rushing low in my body—along with what felt like all of my blood. The sensation was so intense that I slumped forward, bracing myself against the window with my free hand.

I hadn't felt this way in twenty-seven years. Maybe ever.

What was this wicked creature doing to me? I couldn't tear my eyes away from her.

With almost perfect timing to the couple in the adjacent room, she threw her head back and cried out and I felt myself harden instantly.

"No," I snarled, forcing myself to take another step away, and then another.

I would not let this vile demon taint my soul.

Tomorrow, she would die.

GISELLE

I woke with a scream on my lips, sitting bolt upright in my small bed.

Inhaling a shaky breath, I tried to calm my racing heart before it burst clean out of my chest. I didn't need to add heart attack to my emergency room frequent flyer card. I clutched the sheets that pooled at my waist and looked around my dark hotel room, if only to prove to myself that I was really here…

And no longer burning alive.

"It was just a dream," I told myself, blowing out the breath I'd been holding.

The most realistic dream I'd ever had. *Nightmare* was a better word for it.

I ran trembling fingers up and down my sweat-slickened arms, still feeling the heat of the flames licking my flesh. The fire had been everywhere. It surrounded me —*consumed* me. I'd felt the burn of it deep in my soul.

But, as terrifying as it was, it didn't hurt. In fact, it actually felt kind of…good.

"That's it," I grumbled, pushing off the bed and trudging my naked ass to the bathroom, "no more fantasizing about sexy stalkers right before bed."

Talk about a one-way ticket to Hell.

I pressed my forehead to the countertop with a groan, the chill of it a sharp contrast to the heat still radiating from my skin.

In my defense, I hadn't been thinking about my stalker when my me-myself-and-I time had started. My mind just kind of wandered to him all on its twisted own. And then it stayed there. No matter how hard I'd tried, I couldn't get his perfect face or chiseled body out of my head.

And then I didn't want it to go. Quite the opposite, actually. I started to wonder what that gloriously sculpted body would look like naked and hovering over mine, diving into me over and over until I was screaming.

I shuddered, pushing away from the counter and yanking open one of the drawers. I grabbed my hairbrush and started attacking the tangled mess on my head. That's what I got for going to bed with wet hair. I knew better—a light wind could send my hair into a clusterfuck of tangles. Add in some thrashing around and it was the perfect recipe for a hair catastrophe. I briefly considered taking a razor to it.

Maybe that would make my stalker back the fuck off. Or maybe he'd completely snap and kill me. With how my life normally played out, I knew which of the two I'd bet my limited money on. All the more reason to get my ass to the police station.

"I don't have time for this," I growled. I had just over an hour until I had to be at work, and I still wanted to swing by the station to file a report. I didn't know how long that was going to take, or if they'd even believe me.

I tossed the brush onto the counter and flicked on the shower. An entire bottle of hair conditioner would do the trick, and it would be a hell of a lot less painful. As steam billowed out of the curtain and slammed into my face, my mind went back to my nightmare.

Nope, not today, Satan.

I quickly cranked the knob to cold and jumped in. I needed to get moving.

PULLING my still-damp hair into a high pony, I stepped out of my hotel room, straightening the stupid bowtie I had to wear for work. I couldn't complain—at least I had a job. And my uniform was better than what the cocktail waitresses had to wear. Unlike them, my ass and tits were regularly covered. Those girls were saints to deal with drunk gamblers on the regular, getting ogled and groped. I heard the tips were nice, though. I didn't know anything about tips.

As I turned to make sure my door had clicked shut, something on the ground caught my eye.

"What the..." I bent down and picked up the large

white feather. It had to be the length of my forearm, and blindingly white. So white, in fact, that it was practically glowing. Without thinking, I ran my fingers over it. It was the softest thing I'd ever touched.

Something about it felt oddly…familiar.

What kind of bird around here had feathers like this? No, more likely it was from a costume. There were plenty of stage shows in this city, not to mention some of the outfits people wore out on the strip. But why was it in front of my room? This hotel was so far from the main part of the strip. Technically it wasn't even *on* the strip. We typically got gamblers down on their luck, along with the occasional shady hookup.

And then the feather slipped from my trembling fingers as my eyes landed on the window looking into my hotel room. There, streaked into the dirty glass pane, was a handprint.

I took a step back and then another, trying to tell myself that I was making something out of nothing. But there was no mistaking the distinct shape smudged into the glass. Someone had pressed their hand on my window, the print sliding down before disappearing altogether.

Who had been watching me? And *when*?

Did he find me? Deep down, I already knew the answer. Of course, he had.

I spun on my heels and took off in the direction of the nearest police station. There weren't a lot of places to feel safe on the strip, but my own home—albeit a hotel room

—should have been one of them. I wasn't going to be a victim.

Wasting no time, I ran the entire way to the police station, taking advantage of the empty sidewalks this early on a Monday morning. I barged through the station door before promptly doubling over, bracing my hands on my knees and trying to draw in a breath. Despite my rather abrupt entrance, no one paid me any mind. Not even the officer sitting at the front desk.

Pulling in one more ragged breath, I pushed up and moved to the desk where the officer sat staring at his computer screen. Even when I approached, he still didn't look up at me. I tapped my fingernails on the surface of the desk repeatedly.

"Can I help you?" he asked, still not tearing his eyes away from the screen. He must have been playing the world's most intense game of *Tetris*. His lack of attention was starting to piss me off.

"Yes," I told him as calmly as I could manage under the circumstances, "I believe I have a stalker."

That seemed to grab his attention, though when he met my eyes, there was clear annoyance in them. What was this dude's problem? I glanced down at his nametag. Officer Ruiz.

"And you believe this why?"

"Because I've seen the same guy following me three times now—"

"This city really isn't as big as people think," he said, cutting me off. "It's probably just a coincidence. Maybe he works somewhere locally. Three times isn't all that many. Do you have anything else to go off of?"

I swallowed my frustration. "Well, the last time I saw him, he followed me out of my job, down the street, and into a casino before I managed to get away from him. *And,*" I added before he could open his mouth to interrupt me again, "I'm pretty sure he was outside of my hotel room last night."

Officer Ruiz cocked an eyebrow at me. Yeah, this was going nowhere fast. "This is a police station, ma'am. We don't do *pretty sure* around here."

Oh, this asshole did not just air quote me.

"There was a handprint on my window this morning," I bit out. "Go do your fancy forensic shit and pull the prints. I'm sure you'd find out they belong to this guy."

"This isn't *CSI,* lady. We can't do anything without proof of a crime having been committed. From what you've told me, no crime has happened."

Great. We'd gone from *ma'am* to *lady.*

"Yet," I said through clenched teeth. The lights above our heads flickered erratically before one of the bulbs went out completely. "He hasn't done anything to me *yet.* I know he's following me."

His eyes darted up to the light and then back to me. Yeah, he was definitely more concerned about the dead bulb than the chances of me ending up in a similar fashion.

"Until this guy who you *think* is following you does something to break the law, we can't do anything about it. Sorry."

I saw red. "Are you fucking kidding me?" I shouted, slamming my palm on the desktop. A homeless guy on a bench stirred and another officer stepped into the lobby. The lights above us pulsed once more.

"So, I have to wait until this guy does something to me before you actually fucking do anything about it?" I continued. "Are you listening to yourself, right now?"

Officer Ruiz grunted as he stood. "Calm down, miss," he said. "That's just the way it is. I don't make the rules around here. I'm sure it will be fine. It's probably all in your head anyways. Don't worry."

And now he was moving on to gaslighting. Awesome. His naked ring finger made so much more sense now.

"When this guy murders me in my sleep," I said, my rising voice echoing throughout the room, "it'll be on you! Do you hear me, Officer Ruiz? My blood will be on your hands when this guy kills me! Because he's going to. He's coming for me—and it isn't *in my head,* you lazy piece of—"

"Whoa," a deep voice said from somewhere in the room and I glanced over my shoulder to see a third officer step into the lobby. At least, I assumed he was an officer. He wasn't in uniform but there was a badge hanging around his neck. "What's going on here?"

"This lady is crazy," Ruiz spat. "Claims she's being stalked. I told her we can't do anything without proof. She needs to be removed from the building."

I turned to face the new guy. "I *am* being stalked! I know he was outside my hotel last night. And this demon fart of a man," I hissed, jabbing a finger in

Officer Ruiz's direction, "won't do a damn thing to help me."

Demon fart? Where the hell had that come from?

The new officer approached me, his dark wash jeans and polo shirt clinging to his well-sculpted body. That body definitely didn't spend its days devouring donuts like Officer Ruiz's obviously did.

My eyes lingered a moment longer than they should have.

Pretty boy extended his hand to me, which was more than Ruiz had done. "I'm Detective Mark Jenson."

"Giselle," I told him, taking his hand.

"Please, come with me," Jenson said, motioning for me to join him.

"Waste of fucking time, Jenson," Ruiz called after us as we moved out of the main lobby. Jenson chuckled beside me, shaking his head.

He pushed open another door and stepped aside so I could enter in front of him. Almost immediately, I felt his eyes on my ass. My own eyes rolled in response. Then again, I'd done some serious admiring of my own. Guess I couldn't be too upset.

"Don't mind Ruiz," he said as he took a seat at what I could only assume was his desk. "He didn't get his morning coffee and I ate the last donut. Plus, he's just kind of an ass."

He must have seen the absence of amusement on my face because his own smile faded. He sighed, gesturing to the chair across from him.

"Why don't you start from the beginning?" he said after I'd taken a seat. "Tell me what happened."

I took a deep breath and nodded. "I have a stalker," I told him before quickly adding, "And no, he hasn't actually done anything to me yet, but I know he's following me. I've seen him three times already in the past month. Each time he was honed in on me like I was prey. When I saw him watching me yesterday, he'd followed me throughout the strip. He was clearly after me. And I know he was at my hotel last night. He must have followed me from the casino after I'd thought I lost him."

All of my words came out in a rush, blending together until I wasn't sure he could even understand them.

I sucked in a breath, replenishing my aching lungs. I forced myself to meet the detective's eyes. They were a stunning shade of green—unique even. But they weren't nearly as intense as my stalker's.

Probably not the best idea to compare this guy with my sexy stalker.

Should also probably stop referring to him as "sexy." The guy was following me. All the red flags.

"You don't believe me," I said when Jenson didn't respond. I could see it on his face. At least, he wasn't as blatantly rude as Ruiz had been.

The handsome detective shook his head. "No, that isn't true. I just need more information. Let's start with what this man looks like."

Don't say sexy. Don't say sexy. Don't say sexy.

"Tall."

Point for me!

Jenson leaned his elbows on the desk. "He's tall?" he repeated, cocking an eyebrow. "Anything else for me to go by?"

"Tall, dark, and handsome."

Shit. There went that point.

"What do you want me to say?" I continued, trying to play it off and ignoring the ticking of Jenson's jaw. "He's tall, Caucasian, has brown hair, gray eyes, and a muscular build. I wasn't exactly staring at him closely when I was trying to get the hell away from his crazy ass."

Liar, liar, pants on fire.

"Where did you first see him?" the detective asked after a beat. Well, he hadn't kicked me out yet. That had to be a good sign.

"At the bookstore."

"The bookstore?"

"Yeah. He was kind of following me around the store. At first, I thought it was a coincidence—like maybe we were into the same books. Then I thought maybe he was interested, you know?"

Jenson nodded. The way he was staring at me now, he looked like a man who was interested himself. That wasn't going to happen. He might have been damn nice to look at, but he was barking up the wrong tree with me. I steered clear of first responders and military as a general rule. Their jobs were dangerous enough as it was without my shitty-ass luck following them around.

"Did he say anything to you?"

"No," I said, forcing my eyes back to Jenson's face. "He hasn't ever spoken to me."

He leaned back in his swivel chair, lacing his fingers behind his head. "And what's this about him going to your place of residence?"

"Yeah, I rent a room in one of the hotels off the strip. He was there last night, I know it."

"Did you see him?"

I shook my head.

"Hear him outside?"

Another shake.

"Was he caught on security footage? Leave you a letter? Carrier pigeon? How did you know he was there?"

"Do you need another donut?" I asked through clenched teeth. "You're starting to sound a lot like your buddy, Ruiz, out there."

Jenson blew out a breath, scrubbing a large hand over his five o'clock shadow. "Sorry," he muttered. "I've been on the clock since yesterday morning. I'm just trying to find out as much as I can so that I might be able to help you. If we can prove this guy was outside your hotel, we could possibly do something."

He added emphasis to *prove*, if only to make his own point. Yeah, yeah, I got it. I had to have some sort of proof that someone was following me.

I stood and moved behind the chair, starting to pace the small office space. "There was a handprint on my window."

"A handprint?"

I rolled my eyes so hard I felt them stroke my damn brain. "We aren't going to get anywhere if you keep repeating me," I said, and the detective fought the grin tugging at his lips. He really was handsome. Not nearly as good as my stalker, but still.

"Yes, a damn handprint. It was streaked into my window and it wasn't there the day before."

At least, I didn't think it had been. I wasn't exactly inspecting my windows regularly—or ever.

"Could it have been from someone from a neighboring room?"

My mind immediately went to the couple I'd heard walking by my room late last night. The same couple I'd heard all night long having a grand ol' time in the room adjacent to mine.

"It's possible," I found myself saying, slumping back into the chair I'd vacated. "But I know this guy is following me," I rushed to say. "I can't explain it. It's this feeling I can't shake. I don't want to end up on the seven o'clock news."

Jenson pushed up from his chair and rounded the desk. Leaning his tight ass against it, he crossed his arms and stared down at me. "I won't let anything happen to you."

I watched the shock register in his eyes like he was surprised by the words that had spilled out of his own mouth. Nearly as surprised as I was.

"You believe me?"

Reaching into his pocket, Jenson pulled out a business card. Pausing momentarily, he twisted where he sat against the desk and grabbed a pen, jotting something down on the back of the card he was holding. I was fairly certain I knew what it was.

"Here," he said, handing the card to me when he was finished. "If you feel unsafe at any point, or think this man is following you again, you call me. I added my personal cell on the back. You call anytime—day or night—I will be there, or I'll get someone to you if I'm already on assignment. But hopefully it won't come to that. Most times, these guys end up losing interest."

"Do you do that often?" I couldn't help but ask. "Give out your personal number? Doesn't your wife get mad?" Yep, I was fishing. I didn't mess with cheaters. Not that I planned to mess with him, despite his obvious interest. Still, I wanted to know the sort of person I was dealing with. Decent human beings didn't come along often in my line of work—or with my shitty-ass luck.

Jenson flashed me a panty-melting smile and my stomach did a tiny flip. I almost hated that he didn't have the same effect on me as my stalker had. Something about that was so wrong on about a million fucking levels.

"First of all," he started, "I am not married. Except to the job. It's just me and my dog, and we're used to getting work calls around the clock. Second, I would hate for you to become another statistic. And third, well, we'll save third for after we make sure you're safe."

He pushed off the desk and headed toward the door. I took my cue and stood, following him. "If you can, try to snap some photos of the guy, or video even," he said, holding the door open. "Send them to me and I'll run them through our system to see if the guy has any priors. The biggest thing to remember, though, is don't provoke him."

Great, me, the queen of provoking people…

But at least I had someone who believed me. Someone in my corner.

I reached out my hand and he quickly took it. “Thank you, Detective Jenson.”

“Please, call me Mark,” he said. “I’ll walk you out.”

LUCAS

Why in God's holy grace was she at a police station? When she'd left her hotel this morning, she'd all but run here.

She'd never gone to the authorities in any of her past lives. If anything, she enjoyed making first responders' lives a living nightmare, endangering those they'd sworn to protect by raining chaos everywhere she went.

I watched as she exited the station, staying out of sight. If I could catch her on her way to work, I could finally end this.

Before I could make my move, a man stepped out of the building directly behind her. His straight posture spoke of a military background, but the badge around his neck said detective. Why would she need a detective? And why were those fiery eyes of hers darting around the street like a scared little mouse? I'd chased her down hundreds of times in my long life, and even as my blade kissed her neck, she still looked at me with defiance and determination in her eyes. What could possibly have her so afraid now?

The detective led her through the parking lot. His hand danced across the small of her back, the touch far from professional.

Without thinking, my sword was suddenly clutched in my hand, a growl slipping past my lips. Who was this man? And why did he think he could touch her?

He bent down and whispered something into her ear, further encroaching on her personal space. I waited for her to hit him—to do something. Instead, laughter bubbled out of her, her entire body shaking with it. My mind immediately recalled the way that same body had shaken and arched in pleasure last night. Was this who she'd been thinking about while she touched herself?

It didn't matter.

Pushing away from the van, I wove through the many parked cars, keeping hidden.

"I'm off now," I heard the detective say as I got closer. "I'd be more than happy to drive you to your work. If you have time, we can grab some coffee. My treat."

"I think I'll be okay," she said sweetly, nibbling on her bottom lip. Even from where I stood, I could see his eyes track the movement. "I don't really feel comfortable in cars."

"I could walk you," he said a little too eagerly. "You know, to make sure you're safe."

The man had fallen into her wicked charms. She had

more of her mother in her than I'd realized. Succubi were some of the worst creatures to deal with. I'd heard that her mother was a true monster when she still actively roamed the Earth. She was rumored to be the origin of lust itself. All she had to do was walk into a town and every person lost themselves to their sexual desires. She'd also created the first brothel along with many of the sexual diseases that plague the world.

And then one day, she'd just disappeared. Something I wished her daughter would do.

My mark fidgeted with her bag before glancing at her watch. "I don't want to inconvenience you…"

Victory flickered across his face. "No inconvenience at all. It's a beautiful morning and I've been cooped up in that building all night dealing with a case. I could use some fresh air."

She flashed him a genuine smile that had my stomach twisting. With a nod, she turned and headed toward the casino where she worked, his hand still plastered to the small of her back.

I found that no matter how hard I tried, that was all I could see as I followed them.

AFTER BUYING her a cup of fancy caffeine, the detective dropped her outside of her vile casino, reluctantly removing his hand from her back. He said his good-byes, mumbling something about calling if she needed him. But she wouldn't need him.

I'd make sure of that.

She'd given him a hug that lingered longer than was appropriate, and then turned and slipped into the casino, his eyes glued to her backside as she walked away.

I shouldn't have been so surprised. She had a way of luring men to their damnation. She'd had me praying for forgiveness more times than I could count. Like last night…

I watched from the shadows as she settled into her table for her shift. It was early and a weekday so there weren't many patrons in the casino yet. They were likely still up in their rooms, recovering from a night of debauchery and fornication.

If I had my way, we'd destroy these wretched buildings altogether. They were the spawn of Satan, overflowing with sin. Humans thought they were amazing. They loved the unique architecture and fancy décor. But if I'd learned one thing over my many years on Earth, it was that humans were absolutely stupid. They'd been so twisted and corrupted by demons—like her—since the day of their creation.

I'd met very few humans I actually liked. Few of them still had pure hearts or any redeeming qualities.

But I'd still do my part to try to rid the world of evil and make it a better place for those living in it. I had to believe there was still hope for mankind.

If only we could figure out how to permanently remove these demons—especially high-powered ones like her. Their ability to return over and over again was a real pain. And now more and more of the creatures had started popping up around the world. We were outnumbered. But if they stayed dead, maybe we would stand a chance at fixing this broken world for good. It would take centuries to repair the damage they'd caused, but at least we'd have a chance.

A couple sat down at her table and almost immediately started fighting with one another. The man dropped a few bills on the table in exchange for chips. She cut the deck and started dealing cards.

Within five minutes, the couple had lost all their money and were now screaming at the top of their lungs at each other. The demon behind their misery reached under her table and pressed a button. Almost immediately, security showed up and escorted the couple away.

They were quickly replaced by a group of rowdy teachers on summer vacation, all of whom left her table with empty pockets. Next was a hungover bachelor party that spent most of their time hitting on her, spewing filthy comments, and trying to talk her into joining them after she got off work. I felt more joy than I should have when they lost all their money. Even then, that didn't stop the groom from giving her his number before he was forced to leave with his tail tucked between his legs.

Everyone who sat in front of her lost whatever they put down. Some of them lost more than that.

I'd overheard some saying they thought she dealt cursed cards. But it was the dealer who was doing the cursing, not the cards. Some went to her table just to try to beat the unbeatable dealer. They always lost.

"Can I get you something, honey?"

I looked up from where I was sitting at an empty slot machine, surprised to see a cocktail waitress staring back at me. She looked at me expectantly, tray full of poisonous drinks balanced expertly on one hand. She had more skin showing than she had covered thanks to the outfit she was parading around in. What kind of twisted person would choose this for their career?

"Care to order a drink?" she asked again when I didn't respond. I wasn't used to many humans approaching me. They tended to see what they wanted, which meant they didn't see me for what I really was. Typically, the only ones that did try to talk to me were women. I found women in these times were just as lewd and disgusting as men.

"No," I said, turning my attention back to my mark and ignoring the way the waitress stared at me. I believe the humans called it undressing with their eyes.

"You should go over there and say hi," the lady said, obviously not taking the hint. Again, humans weren't the brightest. "Giselle doesn't bite too hard."

"Excuse me?"

She leaned a full hip against the machine I was sitting at, her mischievous eyes moving from me to my mark and then back to me again. She was a few years older than the vile demon—*Giselle*. That was what she was going by this time? "I've seen you in here a few times this month, honey," the waitress said with a grin. "You're always watching her. You look at that girl like she's the only glass of water in a sea of sand. Just go introduce yourself. I'm pretty sure she's single, and you don't strike me as the type who has to worry about rejection."

"No," I said again. I think I'd rather ingest all of the vile concoctions on her tray than fraternize with a demon. Besides, the way that detective had pawed at her, she didn't appear all that single to me. Not that it mattered. She'd be dead the second I got her alone. Because unlike these weak men, the only thing I planned to impale her with was my sword.

"Suit yourself." With a shrug, the cocktail waitress sauntered off, divvying out the drinks on her tray.

My eyes returned to my target. I leaned back, waiting for my moment to strike.

It wouldn't be long. Any minute now, she'd be relieved for her break. And I knew exactly how she spent her breaks: reading her filthy books beside the big fountain that people flocked to this city to see. Even I could admit that the water show was decent. Probably the only thing worth seeing in this godforsaken place.

I just had to wait a bit longer and I could rid her from my life once more.

6

GISELLE

Laurel sashayed over to my table with a tray full of drinks, ready to liquor up my customers so I could take all their money. At least, that was how we referred to it. Neither of us wanted to work at a casino, but a job was a job. As my second-grade teacher used to tell me, *you get what you get and you don't throw a fucking fit.* Okay, so maybe my teacher didn't actually say "fucking," but she definitely was thinking it.

If anyone hated this job more than me, it was Laurel. Though, she was far better at faking it than I was. Her people skills were on point. Which was why she brought in some of the highest tips of all of the waitresses here. Maybe in the whole strip. Customers loved her. She'd tried to find other work multiple times, but there was nowhere else she could make the same kind of money as she did serving at the casino.

And she needed the money. She had two young children at home to take care of, and her husband had passed away a couple of years ago. Without any family, she had to work her ass off to make ends meet. She made sure those kids wanted for nothing.

Laurel was probably the closest thing I had to a friend, seeing as most people realized pretty quickly how piss poor my luck was. Maybe it was because Laurel had already been through her fair share of shit, so the misfortune I brought was minor. Either way, I enjoyed when we had shifts together. It made the time pass faster.

She flashed me a smile and a wink as she set her tray on the edge of my table. She turned her full attention to the players, chatting with each of them as she gave them their beverages, paying them extra special attention. How did she always know exactly what to say to each of them? It was like some sort of magical talent. Or maybe that's just what socially normal people looked like interacting with other normal people. I wouldn't know, I leaned more toward the socially awkward.

One by one, the patrons loaded her apron up with chips.

Seriously, how did she do it? Maybe it had something to do with the fact that Laurel brought them delicious treats for free and I stole all of their hard-earned money.

After serving up the last of her drinks, she stepped behind the table with me and leaned into my space. "You have a handsome, young suitor," she whispered into my ear.

"What?" I breathed. He was here, at my work? I shouldn't have been nearly as surprised as I was.

"He's been watching you," she singsonged. "I think he's too shy to come talk to you. I told him you don't bite. You should go find him on your break. He was at the penny slots. Man is literally sex on legs. Pretty sure I got pregnant just from looking at him."

Laurel fanned herself dramatically and one of the women at my table giggled.

Yep, that definitely sounded like my stalker. Shit.

"Where is this guy?" Giggles asked with a drunken smile. "I like sex."

"You're married," the man beside her bit out. The two of them had been at each other's throats since they sat down. Pretty commonplace at my table. Even newlyweds like them weren't safe from me.

"Doesn't mean I can't put him into my highlight reel," she shot back, and her husband all but growled. He threw back his entire drink and motioned Laurel for another.

"Hey, folks!" a bubbly voice said from behind me. I turned to find Shellie, my replacement, flashing her always-present hundred-watt smile. "I'll be taking over for Giselle for a little while! Are you guys ready to have some fun?"

The mood around the table instantly shifted and one of the guys mumbled something about maybe being able to win back some of his money now. I tried not to take it too personally. People didn't like dealers who constantly took their money. Everyone wanted to win occasionally, and they didn't with me.

I nodded my good-byes and left the table with my zero dollars in tips and Laurel at my side. At least the casino would be happy.

"So..." Laurel drawled.

"What?"

She rolled her pretty blue eyes. "So, are you going to go talk to him?"

"I don't know," I told her. "Maybe."

Nope. Nope. Nopeity fucking nope.

"Laurel," the bartender called, lining up a row of drinks for her to take out.

"Got to go," she said. "Let me know how it goes! At least hit it and quit it for the rest of the female population. A man that fine shouldn't go to waste."

A snort slipped out and she gave me a quick hug before rushing over to the bar. The second she was gone, I glanced around the casino, paranoia rising once more. If Laurel was right, he was here somewhere. Was he watching me right now?

I couldn't exactly leave—not without risking my job. I looked around once more before ducking into the locker room. It wasn't too busy for a Monday; maybe I could say I was sick and head home early. But the guy knew where I lived now—at least, I was almost positive he did. So, what the hell was I supposed to do? And why hadn't I grabbed my stun gun this morning when I'd left for work?

With a groan, I swung open my locker and grabbed my bag, fishing out my phone and the detective's card. I entered his personal number and paused, my thumb hovering over the *call* button. He'd said he'd been working a case all night. He was probably sleeping. I hadn't even seen the guy—maybe it *wasn't* actually him. He wasn't the only drop-dead gorgeous guy in this city. At least, that's what I told myself.

Exiting the pending call, I opened my texts and typed out a quick message. A text was a lot less urgent than a call, right? Like, hey, I might be in danger, but probs not.

It's Giselle. I think my stalker might be at my casino. What should I do if it is him?

Staring at the screen for a whole minute, I finally pressed send and tucked the phone into my back pocket. We weren't supposed to carry cell phones when we were on the floor, but I wasn't about to get caught in a bad situation with no way to call for help. I might have had shitty luck, but I wasn't stupid.

My mind wandered until all I could see was Mark's face. He was seriously easy on the eyes—second hottest guy I'd seen in months. His jaw was nearly as chiseled as the rest of his body, ending in one of those cleft "butt" chins. I'd never found them all that attractive in the past, but on him it fit. About the only thing on him that wasn't hard was the soft curls of his sandy blond hair. They spoke of his playful nature. That and the gleam in his deep green eyes.

The thought alone had me smirking, even through the possibility of my stalker being here. Mark Jenson had a carefree air about him, and he seemed to know just what to say to put a smile on my face.

It was clear he was interested in me. I'd been on this Earth long enough to recognize the signs men gave off.

Plus, he'd damn near come right out and said it when he'd given me his personal number. And then offered to walk me to work. And bought me a coffee. And spent most of the time staring at my ass.

But his interest in me didn't change the fact that he was a cop. It was a real shame, but I didn't mess with heroes. It was a hard limit for me. Not that I hadn't found a few appealing ones over the years—noble, honest, brave men who wanted a go at me. I'd tried once. Years ago, I'd gone on a few dates with a firefighter. Then he got trapped in a burning building and nearly died. His crew said it was the first time he'd ever been injured on the job. I couldn't help but feel like it had something to do with me.

I wasn't stupid. I knew it could have just been a coincidence. But if there was even a chance that I was a danger to someone who already lived in the line of fire, the answer was no. I was better off with my morally gray book boyfriends. They didn't seem bothered by my shitty ass luck. Mostly because they weren't actually real.

But real or not, they could get me off just the same. Well, *almost* the same.

Maybe I could try what Laurel had said. Something casual and quick to fill those baser instincts. It really had been far too long for me. And maybe it would help get my stalker out of my damn mind.

Why did that feel like an impossibility at this point?

A buzzing sound pulled me out of my thoughts and I scrambled to pull my phone out.

Stay around other people. Public places are best. I'll pick you up from work. What time do you get off?

Whenever you get me off. Or at least, that's what the horny teenager living inside of me wanted to say. The adult in me responded with *3 o'clock.*

"Okay," I told myself, tucking my phone back into my pocket. "Stay in public. Right. He isn't going to hurt me in the middle of a crowded place."

A quick look around the locker room told me I was anything but *in public*. In fact, I was completely and totally alone. An easy target. Oops. I really wasn't so good at the whole stalker life thing. In my defense, it wasn't exactly something they taught in school.

Swinging my bag onto my shoulder, I slammed my locker shut and rushed back to the smoke-filled casino before my stalker had a chance to find me and corner me.

Forcing myself to move casually, I strolled through the casino, heading in the direction of my normal lunch break spot. It was about as public as I could get for this city. As the midmorning sun hit my face, I was happy to see there were even more people outside than there were in. Even on a Monday, there would still be crowds in this city.

I kept my pace calm, sticking to the thickest parts of the crowd as I headed toward my favorite reading spot right in front of the Bellagio.

Plopping down on my usual perch in front of the fountain, I pulled out my Kindle and settled in. I spent nearly every lunch break in this spot, catching up on my reading. It was a nice reprieve from the cigarette smoke and noise of the casino. Today, however, I found myself doing more people watching than I did page turning.

I scanned the many passersby for the umpteenth time. He was out there somewhere in the sea of people. I could feel it.

He was probably watching me right this second.

I wasn't even going to begin to psychoanalyze why that sent heat pooling throughout my entire stupid body.

Maybe it was time to switch over to sweet, happily-ever-after rom-coms for a while. Too many morally gray book boyfriends lately. They were a bad influence on a girl. I needed some nice, boy-next-door type of men in my life. Like Mark.

But why did nice seem so totally and completely boring?

Time ticked by slowly and quickly. It felt like I'd been sitting there for hours waiting for someone to attack me and yet, before I knew it, my alarm was going off to get back to work.

I stood, slipping my Kindle into my bag before slinging it over my shoulder. The second I turned toward my work, I felt it. A heavy gaze on my back, piercing me right between the shoulder blades.

Trying to be as discreet as possible, I brushed my ponytail off my shoulder and glanced behind me. I couldn't see him but I knew he was there.

This was getting old. Was this how my life would be now—spending every waking moment looking over my shoulder? I couldn't afford to move anywhere else yet. And besides, this city—as fucked up as it could be at times

—was my home. Was I going to let this asshat of a man run me out of my own home?

No.

I wasn't a damn victim.

I kept my pace slow as I weaved my way back toward my place of work, still feeling my stalker's presence behind me. Shivers raced up and down my spine, telling me he was closer, until soon a massive shadow hovered just behind mine. I scooted to the right and so did the shadow. I shifted left, and the shadow moved left too.

When I could practically feel his hot breath on the back of my head, my brain screamed for me to run.

Predator! Predator! Move your damn ass before he turns yours into a pillow!

But I didn't. Because when the grizzly came for you, you didn't run. You stood your ground. You got bigger, meaner, and tougher. You showed no fear.

Having a few hundred people on the street around me was also a definite advantage. Power in numbers and all that jazz.

Taking a deep breath, I spun around and damn near faceplanted into the wall of muscle that was my stalker. His intense gray eyes registered the briefest moment of shock before hardening once more.

Being the genius that I was, I took a single step back and then jabbed a finger into my stalker's granite-carved chest. I vaguely remembered Mark telling me *not* to provoke the man following me.

Oops. I never was good at following orders.

"Look, buddy," I snapped, shoving my finger into him

again, "I don't know what your deal is, but back the fuck off. If you're interested in me, you're going about it all wrong. If you're planning to wear my head as a hat, well, just…no. I've already alerted the authorities. Find someone else to follow around. Or, you know, don't. It's creepy as fuck."

I finally yanked my hand away from him, not liking the way my skin tingled where it touched his. It felt way too good.

His stormy eyes narrowed on me, a low growl reverberating from his chest. Damn it all to Hell and back if that small sound didn't do many delicious things to my lady bits. Why were growly men so hot?

He reached up and I flinched away from him. His hand hovered a few inches from my cheek, almost like he was afraid to touch me. Was he really ballsy enough to harm me in public like this?

"I see the fires of Hell in your eyes," he finally said, and my knees literally went weak, my toes curling in my work shoes as that deep voice washed over me. Holy hell, he had a voice that could make an angel sin.

"Um, yeah," I said, struggling to draw breath. He was even more breathtaking up close. Despite my body's desire to inch closer to him, I forced myself to step out of his reach. "My eyes are a bit unique in color. Is that why you're stalking me? Because of my eyes?"

"Stalking?" He said the word like it was foreign to him, which only proved how insane and/or delusional he really was.

"Yeah," I drawled, taking another small step back to

put more distance between us. A little farther and I might be able to get away. "That's what it's called when you follow someone around like a crazy person."

Maybe not the best idea to call the person stalking me "crazy." I was a slow learner.

His hand whipped out faster than I could follow. Next thing I knew, he had a death grip on my upper arm, yanking me forward until my front was pressed flush against his. Yeah, that wasn't helping the situation with my lady bits at all.

Seriously, who needed that many muscles? And why the hell did having him pressed against me with said muscles feel so damn familiar? It took everything in me not to arch into him as another growl slipped past his full lips.

"Let go of me," I said through clenched teeth, trying to pull away from him. "I swear to God, I'll scream."

He gave me a hard shake. "You will not use the Lord's name, vile demon."

Demon?

I blinked up at him. Yep, definitely hadn't been expecting that. This guy really was crazy.

"Dude, you've clearly got issues with women," I breathed. "I'd suggest a good shrink if I were you."

"Silence," he hissed and a few people glanced our way. I knew all I had to do was scream and someone would help me. And yet, I found I liked having him so close. It felt as natural as breathing. Like I was created for this messed-up dance we were doing.

Yep, I was going to Hell.

He inched his face closer until his lips grazed the edge of my ear, his short scruff scratching against my cheek. "I will send you back to Hell where you belong," he whispered and I shuddered against him.

It took longer than it should have for it to register in my stupid brain that he'd just threatened me.

Shaking the last of my lust-filled haze, I shoved him away and yanked free of his grip. I reared back, bringing the palm of my hand against his cheek, the slap echoing off the nearest building. That definitely turned a few heads. Everyone loved to see a lovers' quarrel.

I was prepared for his rage; what I hadn't prepared for was the absolute shock on his face or the confusion in his eyes.

"I'm not interested," I all but shouted. "Stay away from me. I'm warning you."

With that I stormed off down the strip, resisting the urge to look back. As if my day couldn't get any worse, I was going to be late coming back from my break.

GISELLE

Just my luck, I clocked back in ten minutes late from my break. Which meant my boss told me I'd have to stay over an hour after my shift to make up for it. How ten minutes equated to an hour was beyond me. They likely just wanted to find a way to keep their big money-maker at a table. Arguing was pointless; I needed the job.

I didn't bother flashing any fake smiles as I dealt cards to my newest group of victims. What was the point? I wasn't going to be getting any tips regardless. And I had enough on my plate as it was with the whole being-threatened-by-my-stalker thing. I didn't have the brain-power left over to worry about pleasing people who wanted to gamble away all their money. All I could think about was clocking out and leaving.

I'd shot a text to Detective Jenson, letting him know about the change in time but leaving out the details of what had happened with my stalker. I had a feeling if he'd known, he would have come over immediately and demanded I leave work early. That or sat and watched over me while I finished my shift.

The idea of him watching me wasn't such a bad one. But I still felt it was best to discuss what had happened in person. I could use the time to process it myself. Years' worth, maybe longer.

"Miss?" One of my patrons tapped a chip on the felt table. It was the only one he had left to his name. He looked at me expectantly.

"Oh, sorry," I mumbled, flipping over my cards. "Dealer wins again," I announced, much to the dismay of those sitting at my table.

"Is my buddy Giselle being mean to you nice folks again?" Laurel teased as she descended on my table like the angel she was with her tray of goodies and her perfect smile. "How about another round of drinks to cheer everyone up? I'll make sure the bartender makes them extra strong," she added with a wink.

One of the gamblers stood, shaking his head. "Nah, I'm out." He tossed his last dollar onto Laurel's tray, glaring at me as he did. Turning on his heels, he stormed off the casino floor, likely heading back to his room.

Laurel flashed me a sympathetic look as she tucked the tip into her apron. She glanced at her watch and then furrowed her brows at me. She knew I was supposed to be off already. I just shrugged in response and she headed off to get more alcohol for those left at my table.

I thankfully only had to endure another few hands before my replacement came. The second he showed up, I rushed to my locker where there were thankfully a few bodies shuffling around, preparing for the early evening shift. I grabbed my things and sent a quick text to the detective before rushing out of the locker room and through the casino.

The second I stepped outside, I took in a deep breath of semi-fresh air before glancing down the way to where I'd confronted my stalker. He was gone, of course. Maybe that was all it took, standing up to him—letting him know I had no interest in him.

I almost laughed. Like anything in my life was ever that damn easy.

A red sedan whipped into the valet parking entrance and Mark stepped out. Like some gallant knight, he rounded the car, opening the passenger side door.

I took a small step back even as he motioned me forward.

"Um, I don't really do cars," I told him for the second time. Bad things tended to happen when I got into vehicles. Or around them in general.

He closed the space between us and took my hand in his. "I promise I'm an excellent driver. A pro, really. That's why they pay me the big bucks."

My eyes traveled from him, back to the car. "I don't know..."

He gave my hand a reassuring squeeze and pulled me forward. "Trust me."

And the scary thing was, I *did* trust him. There weren't many people in this world I could say that about. Maybe it had something to do with his kind eyes, or the fact that he was one of the few who believed me about my stalker. Or maybe it was because he not only believed me, but wanted to protect me.

When had anyone in my life ever wanted to protect me—to stand in my corner?

After another moment of hesitation, I gave him a small nod. He grinned and it eased my growing nerves the slightest bit.

He led me to the car and held the door as I dropped into the passenger seat. Once I was settled, he shut the door and moved around to the driver's side. He'd better be as good a driver as he thought. He was going to need those skills with me as a passenger.

"Was it him?" he asked once he got into the car, getting straight to the point. I appreciated that he didn't try to small talk me about my day or the weather. There were more pressing issues going on. Like the guy following me around and threatening to send me to Hell. "You said you thought he might have been here."

I nodded, fidgeting with my bag as we pulled out of the parking lot. "My coworker saw someone watching me. I took my lunch break in as public of a spot as I could—just like you said to do. He ended up following me there. I might have *maybe* confronted him on my way back..."

"You did what?" His officer voice was coming out. He sounded all business as he swerved around a car that randomly stopped in front of us. I found myself grabbing the oh-shit bar and holding onto it with white-knuckled fingers. I'd been in my fair share of accidents. I really didn't want to add another one to the list.

"I simply told him I wasn't interested and to leave me alone."

Okay, so maybe I didn't use so few words. And maybe I'd called him crazy. And yelled at him. And slapped him.

Semantics.

"Did he say anything to you?"

I nodded again before I realized that he was driving and I didn't want him looking away from the road.

"Yeah," I said. "He called me a demon and said he was going to send me back to Hell."

He made a turn and it dawned on me that I'd never told him where I was staying.

"Where are we going?" I asked, noticing we weren't heading in the direction of the police station either.

"My place," he said simply.

Someone was full of himself. "Um, you could just take me back to my place."

"This guy has officially threatened you," he said, making another turn and heading farther away from the strip. "If there's any chance that you're right and he was at your hotel last night, there's no way I'm taking you there. You can stay with me for the night. If you aren't comfortable with that, I can put you up in a hotel," he added, glancing at me.

"Eyes on the road!" I snapped. With perfect timing, a sports car darted in front of us, running their red light. Mark slammed on the brakes, his arm swinging out to keep me against my seat as his red sedan squealed to a stop.

The detective shot me a look and I shrugged. "I told you, I don't like cars. You can say that I'm a bit…accident prone."

He huffed out a laugh but there wasn't much humor in it as he cautiously eased through the intersection.

"So, what do you want to do? Stay at my place tonight or should I find you a hotel?"

I chewed on the corner of my lip. I didn't really want to tell the guy I didn't have the money to drop on a nice hotel room right now. And I definitely didn't want him offering to pay for a room for me—which I knew he would.

"Your place is fine," I finally told him, which seemed to make him happy. "We can figure out a better long-term solution tomorrow," I quickly added. I couldn't keep paying money for my current room just to avoid staying there for fear of what this creep might do.

Maybe I could convince Chad to let me change rooms. There had to be other rundown rooms he'd be willing to part with. Though he'd probably try to take the opportunity to start charging me more. Plus, there was the whole thing about him claiming I owed him last week's rent. Which I most certainly did not.

"I should probably swing by my place though to grab a

few things," I said, staring out the window. "I don't have any clothes or toiletries with me."

He was quiet for a moment before giving a stiff nod.

I rambled off the directions to my hotel and he flipped a bitch.

We drove in silence until we reached my place. I hopped out of the car the second Mark put it in park, earning a growl from the detective. Sue me, I wasn't used to chivalry.

And I needed out of the metal death trap.

Mark jumped out after me, jogging to catch up. He clearly didn't plan to let me out of his sight. It was endearing and only a little stifling.

"Slow down," he hissed, grabbing my wrist and tugging me back to his side. "We don't know if your stalker is waiting here for you."

I bit back my smart-assed response, knowing he was just doing his job to keep me alive. That didn't stop me from rolling my eyes.

I pulled out of his grip and walked alongside him in the direction of my hotel room. We rounded the last corner and I hit the brakes so hard, I felt my brain smash into the front of my skull.

"What the actual fuck?"

Bright red tape was plastered all over my door, along with an ungodly large eviction notice. Sitting in front of the window were three black garbage bags filled with all of my possessions. That was it—everything I owned fit into three damn bags.

"Son of a..." I mumbled, stomping over to the door.

Whipping out my keycard, I tried to stick it in the slot, despite the fact that there were two new locks along the doorframe. It buzzed red and I cursed under my breath.

"What's going on?"

"What does it look like, Detective?" I snapped and then blew out a breath. "Sorry," I muttered, seeing the mix of pity and surprise in his eyes. It wasn't his fault that my ex-foster brother was being a royal demon dick—whatever the hell that even meant.

I was so pissed I wasn't even thinking clearly.

I stared at the door for another minute like I could somehow open it with my mind. Throwing a fist into the old wood, I spun on my heels and stormed toward the lobby to give Chad a piece of my mind.

"Where are you going?" Mark said to my retreating backside.

"I've got a bone to pick with management," I shot back.

A minute later, I was kicking open the door to the shabby, outdated lobby. It probably wasn't the best idea to be kicking open doors with an officer of the law chasing after me, but I didn't really give a shit at that point. What could the detective do—arrest me? At least in jail, I'd be safe from my stalker for the night.

Wouldn't be the first time I'd spent the night behind bars. And probably wouldn't be the last if I was being honest with myself.

"What the hell are you doing, Giselle?" Chad yelled as he burst out of his office.

"What reason do you have to evict this woman?" Mark

said before I could get a word out. He stepped in front of me, pinning Chad with a hard stare.

My ex-foster brother huffed, stumbling over his words. "She didn't pay rent. When people don't pay rent, they get evicted. I gave her an extra few days."

"I paid!"

"Bullshit, Elle," he shot back, hands going to his hips.

"Don't call me that," I ground out. That nickname was for friends only. Not that I really had many of those, but still. "And you know damn well I paid!"

Mark shifted his full attention to me. Those green eyes were full of pity and I felt my cheeks flush. I didn't need anyone's sympathy for my living or financial situation. I didn't have insurance, and medical bills added up when you were this damn clumsy. The handful of times I'd been robbed didn't help much either. But this was my life and I was used to it by now. I got by. I had nothing to be ashamed of, thank you very much.

"Do you have proof?" he asked.

I was getting sick of that word: *proof.* Sometimes shit just happened and there wasn't a way to prove it.

"No," I told him. "I pay each week in cash. And I'm never late," I added, pinning Chad with a glare.

Chad shrugged, crossing his arms over his growing beer gut. "I gave notice that you were behind and you didn't pay up. So, you can find somewhere else to stay."

"You also said I had until Wednesday!" I shot back at him. The detective's fingers wrapped around my arm, pulling me back a step.

The asshole in the room shrugged a second time and,

if it weren't for the officer standing behind me, I likely would have taken a swing at him. Even with Mark here, I still contemplated hitting Chad. Maybe the detective would turn the other way for me. I just needed five minutes alone with the guy.

"Changed my mind," Chad said with a smirk. "It's my hotel, I can do that. And besides, you don't have a lease. You can either pay what you owe, plus late fees, or you can take your shit and leave."

"Did you give her a seven-day notice?" Mark's voice was deadly soft and all business, sending chills racing down my spine. Would hate to be the perps this man had to deal with regularly. "File a court order? Anything? You can't just change the locks; it's against the law."

"Look here, buddy," Chad started and then snapped his big pie hole shut when Mark whipped out his badge. Yeah, I couldn't lie. Watching Mark assert his dominance over this asshole was a glorious sight.

"She doesn't have a lease," Chad sputtered, turning red in the face. "She isn't even a tenant."

Bold. Faced. Lie.

"I've stayed here for *years*," I snapped.

Chad seemed to regain a bit of confidence. "There's no record of you being here that long, and you have no proof of payment. Face it, Giselle, you got nothing. So, you can either pay up, along with the five hundred dollars in fees, or you can get. The. Fuck. Out."

"Five hundred dollars?" I shrieked. What the hell was he smoking?

Mark bent low, his lips grazing my ear. While the

subtle touch felt good, it didn't have nearly the same effect on me as it had when my stalker did it. "Deal with him in court," he told me. "Let's get your stuff and go."

I blew out a breath. I knew he was right. Chad didn't keep records of anything. It was currently his word against mine. And my word came with some horrible luck.

Jabbing a finger at Chad, I narrowed my eyes at him. "This isn't over, you gambling piece of shit. You'll pay for this."

"Bitch," he spat. "That's why no one has ever wanted you. Even as a child."

He barely got the words out before Mark had him pressed against the wall, one large hand fisted in Chad's shirt.

"Watch your mouth," he hissed, shoving Chad into the wall once more before releasing him and taking a step back. "You won't talk to her like that."

Ignoring Chad's empty threats and slew of curse words, Mark wrapped an arm around my shoulders and pulled me out of the lobby.

The second we got outside, I turned to face him. "He's going to try to sue you for that."

The detective snorted. "Let him try. His slimy word against mine."

With a wink, Mark took my hand and led me back to my old room. He scooped up my three pathetic-looking bags of stuff and carried them back to his car, never once releasing my hand. Tossing the bags into the backseat, he held open the passenger door for me.

"Let's get you out of here," he said, flashing me that panty-melting smile of his. But even that smile couldn't hide the pity that still shimmered in his green eyes. "One problem at a time," he continued. "First, we deal with the stalker threat. Then I'll help you destroy that piece of shit hotel owner."

GISELLE

"You can stay with me for as long as you need," Mark said as he pulled up to his condo.

"I don't need handouts," I muttered, unable to meet his eyes as he turned to face me.

He put a hand on my thigh and gave it a light squeeze. "I didn't mean it like that," he assured me. "If you want to get a hotel for a while, that's fine too. I just mean that I'm here if you need me. Unless you snore, in which case the offer is rescinded."

I couldn't resist the smile tugging at my lips at his attempt at lightening the increasingly darkening mood.

"One night," I told him before adding, "Thank you."

He slipped out of the car and moved around quickly to open my door for me before I got the chance to open it myself. After I stepped out, he reached into the backseat and grabbed my bags.

"I can carry those," I said, reaching for the bags that held my entire life. I wondered if my stun gun was somewhere inside of one of them. After my encounter with my stalker, I wasn't sure I wanted to go anywhere without it ever again.

"I've got it," he said.

He led me to his condo and unlocked the door, ushering me inside.

"Sorry," he said, scratching at the back of his head as we stepped into the small but modern condo. "There's only one bedroom. I might have exaggerated when I said they paid me the big bucks."

The dirty bookworm in me smirked at the thought of one bed. It was my favorite trope. It was almost enough to make me forget about having a psychopathic stalker who wanted to send me to Hell and a piece of shit ex-foster brother who was tossing my ass to the curb.

Almost.

"So, who was that guy anyway?" he asked, setting my bags down and locking the door behind me.

I peeked down the short hallway into his living room. It was cleaner than I expected, with very few personal effects. In fact, it felt a bit cold—like one of the many hotel rooms on the strip. There weren't even any photos on the walls. I got the impression Mark probably didn't spend too much time here.

"He's my ex-foster brother," I finally said.

"He's family?" The surprise in his voice was evident.

I snorted. "No. Hence the *ex*. I really shouldn't even label him as that. His family took me in for less than a year when I was a teenager. He let me stay at the hotel since he felt bad about his parents not adopting me. It isn't even the first time he's pulled this shit."

Chad had tried to get more money out of me a few times. Each time had been when he'd fallen back into his old habits. He liked to play the ponies. This was just the first time he actually followed through with his threats to kick me out.

It hurt more than I cared to admit. Because as much as I said otherwise, Chad really was the closest thing I had to family. Even if he was a prick.

"Fuck him," Mark muttered, moving farther into the condo. I followed him through the living room and into the kitchen, watching as he went straight to a cabinet above his fridge. He opened it and pulled down a bottle of whiskey.

"Do you drink?" he asked, glancing at me over his shoulder.

I hopped up on one of the three barstools and planted my elbows on the counter. "Have you not seen the state of my life?" I said, cocking an eyebrow at him.

He chuckled, reaching back up and grabbing two shot glasses. Closing the cabinet, he turned and set the glasses on the counter in front of me. He opened the whiskey bottle and poured two very heavy shots before placing the bottle on the counter, leaving the cap off.

I rested my chin on the backs of my hands. "Trying to get me drunk, Jenson?"

"I told you to call me Mark," he said, picking up his glass.

Grabbing my own glass, I clinked it against his and tossed it back.

I nearly moaned as the liquid fire burned going down my throat. Then I recognized the sweet aftertaste.

"Peanut butter?" I asked and he smirked, downing his own shot and pouring each of us another.

A strange sound—low and rumbly—came from somewhere in the condo and I jolted where I sat, much to the obvious amusement of the detective standing across from me.

"Don't worry," he said. "That's Sasha."

"Sasha?"

"My dog," he responded casually. I'd forgotten he'd told me back at the station that he shared his place with a furry critter. "She's in her crate in my bedroom."

"That wasn't a dog," I shot back. "That sounded like a fucking velociraptor."

Mark laughed. "She's a big girl, but harmless to those on the right side of the law," he added with a wink. "She's probably pissed that I haven't let her out yet. She likes to be the center of attention in my life. Plus, you used the name of her favorite snack. I'll let her out a little later and you can meet her."

As if the beast could understand him, she calmed, her deep barks and growls turning into whines. I still wasn't convinced it was a dog. I loved animals, really, I did. But I'd been bitten numerous times in my life. I was pretty sure if Mark let Sasha out, she would instantly decide I was a perpetrator and eat my heart for dinner.

"Tell me about yourself," he said once Sasha settled

back down. He leaned a narrow hip against the counter, green eyes boring into me. "What do you do when you aren't being chased around Las Vegas by a deranged stalker or working in a casino?"

"Or being blatantly hit on by the detective helping me with said stalker?"

He didn't bother correcting me, a grin stretching across his handsome face. He really did have a nice smile. What would my stalker's smile look like?

Nope. Not going there.

"I read," I finally told him, taking the second shot. This time I did moan, my eyelids fluttering closed as I savored the amber liquid. Damn, that stuff was good.

When I opened my eyes, Detective Jenson was looking at me intently, his pupils dilated. I caught my lower lip between my teeth and he tracked the movement.

Why did that feel so familiar? And why did it make me once again think of my stalker?

I cleared my throat, pushing my glass in his direction. I lived in Vegas—I could hold my liquor. He grabbed the bottle and quickly refilled me.

"What about you, Detective?" I asked, knocking back my shot. The whiskey hit my stomach, sending tendrils of heat spreading throughout my body. "What do you do when you aren't being a hero and hitting on the woman whose case you're working?"

The smile slipped from his lips and I worried I'd taken it too far.

Mark set his shot glass down. "Giselle, I don't do this with everyone. This is a first for me. I want you to know that. If my boss knew I was doing this, I could lose my job."

That hadn't been the response I was expecting.

"Then why are you doing it?" The words came out as no more than a whisper.

"I don't know," he said and I could hear the truth in his words. "Do you believe in fate?"

All I could do was shrug. I wasn't really sure if I believed in it or not. Nothing in my life ever really seemed to work out for me. Fate was always just out of reach, working its elusive magic for others. Never me.

"There's something about you," he continued, scrubbing a hand down the side of his face. I noticed for the first time that he'd shaved. "It's something I can't put my finger on. You feel…familiar. *Right.* I know it sounds crazy, but it's like I was meant to find you. Like we're connected somehow.

"And this is probably the absolute worst thing to say to someone who's dealing with a stalker right now," he rushed to say, panic flickering through his kind eyes. "I'm not trying to creep you out, I promise. I just… I feel like maybe this is where we are both supposed to be right this moment."

The sincerity on his face was something I wasn't used to seeing in my life. It sent a warmth spreading through my chest. A foreign sensation for me.

"You wear your emotions right on your sleeve," I said when I found my voice. "I've never met a man like that before."

He flashed me a smile but it seemed forced. "Major turn-off?"

"Not at all," I replied. "It's refreshing. I wish more were like that."

He poured us each another shot, cradling his in one big hand and staring into the amber liquid. "When I was just a little kid, I nearly died. It was a freak accident I never should have walked away from. My mom always used to tell me that an angel saved me. She instilled in me that each day I spent on this Earth was a blessing, and that I should live it like it was my last because angels didn't always come twice."

"Your mom sounds pretty amazing."

"She was," he said with a sad smile. "She passed a few years ago. Cancer."

I grabbed the shot he'd poured for me and held it up. "To living each day like it's our last."

He clinked his glass to mine and we quickly threw them back. Setting his shot glass down, Mark rounded the counter. In three long strides, he was standing in front of me, taking my hand and pulling me from the barstool until my body was flush against his. I was surprised to feel his rather impressive length digging into my lower stomach.

And that wasn't the only part of him that was hard. Though I noted that his muscular body wasn't quite as chiseled from granite as my stalker's was, and he wasn't quite as tall. And my skin didn't light up wherever it touched his.

What would it feel like to have my stalker's hands plastered to my naked flesh? Would he be bigger in every aspect?

I forced those thoughts away, scolding myself for thinking about another man—a *psychotic* one at that—while standing pressed against Mark. A man who clearly wanted me and whose touch most definitely still had some effect on me if the moisture building between my legs was any indicator. Or was that because my mind kept wandering back to my stalker?

"If you don't want this," Mark said, putting one hand under my chin and tipping my head back so I was forced to meet his eyes, "tell me now. I won't do anything you don't want. But if you'll let me, I'll do my best to distract you from everything you've got going on."

A distraction was exactly what I needed. Anything to keep my mind off the man following me. Bonus that it was a distraction with someone like Mark.

I answered by reaching up and tangling my fingers into his sandy curls, yanking his face down until his lips crashed into mine.

I don't know what I was expecting to feel when I kissed Mark, but nothing wasn't it. And that was exactly what I'd felt. *Nothing.* No butterflies, no rush of heat. Not even the slightest spark. Even my stupid stalker had set off a whole slew of sinful fireworks deep inside me. And that was just from one touch. It was as if my ridiculously high sex drive had just…shut off for the first time in my life.

Mark didn't seem to be as unaffected as me. He caught up quickly, his mouth moving over mine with wild fervor.

His large hands slipped down my hips, splaying over my ass and pulling me tighter to him. His tongue slipped into my mouth and I wiggled against him, hoping to feel something—*anything*.

But I didn't need fireworks right now. I just needed to forget the shit show that was my life for a little while. Mark was giving me that opportunity.

I arched into him, grinding my hips over the bulge in his jeans. His fingers dug into the flesh of my ass, a groan slipping past his lips. I couldn't help but wonder if I'd elicit the same response from my stalker.

"No," I breathed and Mark froze.

His mouth left mine almost immediately. "Do you want me to stop?" he asked, his voice thick with desire. He most definitely didn't want to stop. But I knew he would if I asked him to. Because he was the boy-next-door. A good man. The kind of guy I *should* be with.

Even if that wasn't what I found myself wanting.

"Should I stop?" he asked again, his breath hot on my face.

Yes, I wanted to tell him. But my stupid mouth said, "No."

Mark reclaimed my lips the second the word left them. He backed me toward the leather sofa, breaking the kiss to gently push me onto it. He sprawled his big body on top of mine before kissing me again. Where I expected more fire and urgency, his lips moved over mine languidly—soft and sweet. Like we had all the time in the world.

The entire atmosphere in the room changed with that

one kiss. In an instant, we went from a hot and heavy fling to… Something I wasn't ready for.

I wasn't ready for any of this.

I didn't date first responders. Hell, I hardly dated at all. No one was safe from my shitty life. This was just supposed to be a fun distraction. A quick fling.

I wrapped my arms around the back of his neck and tried to pick up the pace, but he was having none of it. His mouth moved from my lips to my neck, each kiss feather light as his lips trailed lower and lower.

It was too much. I wasn't sure I could handle much more intimacy. I needed fast and hard and rough. This was bordering on lovemaking. I did *not* make love. Ever. It wasn't in my nature.

Mark's hand slid under my shirt and my eyes fluttered shut, my mind wandering to my stalker once more. And this time I let it. I was sick of fighting it. I needed his wild intensity to distract me from what was supposed to be my distraction from *him*.

I found myself wondering what it would feel like if it were his hands on me instead. Mark's touch wasn't bad, don't get me wrong, but it didn't make my skin tingle like my stalker's had. A moan slipped past my lips as I remembered the way his rock-hard body pressed up against mine when he'd found me on the strip, my body arching off the sofa.

I felt Mark grin against the hollow of my throat, clearly thinking it was in response to him. I should have felt a lot guiltier than I did. In fact, I didn't feel guilty at all. All I felt was my skin heating as I imagined my stalker's piercing gray eyes watching me, his big hands working me higher and higher.

A low growl reverberated through the condo, and at first, I thought it came from the detective until I realized it was coming from the direction of the bedroom. Mark froze where he was, his fingers hovering over the button of my pants.

The growl grew more menacing and the man on top of me leaped into action, hopping off the sofa and diving for his entertainment center. A second later, there was a pistol gripped in his hand.

"What's going on?" I asked, shooting upright.

"I don't know," he said right before glass shattered somewhere in his condo. Sasha started howling and I could hear her banging against her crate, trying to break free.

Mark grabbed me and hoisted me up off the sofa. Almost immediately, he shoved me to the ground, tucking my body between the edge of the sofa and the wall.

"Stay here!" he hissed before taking off.

I scooted back until I collided with the wall. Tucking my knees into my chest, I waited, listening for any little sound coming from Mark's condo. The pounding of footsteps coming toward the sofa had my heart racing and my eyes searching for anything I could use as a weapon.

Something large and furry lunged for me and I spun away from it, shielding my face. When an attack didn't come, I peeked out from the ball I'd curled into. Big brown eyes met mine, the behemoth of a dog sitting on the floor staring at me like it was ready for playtime.

"Um, hi?"

"All clear," Mark said as he stepped back into the living room, tucking the pistol into the back of his jeans and pulling his shirt over it. "Sasha, come."

The dog yipped once, rushing over to sit obediently at Mark's feet. Her eyes watched him carefully, waiting for his next command. I wondered if she used to be his K-9 when he was still a cop. He reached down and gave her a pet, his eyes glued to me.

"What happened?" I asked, scrambling to get off the floor.

Mark's face was grim, eyes hard. I was dealing with Detective Jenson now. "Someone smashed in my bedroom window," he answered.

"Shit," I breathed. "Do you think there's any chance it's a coincidence?"

Even as I said the words, I knew it wasn't. It was my stalker—it had to be. He'd followed us here. He was getting bolder.

"We should check you into a hotel," Mark said instead of answering me. "I'd rather be safe than sorry when it comes to you. I told you I'd keep you safe and I intend to do just that. Let's go."

I took a shaky breath and followed him toward the front door. My feet faltered in front of his open bedroom door, my eyes landing on the shattered glass all over his bedroom carpet. The window was all but gone.

"I'm so sorry, Mark," I whispered, grabbing my bags from where we left them by the front door. "This is all my fault."

He whirled around on me. "Don't," he snapped, and I took a small step back. "This is *not* your fault. This is that piece of shit's doing. He's doing this *to* you. None of this is on you. You're the victim here. So, don't start apologizing. I don't regret anything—not bringing you here, or what we did. Or almost did," he added. I knew men enough to tell he was definitely regretting us being interrupted.

He forced a smile and took my hand, squeezing it.

"It's going to be okay," he told me. "Let's get you somewhere to stay for a few nights. I'll put a protective detail on you. Someone will guard your door at all times."

"You aren't going to stay with me?"

Mark leaned forward and kissed my forehead, taking my bags from me like the perfect gentleman he was. "I have to go to the station and deal with all this first. Reports need to be filed. I'll come check on you after, but it might take a while."

He paused, looking at his dog and then back to me. "I want you to take Sasha with you."

I opened my mouth to protest but he held a hand up. "Please. It would make me feel better knowing she was with you. She'll keep you safe until I get back to you. Besides, I can't keep her here with the place like this."

The dog at his feet smiled up at me, her tongue hanging out to one side. She wasn't nearly as scary looking now as she'd sounded before. I was pretty sure she was a German shepherd, but I wasn't positive. I didn't know the first thing about dogs or how to take care of them. I didn't dislike them; I was always just too afraid to have one, worried it would attack me or end up getting hit by a car.

Pursing my lips, I blew out a breath and nodded. As if the dog knew, she trotted over to me and sat at my feet.

Guess I was a temporary dog mom now.

LUCAS

I'd never experienced rage like what I'd felt when I watched "Giselle" walk into the detective's condo with him. Once again, his hands seemed to have been glued to her.

What had she been thinking? Allowing herself to be alone with him like that? He'd clearly had only one thing on his mind. And he'd nearly gotten it. If it weren't for me, he likely would have.

I really shouldn't have been surprised. She was her mother's daughter—a vile temptress. The woman could make a saint sin. She'd done it many times before. This was nothing new. Besides, she was there with him by choice. She knew exactly what she was doing. She was luring him to his doom—corrupting his soul. That was what she *was*.

So, why had it filled me with so much anger? And why

did seeing him with his hands on her body make me want to burn the whole world to the ground to ensure that no man ever touched her again?

When he'd laid her out on the sofa, it had taken everything in me to resist breaking through his sliding glass door and tearing him off her. The only one touching her should be me.

With my blade.

But when she'd arched into him—just like she'd done to me so many years ago—I saw red. My control shattered, just like his window. It took everything in me to move to his bedroom. It was that or risk killing an innocent in my blind rage. Though the detective had proved he was anything but innocent.

The second he'd stepped into the bedroom to check what had happened, I'd circled around to the back door again. I needed her alone so I could end her. I needed to get the task over with and shake whatever this was that she was doing to me.

But what I had seen in that sliding glass window had stopped me in my tracks.

She'd looked absolutely terrified. Even from outside, I'd been able to see how her body trembled.

But what had really gotten me were the tears pooling in her wide eyes. Hundreds of years I'd chased her down and killed her—*hundreds*. Never in that time had I seen her cry. I didn't even know demons *could* cry.

Maybe it really *wasn't* her…

And if I killed an innocent instead of my mark—could I live with myself if I made that sort of critical mistake?

And what chance would I have at gaining the archangel position if I did? Then again, if it really was her and I didn't send her back to Hell, then I was failing at my God-given task.

I groaned from where I stood in the shadows across the street.

She was messing with my head yet again. I just needed to kill her and be done with it. Zain had already called me two more times in the past hour. I'd sent both calls to voicemail, not wanting to hear whatever it was he had to say. It wasn't his job to check in on me—not yet at least. And I'd make sure it never would be.

That archangel position was going to be mine, not his.

I watched as the detective escorted her out of his place, her bags clutched in one of his hands and a phone in the other. A large dog stepped out of the building behind him. With a nod of his head, the animal trotted over to my target and sat at her feet. She gave it an absent pat on the head.

"Yeah, send someone out to my place to keep an eye on it," the detective said into the device pressed to his ear. He locked the door and glanced at his broken window. "And call a glass company to get my window fixed too. Thanks, Ruiz. Yeah, I'm going to take her somewhere safe and then I'll be there. I'm going to shoot you the hotel information. Have Lance head over. I want him outside her room at all times, got it? Good."

Giselle stood at the bottom of the porch steps, eyes darting up and down the dark street. She knew it was me. She was a monster, but she wasn't stupid.

Even if she was playing dumb.

I took a slow step back, tucking farther into the shadows.

Maybe she really didn't remember. Was that possible? Could a demon be reborn without the knowledge of what they really were? As I watched her fumble with the car door handle, her hands shaking too hard to open it, I started to seriously consider that possibility.

No one was this good of an actor. Not even a demon of her power level.

But what would trigger that? Had it just happened, or did she have some sort of accident? Could demons suffer from amnesia like humans?

It didn't matter. She was still a demon. Her presence alone in this city was wreaking havoc on it, whether she was actively trying to or not.

She needed to die.

I just wasn't sure if I could complete the task with her in her current state. Which left me with only one option. I'd have to *make* her remember.

The detective stepped behind her, reaching around her and stilling her shaking hand. My stomach twisted as he bent low, whispering something into her ear. She visibly relaxed, blowing out a breath and nodding. He pulled the door open and helped her into her seat before tossing the bags in the back and letting the dog hop in.

A minute later he was peeling out of the driveway and speeding down the street. I didn't know where he planned to take her, but it didn't matter.

There was nowhere she could go that I couldn't find her. I'd always find her.

I took to the skies, following the red car through the darkness, heading back in the direction of the busy Las Vegas strip.

GISELLE

I was so damn bored.

There was only so much one could do in a fancy hotel room when they were alone. Well, mostly alone.

Sasha looked up at me from where she lay at the foot of the perfectly-made bed, her big head resting on her crossed paws. She seemed nearly as bored as I was.

Mark had insisted on booking me a room at the Cosmopolitan. He liked the level of security they had, plus they were dog-friendly with no size limit. Which was a good thing, seeing as Sasha was about the size of a small cow. I told him I'd pay for the room myself but he refused. He didn't want me using my cards anywhere in case my stalker was tracking them somehow. Which, at this point, was a likely possibility.

Not only had he covered the cost of the room, but he'd

booked me a room on the forty-fifth floor with a view of the Bellagio fountains. The man was by far too good for me.

He'd still been a bit on edge when he'd left me in the room. I knew he'd wanted to stay with me. Even with one of his officers standing guard outside my door and his behemoth dog on my bed, he didn't want to leave me. I also knew it was still bothering him that my stalker had been able to find his condo. And who wouldn't be upset about something like that?

There was something about knowing someone had broken into your safe space—your home. It was a violating sort of feeling. It was how I'd felt when I'd realized my stalker had figured out where I was living. I had no doubt the fucker would find me again here, but at least here there was added security.

Outside of general hotel security, he'd have to find my room and get past my protective watch—quite the task because Lance was a brick shithouse. That or he'd have to grow wings and fly because my balcony was the only other way in.

I was as safe as I was going to be here.

"And bored out of my fucking mind," I grumbled, huffing out a breath as I plopped down on the bed beside Sasha. I gave her a scratch behind the ear, grateful she had decided not to eat me for dinner. If things continued to go well with her, I might have to finally pull the trigger and get myself a pet. Maybe a goldfish to start.

"Speaking of dinner," I said, glancing at the bedside clock. It was already eleven. Mark had been gone for over three hours and the adrenaline had officially worn off, leaving me with some serious hunger pangs.

"Think Mr. Hulk out there would let me order some food?" I asked the dog. Her tail wagged once. "I'll take that as a yes."

I headed for the door and flipped the additional locks before poking my head out. Lance whipped his head my way, hand falling to the butt of his gun.

"I'm okay," I rushed to say, resisting the urge to scurry back into the safety of my room. He was a big man with muscles on top of muscles on top of more muscles. Dude could probably crush a person with a single finger. Mark assured me he was a big teddy bear. Right, more like a grizzly.

At least I didn't get stuck with Ruiz and his permanent scowl.

"What do you need, miss?" Lance asked.

"I'm pretty hungry," I told him, fidgeting with the door handle. "Do you think it would be okay to order some room service to be brought up?"

Hopefully he'd be smart enough to realize I wasn't actually asking. I was going to get food one way or another. Otherwise, he was going to have to deal with Hangry Elle. And that was far scarier than any stalker.

Lance cocked an eyebrow at me before glancing up and down the hall. "I guess that would be okay. I'll bring the cart in to you after I make sure it's safe."

"Want me to order you anything?" I asked. "It's on Jenson."

That earned me a snort—it was the closest I'd gotten

to a smile since the officer arrived. He was a hard one to crack. These were the most words he'd spoken to me. I'd tried a couple of times to strike up a conversation with him. The first time he'd told me to get back inside for my own safety. The second time he'd ignored me until I took the hint.

Which left me with the dog to talk to.

At least he took his job seriously. I should have been glad for that, seeing as his job was currently to keep me safe.

"I'm fine, miss," he told me. "You should go back in. I'll bring your food in when it comes."

With a nod, I slipped back into the room, flipping the extra locks back into place.

"All right, pooch," I said as I passed Sasha, "what do you want for dinner? Your daddy said you like peanut butter. What about bacon?"

Her big ears perked up at that one word. She lifted her head and gave me a soft woof.

"Breakfast for dinner it is," I said with a laugh. At least she had good taste. And she wasn't choosing to taste me. We were getting along just fine.

After ordering a smorgasbord of food for myself and the dog, I hopped onto the bed and grabbed the remote, flipping through the channels without really seeing what was on. It was something I'd done a few times since checking into the hotel. There wasn't much else to do.

Pace.

Channel surf.

Pet the danger floof.

Watch the pretty dancing fountain.

Fantasize about morally gray men who wanted to send me to Hell.

Scold myself for being an idiot.

Pace some more.

If Mark were here with me, I could think of many other—*more fun*—things I could be doing to pass the time. But he wasn't. Not yet at least. I wasn't sure how much longer he'd have to work before he'd be able to meet back up with me. Though, if I was being honest with myself, I wasn't sure I was ready to pick up where we'd left off. Not unless he was ready to drop the intimacy.

It probably didn't matter anyway. My stalker breaking into Mark's house was likely a permanent mood killer. Just my luck.

I found that didn't disappoint me nearly as much as it should have.

A knock on the door had me nearly jumping out of my skin. Sasha didn't even lift her big head.

"Some guard dog you are," I muttered, shoving off the bed and heading to the door. A quick look out the peephole showed Lance's well-shaved chin.

I fought with the locks and yanked the door open, my stomach growling as the smell of food crashed into me.

"Your food is here," he stated the obvious, pushing the silver cart into the room. Before it even stopped rolling, I had the cover off one of the many plates. My mouth watered at the sight of bacon.

"Wow," Lance said, inching his way back to the door.

"Wish I could find me a woman who looked at me the way you look at that bacon."

I flashed him a grin and shoved one entire piece into my mouth and groaned as it all but melted on my tongue. Now *that* was heaven.

"You sure you don't want any?" I asked around a mouth full of meat.

"I wouldn't dare come between a woman and her food."

I snorted. "Smart man."

Without another word, he closed the door. After a solid ten seconds, I heard him call in, "Lock the damn door."

Rolling my eyes, I flicked the locks into place and then turned my full attention to the steaming plates of deliciousness, the glorious scent of breakfast wafting through the room. It was a smell so wonderful that even Sasha, the world's laziest guard dog, perked her head up. She hopped off the bed and trotted over to me as I pushed the cart farther into the room. I clearly wasn't the only woman in the room who was bordering on hangry.

I set out the plates of food on the coffee table and Sasha made herself comfortable, sitting expectantly beside me. Her jaws snapped shut on the piece of bacon I tossed at her.

"You're lucky I like you," I told her.

A vibration tickled my backside and I reached into my rear pocket and pulled out my cell phone. Mark's name flashed across the screen.

"Hey," I said, biting into a piece of toast as Sasha whined next to me.

"How are you holding up?"

"I'm fattening up your dog," I said, handing said beastie a sausage which she happily took. "You clearly never feed her."

"She doesn't eat table scraps," he shot back.

"You mean like peanut butter?"

"Touché." I could hear the smile in his voice. It calmed my nerves and I exhaled the breath I didn't realize I'd been holding. "How are you doing? Are you okay?"

"I'm clearly not meant for solitude," I told him as I dove into the pancakes, rolling one up and dunking it into the cup of syrup. "I'm about an hour away from death by boredom."

"I'll be there as soon as I can," he replied, and I could tell how exhausted he was. "My guys didn't find any fingerprints or evidence at my place. We have no leads. Not sure where we go from here."

"I can't stay here, Mark." I didn't want to sound ungrateful, but I wasn't going to spend my life in hiding. As much as I was starting to feel like one, I was no victim. "I have to be back at work in a couple of days."

I refused to stop living my life. The second I did, this guy won.

"What you have to do is stay safe," Mark shot back and then sighed. "Sorry. I know this isn't easy. But clearly this man is unstable."

"How come we didn't see him following us?" I asked, pushing the food away. It was something that had been on my mind since I got to the hotel. My stalker had clearly followed me from either work or my old hotel room all the way to Mark's condo. How did neither of us notice someone tailing us? I mean, Mark was a damn *detective.* He'd been checking mirrors constantly as we drove. I knew because I'd kept yelling at him to keep his damn eyes on the road.

"I don't know," Mark finally answered. "I never saw anyone behind us."

A voice called out his name in the background.

"Shit," he muttered. "I have to go. Get some sleep. I'll try to get there by morning and we can figure out our next move. You might need to leave town for a while."

He hung up before I could say anything else, including telling him that I wasn't going anywhere. This fucked-up city was my home and always had been. Sure, there were other places I could go, but this city called to me. I couldn't explain it, I just knew this was where I belonged. I didn't want to leave. Besides, even if I did want to, I didn't have the funds to go somewhere.

I groaned, crawling to my feet and pacing the room for the umpteenth time, starting to feel like a caged animal.

How the hell was I supposed to sleep after Mark dropped that bomb on me? After *any* of this? Yeah, that wasn't going to happen.

Leaving the literal table scraps for Sasha to clean up if she wanted, I strode into the bathroom to do something I never got to do at my shitty, rundown hotel. I cranked the faucet handle to molten lava and started to fill the bathtub. Shuffling through the mini bottles on the marble countertop, I grabbed a container of lavender shower gel and dumped the entire contents of the bottle into the tub, watching as it frothed and foamed, bubbles taking over the tub.

Bacon and a bath? I'd clearly died and gone to Heaven. It was one thing I could definitely thank my stalker for.

Kicking the door closed out of habit, I quickly stripped out of my work clothes and tossed them to the floor before stepping into the tub.

A sigh escaped my lips, my head dropping back as the heat consumed me. It was glorious. The scalding water enveloped my body as I eased into the tub. It burned in the best way, the liquid flames of hell wrapping around me, searing my skin and tinting it red. Within seconds, my body disappeared beneath the thick layer of bubbles floating along the surface.

I rested my head against the rim of the tub and let my eyes flutter shut, the stress of the night having no choice but to melt away. Inhaling deeply, I took in the calming scent of lavender and forced my mind to go blank. I didn't want to think about anything for five whole minutes.

Not about my stalker. Not about his smoldering gray eyes, or the way they pierced through my damn soul. I didn't want to think about his carved-from-stone body and how it felt pressed against mine. Or how his touch affected me far more than Mark's had. I didn't want to think about Mark's condo window or our interrupted moment together. Or about Chad kicking me out of the only place I'd called home for years, or my shitty job, or my piss-poor luck.

I just wanted one solid moment of peace. Was that too much to ask for?

A growl coming from the hotel room was a resounding yes.

My eyes popped open and I sat up, water sloshing over the side of the tub and splattering on the floor. Sasha's growls grew increasingly louder and my heart started hammering against my sternum.

Just as quickly as the growling began, it stopped.

I squinted at the closed bathroom door, listening for any sounds coming from outside the door. All I could hear was the muffled sound of the television I'd left on. Maybe the dog had heard something on TV she hadn't liked? But even as that thought crossed my mind, something about it didn't settle right with me.

"Sasha?" I called out. Yep, I was officially the annoying character in a horror movie that was too stupid to live. Great.

Sure, just give away your location to the crazy stalker, dumbass.

I listened for another full minute, not hearing anything out of the ordinary. Slowly, I eased back into the water, telling myself it was fine. I was just on edge, that was all. The only way in the room was through the door and I was positive it hadn't opened.

If I didn't need a good therapist before all of this, I was definitely going to need one now.

"No shame in that," I muttered to myself as I closed my eyes once more. The second they drifted shut, the floor just outside the bathroom door creaked and my heart stopped.

I was standing before I realized I'd moved. My chest heaved with each breath I took, my eyes glued to the still-closed door. I leaped out of the tub, nearly landing on my ass as I slid across the small bathroom, catching myself on the counter. Once I regained my footing, I yanked one of the two plush robes from the counter and wrapped it around my body, loosely fastening it at the waist.

My hand lingered on the doorknob and I pulled in a deep breath.

I'm not a victim.

Cracking the door open a sliver, I peeked outside to see nothing but the wall facing the bathroom door. I pushed it open a few more inches but didn't see anyone. Stepping out of the bathroom, I peered into the main part of the hotel room. It appeared empty. Too empty.

Where was the dog?

"Sasha?" My voice was no more than a whisper.

But the giant dog didn't come.

My heart pounded loudly in my ears.

"Miss?" Lance's voice traveled into the room from the hallway. "Everything okay in there?"

I opened my mouth to respond when a soft woof came from the other side of the room. I blew out a breath, my entire body sagging with relief.

"Everything's fine," I called. "Except my ruined bath," I grumbled to myself, fiddling with the tie of my robe.

I moved further into the room to check on Mark's dog, half expecting to see her standing on the coffee table, licking it clean. But she wasn't there. I froze when I saw where she was standing instead.

Outside. On the balcony. She gave another muffled bark, batting at the glass.

"What the..."

A hand came around me, clamping over my mouth as I tried to scream.

GISELLE

He'd found me. But how the hell had he gotten into my hotel room? I knew Lance was still outside the door, and we were forty-five floors off the ground.

I struggled against his hold, clawing at the hand he had over my mouth. His other arm shot out, wrapping around my middle and holding my back flush against his front, effectively pinning one of my arms to my side.

Everywhere he touched me, my skin came alive, electricity pulsing between us. It felt so damn good as it washed over me. I'd never felt anything like it before. It took every shred of control I had in me not to arch my ass back into his solid body.

Dammit all to hell and back, why did he have to be crazy?

Sasha started barking from where she was locked out on the balcony.

"Miss?" Lance called into the room again and I tried to scream through my stalker's big hand. Sasha's barking increased until it was more like a savage howl. "Giselle?" he shouted when I didn't answer, using my name for the first time since I'd met him. He pounded on the door twice. "Open the door. Now."

"Be good," my stalker breathed into my ear and I shuddered. God clearly had a sense of humor when He made this man. That voice was pure sin. "I don't want any innocents to die tonight. You behave and the humans can live."

Innocents? Humans? What the hell was wrong with this guy? Who even spoke like that?

"What's going on?" Mark's familiar voice traveled through the door and my breath caught in my chest.

Prying my mouth open, I bit down on the meaty part of my stalker's hand, clamping my jaw shut until I tasted blood. The man pressed against me hissed, yanking his hand away.

"Mark!" I screamed. "Help!"

Something crashed against the door and I knew I needed to get out of my attacker's hold. I refused to be used in some sort of hostage situation. I slammed the heel of my foot into the top of his and then threw my one free arm back, driving my elbow into his ribcage hard enough that I thought I heard one crack.

You didn't have my kind of luck and not learn how to defend yourself against handsy men.

He grunted and stumbled back a step, his hold on me

loosening just enough for me to slip out of his arms. Almost immediately, he lunged for me, his fingers hooking around the belt of my robe as I jumped away from him. Cool air caressed my skin and I glanced down to find the top of my robe splayed wide open, my breasts on full display.

Instead of reaching for me again, my stalker shocked me by whirling away from me, shielding his eyes.

I mean, I'd heard somewhere that a woman's breasts were basically a weapon, but damn.

Another bang came to the hotel door before it flew open, slamming into the wall with a loud crash.

Mark's eyes immediately fell to my naked breasts and I could see the rage forming on his face. I scrambled to close the robe.

The next sound I heard was one I'd never heard before —not in real life, at least.

My eyes shot to my stalker who was facing me once more, a fucking *sword* in his hand.

"Giselle, get back!" Mark ordered, stepping into the room with his gun drawn. He pointed the weapon at my stalker, putting his body in front of mine. My stalker didn't even bat an eye at the gun fixed on his chest.

"Put the weapon down or I will be forced to shoot you."

"There's no use, bullets can't kill him!" I shouted and then gasped. Both Mark's and my stalker's eyes snapped to me. Confusion flooded Mark's face, but not my stalker's. His eyes narrowed on me, suspicion clouding those stormy grays.

Panic filtered through me. What was I even talking about? Of course, bullets would kill him. They were freaking *bullets*. But deep down, I knew that wasn't true.

Why wasn't it true—and how the hell did I know it wasn't?

"She's mine," my stalker growled, and my lady bits denied all sense of rationality by clenching at his proclamation. "Hand her over and I will spare you, *Detective*."

"This dude is crazy," Lance grumbled. I hadn't realized he'd followed Mark into the room. His gun was also trained on my stalker.

But my stalker wasn't looking at either of the two men. Instead, his intense gray eyes were glued to me and I couldn't seem to tear my gaze from his no matter how hard I tried.

He took one step forward, sword still raised, and both Mark and Lance opened fire.

My hands clamped over my ears as the scream tore out of me. On the balcony, Sasha was going wild, slamming her entire monstrous body into the glass. My whole body shook as I curled in on myself, shielding myself from the scene unfolding in front of me.

I couldn't look. I couldn't bear to see the holes in my stalker's body. He was crazy—absolutely batshit—and he clearly wanted to harm me, but something about him still felt unsettlingly familiar. I didn't want to see him bleeding out on the hotel floor. And I certainly didn't want anyone to die because of me.

But better him than me if it had to be one of us, right?

"What the fuck?" Lance hissed. The panic in his voice forced me to look up.

My stalker was still on his feet, bullet holes in the center of his shirt. But there was no blood.

"Why isn't there any blood?" I shrieked.

He growled, fingers flexing on the hilt of his sword as the bullets popped out of his skin and rolled across the floor.

Mark's eyes, full of fear, met mine. "Run!"

I bolted out of the room, slamming into the wall across the way. Commotion behind me had me pushing off the wall and sprinting down the hallway toward the elevators, my bare feet slapping against the thin carpeting.

I slid into the elevator area and, with all of the luck I was used to, the lights above the elevators flickered out. I punched the down button repeatedly but nothing happened.

You've got to be kidding me.

Darting back into the long hallway, I headed for the flickering *Exit* sign. I hit the brakes at the stairwell door and groaned. Forty-five flights of stairs.

Maybe I should have just let Mr. Sword Fighter kill me. It would have been far less painful.

Footsteps barreled down the hallway and I didn't even bother to look behind me. I kicked the metal door open and dove through it, taking the first three flights of stairs two at a time, trying to put as much distance between me and my attacker as possible.

If he was chasing me down, where were Mark and

Lance? Were they okay? I wasn't sure I could forgive myself if something happened to them because of me.

The floor level signs appeared less and less frequently as I started to run out of steam.

"Fucking stairmageddon," I panted, rounding yet another corner. My head spun around the word, my feet briefly faltering as a pang shot through my temple. I felt like I was going in circles. This had to be the *Nine Circles of Hell* everyone talked about. Only instead of nine, there were forty-fucking-five.

I was really starting to think I would be better off taking my chances with my stalker instead.

But as that thought hit me, pounding footfalls echoed throughout the stairwell, coming from somewhere above me.

"Shit," I hissed, forcing my legs to keep going. I wasn't going to let a damn charley horse lead to my demise again.

Again?

I stumbled down the next three stairs, nearly catapulting down the remaining flight. I gripped the railing with white-knuckled fingers, trying to fill my aching lungs. A glance at the next floor level sign showed me I still had twenty-six more flights to go.

"Oh hell no."

I barreled through the next door, tumbling out into another long hallway lined with hotel rooms. Each door handle was draped with a *do not disturb* plaque.

"Help!" I tried to scream but it came out as more of a strangled cry. I started pounding on doors desperately.

The guests on the other side, if they said anything at all, yelled at me to go away, some of them calling me a crazy drunk.

Normally that would be pretty accurate for this city, but not this time.

I slammed my fists into the next door, changing my tactic.

"Fire!" I shouted at the door. "Help, please! Fire!"

Almost immediately, the door swung open and a man in his mid-thirties wearing a baggy white T-shirt and a pair of boxers stood in the frame. His eyes—bloodshot and glossy like he'd been drinking—ran over me.

The stairwell door creaked open down the hall and a whimper left my lips. Where the hell was Mark?

"You have to help me," I rushed to tell the man. "There's someone after me. Please, I need to use your phone!"

After the world's longest second, he stepped aside, letting me into the room before closing and locking the door.

I rushed straight to his phone and fumbled with the keypad, trying to dial out as I called 9-1-1. The second the dispatcher answered I started spewing out words in rapid succession.

"I'm at the Cosmopolitan and my stalker found me. He has a weapon! There was an officer guarding my room and Detective Jenson was there—I'm not sure where they are now or if they are okay. Please, send help!"

"Miss, you need to calm down," the woman on the

other end of the line told me. "Take a deep breath. I've got help coming your way. What room are you in?"

"What room is this?" I asked the man whose room I'd barged into. He was leaning against the wall, a mini bottle of tequila in his hand. His eyes raked down my robe-covered body and I resisted the urge to cinch the belt even tighter

After taking another swig, he rambled off some numbers and I relayed them to the dispatcher.

"Okay, sit tight, we have help on the way."

I didn't wait for her to tell me to stay on the line, hanging up the phone before she had a chance to ask any more questions. Not my most polite moment, but I was in full panic mode.

"Thanks," I finally said, realizing I hadn't thanked him yet for being the only person to open the door for me. Or maybe it was just true what people said: when you needed help, yell *fire* instead and someone will come running.

Humans sucked.

A grin tugged at his lips. "No, thank *you*."

He set down the now empty bottle, joining it with a plethora of other bottles. All empty.

Shit. This guy was really wasted.

He took a clumsy step forward, his predatory eyes fixed on the top of my robe. "What you got under there?"

"Excuse me?" I shot back, hand automatically going to the seam of my robe, holding it together. There was a rather small and pathetic bulge growing in his boxers, tenting them out a few inches. Hello, whiskey dick.

"Come on, baby," he practically purred, making my

skin crawl. "Let's have a little fun while you wait for the cops. You owe me a little something for helping you."

Owed him? Of all the rooms on this massive floor, this was the type of person I got? I shouldn't have been so surprised.

I took a small step back, bumping into the nightstand. "I don't owe you shit, buddy. Look, you've obviously had a few drinks. Let's just wait for the cops to get here and I'll be out of your hair so you can take care of...*that*."

He was drunk, I had to remind myself of that. He wasn't thinking clearly. Then again...

Drunk words, sober thoughts.

He struggled to yank his shirt off. "Oh, I think I'll take care of it right now," he said, his words starting to slur together as the most recent bottle of alcohol combined with what he'd already consumed. "With you."

I found I felt safer trapped in my stalker's arms than I did standing in this room. I should have taken my chances with sword boy. This guy was trying at a whole different sword game—one he most definitely wasn't going to win.

He moved closer, trapping me between the bed and the wall. Thinking fast, I leaped onto the bed, trying to roll away from him.

The man grabbed my ankle with surprising speed and yanked me back, eliciting a cry from me. He twisted my leg, rolling me over. I kicked out at him with my free leg, sending my heel into his nose with a satisfying crunch.

He howled, releasing me to hold his bleeding nose. I scrambled off the bed and darted for the door.

"You're going to pay for that, bitch!"

His nose already forgotten, he lunged for me, slamming his body into mine and shoving me into the wall. Next thing I knew, the back of his hand connected with my face, making the room spin. Blood filled my mouth and he chuckled.

"You like it rough, eh?"

He grabbed a fist full of my robe, yanking it down to expose one breast. I jerked my knee up, aiming for his groin and hitting his thigh instead, earning a snarl from him. Shifting his weight, he pinned my legs against the wall with his until I couldn't move an inch. Panic swelled within me as one hand came around my neck. The scent of alcohol on his breath was so strong that even my head started to spin.

This was not happening.

As his mouth swooped toward my face, I slammed my forehead into his. Pain exploded in my skull, black dots dancing around the corners of my vision. My attacker released me, groaning as he stumbled back a couple of steps, grabbing his head.

The door behind him flew open, flying off the hinges. I looked up, expecting to see Mark, or Lance, or the police.

My stalker stood in the doorway, his muscular body heaving with each breath he took.

His gray eyes immediately went to me. They trailed up my body like a physical touch that had me squirming against the wall. His gaze reached my open robe, not shying away as he'd done before, and a fire ignited in his eyes that wasn't entirely sexual. He was pissed. Those angry eyes darted to my face, landing on the blood I felt trickling from the corner of my mouth.

A growl slipped past his lips that had me clamping my trembling thighs together. If he asked who did this to me, I was going to physically combust.

My stalker's eyes narrowed, his rage palpable in the small hotel room. He turned that rage on my most recent attacker, and I nearly pissed myself for the drunken asshole.

"Who the fuck are you?" the drunk slurred, facing off with the man who'd had me running into this room to begin with. Clearly, the alcohol had given him some serious liquid courage if he thought he stood a chance against the man towering over him.

"You touched what doesn't belong to you," my stalker's deep voice declared, and my breath caught in my chest.

"What are you—"

The drunk's words were cut off as he lost his head —literally.

I screamed, watching the man's headless body collapse to the hotel floor, blood pooling around him at an alarming rate. I scrambled back farther into the room, trying to get away from the blood. There was so much blood.

"What did you do?" I shrieked, feeling my breaths coming faster until the room started to spin around me. My hand shot out, grabbing the edge of the bed to steady myself, my body shaking violently.

My stalker took two long strides toward me, quickly closing the distance between us. "Silence," he barked and my jaw clamped shut, eyes darting to the blood-stained sword still clutched in his hand. "This is all your fault, *demon*," he spat.

"The demon you just saved," I breathed, not knowing what had possessed me to say such a stupid thing.

Whatever air was still in my lungs left in a whoosh until it felt like my lungs were constricting in my chest. I blinked away the image of a bright light rushing toward me—the sound of a train horn blaring in my head. If I had any breath left, I would have screamed again.

What was wrong with me? I stumbled away from the bed, landing on my butt.

"I can't breathe," I said, trying to pull in air with no success. I flipped onto my hands and knees, watching the world teeter around me.

My stalker's booted feet appeared next to me and I made a feeble attempt to crawl away from him. I'd just watched him *kill* a man! Whether he'd done it to save me or not, he was still making my life a living hell. And I was likely next. He was probably just saving me so he could do the deed himself.

"Get away from me," I rasped, hating the tears that pooled in my eyes.

A strong hand gripped my arm, yanking me to my feet. Without a single word, he started to drag me toward the sliding glass door that led to the balcony.

"What are you doing?" I shrieked, trying to pull away from him with no success. Was he going to throw me over the edge?

"You are coming with me," he said in his silky deep

voice. "I am going to keep you until you remember exactly what you are."

"And then what?" I wasn't sure I wanted to know the answer to that question.

He threw open the slider and shoved me onto the balcony in front of him.

"Then I'll send you back to Hell."

That was what I was afraid of.

His intense eyes met mine, and then he reared back his hand and brought the butt of his sword into my temple. The world around me went black.

LUCAS

I needed to get her out of my arms. I couldn't take another minute of being this unbearably close to her.

It felt far too good—like nothing I'd ever felt before. No, that wasn't entirely true. It was like what I'd felt twenty-seven years ago in that dark subway tunnel.

I landed in the middle of the desert, the early morning sun already beating down on my shoulders. But even the heat of the day didn't compete with the woman in my arms.

Her limp body was like molten lava against mine, the fires of Hell pumping through her veins. Her bare skin burned mine wherever it touched me, which was practically everywhere seeing as her already miniscule robe had slipped open on the long trip here. It made for an extremely distracted flight.

My heart beat wildly within my chest as I carried her into the tiny, secluded cabin. I was eager to set her down and wash away the sinful thoughts she was planting in my head.

This vile woman could twist my mind even when unconscious. She was too powerful for her own good. It was no surprise that she'd ended up in the predicament I'd found her in when I'd barged into that man's hotel room. The succubus side of her made men lose all rational thought. Myself included if the uncomfortable bulge in my pants was any indication.

I carefully laid her on the bed, averting my eyes as I attempted to fix her robe. My fingertips brushed along the tops of her breasts and down the flat plane of her stomach as I fumbled with the fabric, frantically tugging it together. I cinched the tie in place and prayed that this time it would hold. Only when I knew she was covered did I stare down at her. And what I saw had my breath catching in my throat. In the white garb, with her hair splayed around her body like a fiery halo, she almost looked like an angel.

Almost.

But I knew the truth. She was anything but innocent. There wasn't a holy bone in that woman's body. It didn't matter how angelic—or otherworldly—she looked sprawled out against the crisp white sheets with that serene look on her face. She was pure evil.

My eyes lingered far longer than they should have.

Forcing myself to move, I grabbed one of her wrists and clasped the open handcuff around it. Lifting her hand over her head, I secured the other end to the bedpost and made sure both were tight, but not tight enough to hurt her.

It had been hard enough knocking her out before taking her from the hotel. Unlike in the past, I found I took no joy from seeing her in pain.

Once again, I found my eyes falling to her still frame. Her full lips parted as she stirred and my mind went right back to that day in the subway. The feel of her lips on mine had haunted me—it plagued my every waking thought. No matter how much I prayed, I still felt her mouth crashing into mine in the dark recesses of that subway tunnel.

I tore my gaze away from her and stepped out of the cabin, taking a deep breath of the hot desert air.

We were in the middle of nowhere, far enough into the heart of the desert that no one would likely stumble upon us. And no one would come to her aid if she managed to escape. There was nowhere she could run out here. Nowhere to hide. She was mine.

I'd keep her here as long as it took for her to remember her roots. And the second she did, I'd remove her like the weed she was.

I'd nearly completed the task when she'd told the detective that I couldn't be killed, and again when she'd told me I'd saved her despite what she was—just as she'd done years ago. The pure fear in her eyes was the only thing staying my hand. She looked like no more than a scared human. No matter how much I'd tried, I found I couldn't do it.

What was wrong with me? I'd never had this problem in the past. I was one of the best of my kind. A warrior. A demon slayer. So, why now?

What was it about her stopping me this time?

A pang shot through my chest as I thought about the look in her eyes when I'd stormed in on the man trying to…violate her. Her teary eyes had begged me to save her —*me*. She'd looked to me for protection. And then there was the blood on her face. I could hardly stand it.

I saw red. I'd completely snapped.

I rarely lost my temper like that. The woman brought out the worst in me. Just like she'd probably brought out the worst in him. But even her wicked ways had their limitations when it came to corrupting a soul. He likely already had evil lurking within him.

Still, I shouldn't have killed him. But he had crossed a line that he couldn't come back from. That *I* couldn't let him come back from. He'd hurt her. And he'd planned to do far worse if I hadn't shown up when I had. He deserved to die.

It was my job to make him pay for his many sins.

Vibrations pulsed against my thigh and I groaned, fishing out the phone. I'd been avoiding this call, letting the missed calls pile up until I worried the headstrong angel would show up on my doorstep demanding answers. That was an added problem I didn't need at the moment. I hit the answer button.

"What do you want, Zain?" I said the second the phone touched my ear.

"Is that any way to talk to your superior?"

My feet faltered in the desert sand. "They would have made an official announcement if you'd been given the archangel position," I replied, swallowing the desire to call him a liar.

He chuckled on the other end of the line. "The job is all but mine, they practically told me as much. They will be announcing the good news soon, I'm sure. I'm working on something they are very interested in. Something big. I can't give you the details yet, but they want what I have. It is so nice to know that good work still gets rewarded, isn't it, Lucas?"

My teeth hurt with how hard I was clenching them. I had to keep myself from saying anything I would regret, especially if he really had been given the position. Archangels outranked us tenfold—they were deemed the holiest and most superior of the angels. They led our war against the growing demon populace and they were a direct line to the Almighty.

I couldn't imagine Zain with that sort of power. Not when I'd worked so long and so hard to get the promotion myself.

"Speaking of good work," he continued, the smirk in his voice making my wings twitch behind me. "The Arches were not all too happy to hear that you still haven't taken care of your target yet."

"Kind of you to keep them informed of my status," I bit out.

"Just preparing for my future position," he said casually. "I'm sure you can understand that, brother."

I couldn't stop the growl in my throat, my fingers tightening on the phone until I heard the outer case crack.

"I did remind them of your track record and explained that this was your first time failing to remove your mark. I told them you needed more time to complete the assignment, but they were having none of it. They are growing impatient with you—it has never taken you so long to find and remove a demon. I did all I could to placate them, but they want her gone."

More like he'd done all he could to make me look poorly in front of the Arches so he could take the position I'd been working toward for centuries.

"I told them it would be my great honor to assist you in this—as my first unofficial task as the new archangel—and they agreed. Just tell me where you are. I will help you end this, brother."

"I don't need your help, *brother*," I seethed.

"Come now…" he replied, and I hated the way he was talking down to me like I was no more than a youngling. "There's no shame in asking for help from those with the skills to do so. I have been helping the trainees for years."

I'd been hunting down this particular demon for hundreds upon hundreds of years—not to mention sending thousands of lower-levels back to Hell. I didn't need the likes of Zain swooping in to finish my job for me. If I allowed him to step in, I'd never stand a chance at any future archangel promotions. I'd be the laughingstock of my kind, and he knew it.

"It is taken care of," I told him, my voice dangerously low.

I hung up before he could get another word out, resisting the urge to throw the device across the vast wasteland in front of me.

Tucking the phone into my pocket, I unsheathed my sword and stormed back into the cabin. I was going to end this before this wretched creature—or Zain—made my life any worse.

The kiss we'd shared a quarter-century ago had obviously messed with my head. Her teary eyes and unusual behavior had made me weak. But no more. It was not my fault she didn't remember what she was. *I* knew the vile monster she was and that was all that mattered. She was a plague on this Earth and I would rid the world of her presence like I always had.

I'd already lost so much because of my hesitation. I should have ended her the second I'd finally found her. If I had, maybe it would have been me getting the promotion instead of Zain.

That position should have been mine.

I stood beside the bed and raised my blade.

Her body trembled where it still lay, sweat coating her exposed skin as she tossed and turned on the bed, pulling against her restrained arm. A whimper left her lips, eyes scrunched closed.

I slowly lowered my sword, watching her. I'd never watched someone have a nightmare up close before. She looked terrified, her chest rising and falling rapidly.

"No," she muttered in her sleep. "Please, no."

Tears fell from her closed eyes, spilling over her cheeks and into her hair. Before I realized what I was doing, my sword was gone and I was sitting beside her on the bed. I reached out, wiping the moisture from her flushed face. Her skin tingled under my fingertips. It was a strange sensation, one I only felt when she touched me. What scared me was how *glorious* it felt. Probably some sort of demon, succubus, magic.

Another whimper slipped past her lips that quickly turned into a pained cry. More tears replaced the ones I'd removed.

"It's okay," I found myself whispering, smoothing her hair back. "I've got you."

My hand froze, fingers tangled in her long locks. Those three words echoed in my head. What was I even saying?

Her free arm shot out and before I could react, her hand found mine. She clutched onto me for dear life, her fingers tightening around my own. Almost immediately, her body relaxed into the bed. With a shaky exhale, her breathing started to normalize. The rise and fall of her chest slowed until she appeared just as serene as she had when I'd first laid her on the bed. Except this time, she was clinging onto me like I was her only lifeline.

And so instead of killing her, I sat beside her, her small hand tucked in mine. I watched over her as she slept, keeping away the nightmares that seemed to plague her.

If only she knew that I was soon to be one of her nightmares. Because whatever she was doing to me, I couldn't let it last.

I couldn't fail.

GISELLE

I was sure someone had beaten me over the head with a sledgehammer.

My eyelids felt heavy as they fluttered open only to quickly slam shut. The early morning sunlight was blinding as it shone through the window beside me. Why had I left my curtains open? I never did that. Too many freaks out there.

I groaned as I tried to shield my eyes with my arm. Only my arm didn't move.

Panic exploded within me as my eyes snapped open again, darting to where my wrist was cuffed to a bedpost I most certainly didn't recognize. I frantically yanked on the metal to no avail. That's when I noticed my other hand was encased in something warm. Something that made my skin tingle.

My breaths came faster as I forced my gaze to the left,

meeting my stalker's piercing gray eyes head-on. My hand started to tremble where it rested neatly in his much larger one. Almost as if I'd burned him, he released me, jolting to his feet and leaving a dip in the bed where he'd been sitting beside me.

He was holding my hand?

He was probably just deciding which of my fingers he wanted to eat first.

"Where's Mark?" I rasped, my throat feeling like I'd swallowed a box of nails. "Lance?"

My stalker stared at me intently, his scowl deepening, especially at the mention of Mark's name. After a painfully long minute, he uncrossed his arms. "They are alive" was all he said.

I should have felt some relief knowing Mark and Lance were okay. Mark had gone above and beyond to help me. If he'd been killed because of me... Well, I'd never forgive myself. He was a good man—far too good for me. If I ever got away from Mr. Screw Loose, I'd find some way to make it up to Mark. Hell, maybe I'd even break my no heroes rule. It was about time I found myself a nice, honorable, *sane* man.

It'd be a first for me.

I was swearing off morally gray men from now on. It was only good ol' boring boys next door for this gal from here on out.

If I lived.

I tracked my stalker as he turned his back to me, moving that perfectly sculpted ass across the small room to an even smaller kitchenette. He leaned a narrow hip against the counter, his muscular arms flexing as they crossed over his broad chest, his too-tight shirt hugging him like a second skin. Damn, he really was built like a god.

Maybe I'd swear off morally gray men tomorrow.

I took a moment to glance around the room. It was some sort of cabin. A ridiculously small one where the entire cabin was just one room, minus a door that I imagined led to a bathroom. One I hoped to hell had running water. Preferably hot.

Not to say my stalker was going to let me shower. Or eat. Or *live*.

He watched me, keeping his eyes carefully fixed on my face as I grabbed the edges of my robe, holding them together with my free hand. A brief flash of fear flickered across his eyes, like he was worried I might throw the fabric open. The guy apparently had a serious hang-up with naked flesh. Good thing for him I wasn't a nudist. Then again, maybe he'd keep his hands off me altogether if I was.

Beware of the titties, dude.

"And the dog?" I finally asked, remembering Sasha on the hotel room balcony, slamming her large frame into the glass door. I'd grown rather fond of that giant danger floof. I didn't tolerate animal abusers. There was morally gray, and there was fucked-up monster. If he'd hurt that dog, it didn't matter how many abs he had, I'd find a way to kill him myself. *Slowly.*

"The beast also lives," he said. "Animals tend to have purer souls than humans. She was innocent."

There was that weird-ass lingo of his again. What was with this guy? I reminded myself to shy away from calling him crazy again.

I scanned the room a second time before looking down at the queen-sized bed I was sitting on. It, a small table, and two chairs were the only pieces of furniture in the cabin.

"One bed," I muttered with a snort, rolling my eyes into the back of my head for good measure. "Yep, God *definitely* has a sense of humor."

My stalker closed the distance between us in three long strides until he was towering over me, his muscular body blocking out the sun. "Do not speak of the Lord," he snarled. "You will not speak His holy name, demon."

I tried to lean away from him without success, pulling on my restraints and wincing when the metal of the cuffs bit into my wrist.

Something flashed in his eyes, but before I could decipher what it was, it was gone. He took a step back and I relaxed the smallest bit, managing to pull in a breath.

I held up my hands—well, one of them. "Sorry," I said, though it came out as more of a question than an apology. What was his deal anyway?

Oh, that's right, he was a psycho.

"What do you want with me?" I asked, struggling to swallow. I was sure I didn't want to know the answer. I'd seen the guy's face. I highly doubted he had any intention of letting me waltz out of here—wherever *here* was. I'd need to find a way to escape. Preferably before he decided to murder me with a chainsaw and make my skin into a coat.

"I told you," he bit out, his eyes narrowing on me. "I am going to make you remember what you are."

"Right," I drawled. "Which is?"

"A demon," he said with such certainty that I felt bad for the laugh that bubbled out of me. A laugh that earned me a growl.

I sucked in a sharp breath at the sudden pulsing between my legs.

"Yeah, you need to stop with all the growling if we're going to be sharing a bed," I told him, biting my lip to keep the small moan from slipping out. I hated the effect he had on me. There was so much wrong about being turned on by my captor.

This shit only happened in books—books that most definitely were my weakness. Until now, I'd never met a growly man in real life. I'd assumed they were purely fiction. It was like this man standing over me had walked straight out of one of my favorite stories.

Just my luck he was a raving lunatic who thought I was a demon.

All. The. Red. Flags.

"You will not lure me into your bed, temptress."

Another humorless snort of laughter tumbled past my lips. Now I was a temptress? This guy had serious issues with women—or at the very least, *me.* And he most definitely wasn't amused with my laughter if the look in his stormy eyes was any indication. I was going to get myself killed if I didn't shut my stupid mouth and fast.

"Don't flatter yourself, asshole," I shot back, glaring right back at him like the slow learner I was. I'd never been very good at keeping my word hole shut. It was always getting me into trouble. But if I was going to die anyway, I might as well go out in a blaze of glory, right?

"Watch your mouth!" he raged, and again I found myself cowering, yanking on my restraints despite the pain it caused me. Okay, so he didn't like cursing. Noted.

"What do you plan to do with me?" I whispered, watching as his eyes flicked to my wrist once more, his brows furrowing. He looked conflicted but I wasn't sure why.

"Once you remember," he said, taking another step back, eyes still on my wrist, "I will send you back to Hell like I've always done."

Right, of course.

"Two flaws with your little plan," I told him, ticking off fingers on my unrestrained hand. "First—because I'm not a demon—what if I never remember? And second, even if your delusion was somehow real, why the hell would I ever admit it?"

"I'll know," he said. And once again, he said it with such confidence like he truly believed he knew me. The arrogant asshole.

"Well, you might as well just kill me and get it over with," I snapped. "Because—and I say this with all due respect—I'm not a goddamned fucking demon, you psychopath."

So much for the no more growling. My stalker was practically foaming at the damn mouth as the words fell from my lips. His shoulders climbed to his ears, one hand going to the sword I hadn't realized was hanging from his waist. It was the same blade he'd used to kill the drunk at the hotel. A shudder ripped through my body as the image of the drunk's headless body flopping onto the hotel floor rushed back to me.

Holy shit. I *really* needed to keep my fucking mouth closed. This man was dangerous. So, why did I feel like this was all a game—one that had my heart racing in the best of ways?

"Vile creature," he hissed. "You will stay here for as long as it takes. You will admit what you are."

"You can't keep me here forever," I breathed, hating how my voice trembled as I spoke. "People will realize I'm missing. They'll come looking for me."

Apparently, it was his turn to laugh. He chuckled darkly, eyes once again going to my restrained wrist. "First, I can and I will," he sneered, inching closer to me once more until his legs brushed the edge of the bed. I didn't miss the mocking tone of his deep voice. "Second, we are in the middle of nowhere. Even if you manage to escape, there is nowhere you can go in this desert waste-land. No one will hear you screaming for help out here. No one will come to find you.

"And thirdly," he added, cutting me off before I could get a word out, "I have watched you for over a month. You have no one close to you. No one will bother to come looking for you—"

"Mark," I blurted out. "The detective will come for me."

Again, he bristled at the mention of Mark. "By the time he finds you—*if* he finds you—it will be too late. He should thank me; I'm doing him a favor. I am saving his soul."

My mouth hung open, struggling to draw breath.

"Who the hell are you?" I practically shrieked.

"I'm the angel sent to destroy you," he said, his voice dangerously low. The way he looked down at me—this was the predator I'd seen in the liquor store. And apparently, I was his prey. "I have killed you hundreds of times. And I will do so again. I will not fail in my mission. Your time wreaking havoc on this Earth is about to end."

An angel?

The dude thought he was an angel and I was a demon? My mind spun around that new little tidbit of information.

"You're insane! Are you serious? You seriously think I'm going to believe you're an angel sent to *kill* me? That's the shit serial killers say! Let me go!"

Okay, so I knew that *let me go* was about as cliché as him saying it was his purpose in life to kill me. But I couldn't help myself. The guy had a sword and thought I was a demon to eradicate.

"I am no killer," he ground out, his hand still gripping the hilt of his sword. "My purpose is to protect the humans of this world."

Was he serious? "Protect?" I couldn't help the anger creeping into my voice. "You just said you want to kill me!"

"You are not human, *demon*. Killing you is no sin. In

fact, it is an honor bestowed upon me to remove you from this Earth. The world will be safer without you in it."

This dude was painting himself a perfect insanity case if he ever got caught.

"And the guy you killed? Was he supposed to be a demon too?" I pushed. "Is everyone a demon, Mr. Holy Man?"

My stalker was silent for a moment, his jaw ticking. "He was a sinner," he said slowly. "He was going to do vile things to you. He needed to be stopped."

I'd almost forgotten that my stalker had saved me. The whole reason he'd attacked the drunk was because of what the man had been trying to do to me. Though he probably could have done it without *killing* the guy. Still, I was shocked at the level of relief I'd felt seeing him standing in the doorway of that hotel room. It was like something in me knew he'd fix it.

I yanked on the handcuff again, wincing as the metal once again bit into my wrist, starting to leave an angry red line. As I expected, his eyes again tracked the movement, darkening.

Interesting.

"So, you saved me from him just to kill me yourself?" I finally said. It didn't make sense. Any of it. His claim to want to kill me while looking conflicted over my physical pain. How he wanted me dead and yet he'd swooped in to rescue me from the drunk before I could get hurt, or worse. He said one thing but did another.

I pursed my lips and sat up a little taller on the bed,

hardening myself as I stared up at him. "If you're going to kill me, just get it over with."

I was about to play a dangerous game with a dangerous man. But I had to test my theory that he wouldn't actually kill me. Not yet, at least.

The rise and fall of his chest increased until he was breathing nearly as heavily as I was. "Do you admit what you are?"

"Why do you need me to say it?" I countered. "You've clearly made up your mind about what you think I am. What are you waiting for? If you're so sure, then do it."

He moved away from the bed, gray eyes never leaving mine even as he physically backed down. A second later, he spun on his heels and stormed out of the cabin, slamming the door behind him.

I slumped into the bed, taking a shaky breath as the tears began to fall. But I couldn't let myself completely fall apart. No, I had to get out of here.

I had no doubts in my mind that my stalker thought he was supposed to kill me, but he was clearly struggling to complete the task. And I needed to make sure it stayed that way until I was able to escape.

One set of handcuffs wasn't going to keep me in this cabin with him.

I *was* going to escape. And I was going to do it before he decided it was time to send me to Hell.

GISELLE

It had been days and he still hadn't returned to the small desert cabin.

Okay, so maybe it hadn't actually been days. More like hours. But those few hours had felt like days in the blistering midday heat. Despite the hum of the generator running outside the wall, the cabin lacked any sort of adequate air-cooling system. Growing up in Nevada, I was used to the heat—and the lack of modern conveniences like air conditioning. Still, the desert was a whole different beast. I could only imagine this was what Hell would feel like.

My stalker would say I knew exactly what it was like.

A thin layer of sweat coated my skin as I sprawled out on the bed. Using my one free hand, I flipped open the robe, enjoying the briefest moment of fresh air kissing my overheated skin.

For the hundredth time, I glanced at the only door in and out of the cabin. It hadn't opened since he'd stormed out. Was he standing outside? Was he nearby? Did he leave me here to die?

I wasn't sure how many opportunities I'd have to try to escape—or how long he'd be able to resist actually killing me. And I refused to be a victim.

"Come on, chicken," I told myself, still watching the door.

Taking a deep breath, I sat up and scooted against the headboard so I could check out my handcuff situation.

It was a basic, standard issue set of cuffs. I would know; I'd worn a few pairs in my life. Sometimes misunderstandings and wrong-place-wrong-time situations could end with a pretty set of silver bracelets. But this wasn't a simple arrest, not by a long shot.

If I had something long and thin, I could pick my way out of the cuffs. But I didn't. Instead, I shifted my attention to the headboard that my handcuff's twin was attached to. Just my luck, it was made of thick wood and looked like it could withstand a damn tornado.

Awesome.

Why couldn't it have been some cheapy bed from the local chain store that broke with one zealous romp in the sack?

I twisted around, stretching my chained arm as far as possible so I could get my legs between me and the headboard. With my knees tucked into my chest, I carefully lined up my feet a few inches from my target, straining to keep my cuffs out of the way.

With a deep breath, I kicked out as hard as I could.

A cry slipped past my defenses as my heels slammed into—what I hoped was—a weak spot where the cross beam connected with the bedpost. While the pain traveled up through my feet, into my legs, and destroyed my very soul, the wood didn't even budge.

"Shit," I hissed.

I shifted my weight, stretching my arm out a little more until I was sure it would pop out of the socket. Lining my feet up again, I kicked the wood a second time. The tiny cracking sound had my heart racing.

Kicking out again and again, I drove my heels into the beam until I wasn't sure what would break first, the wood or one of my feet. I grunted as I struck the headboard one last time, gasping as the beam snapped free of the post and slammed into the wall, jerking my arm with it.

I stared at the broken headboard, my panted breaths and the hum of the generator the only sounds in the small cabin.

"I did it," I whispered. I was free. Well, a step closer at least. I needed to get moving.

My body swiftly got on the same page as my brain. I scrambled to my knees, sliding the handcuff off the broken headboard and pulling my arm into my chest. Flexing my fingers, I winced as the blood rushed back into them.

Ignoring the prickling pain, I hopped off the bed, the wooden floorboards rough against the soles of my feet. I glared down at the two naked offenders. I couldn't go parading around the desert without shoes. I'd always had a great tolerance for heat, but the desert sand wasn't just hot—it was home to some bite-happy critters.

The goal was to escape with my life, not to get bitten by something venomous and die in the process.

I cinched my robe shut and tied it off in a knot as I scanned the room. The guy had to have some sort of clothes here for himself. Thankfully, the cabin wasn't all that big and my eyes quickly landed on a bag under the small dining table. I dove for it, dragging it out and tossing it onto the bed.

The second I peeked inside, I sent a silent prayer up to the god I apparently wasn't supposed to mention by name when I spotted the pair of black boots.

I yanked the boots free and my eyes grew three sizes bigger.

Speaking of big...

"Holy fuck me running," I mumbled, looking at the size of them. Dude already had some large hands, and apparently his feet weren't any different. I couldn't help the horny teenager inside of me from wondering if *everything* on him was just as enormous...

"Snap out of it, Elle," I scolded myself, sitting on the edge of the bed. I refused to be part of a serial killer nightly special just because of my abnormally high sex drive.

I shoved my foot into the first boot and worked the laces to tighten them as much as I possibly could around my ankles to keep them on my feet. There was no way I'd be able to run in them, but they'd at least protect me from the elements. Doing the same with the second boot, I stood and searched the room for anything else I might need.

Spotting the mini-fridge in the corner of the room, I hobbled over to it, the boots slapping loudly against the wood floor. I yanked the door open and sent another prayer heavenward before grabbing a couple bottles of water, sticking one in each of the robe's two pockets.

I sucked in a deep breath as I made my way to the front door. I could relieve my aching bladder once I got far from this place. I didn't want to linger here any longer than I already had.

Cracking the door open, I peeked out into the blinding light of day, the wave of heat slamming into me and filling me with an unexpected sense of homesickness.

Only I didn't exactly have a home anymore.

When I didn't see my stalker outside the cabin, I threw the door open and stepped into the wall of heat that was the desert. Shielding my eyes, I scanned my surroundings.

"Satan's left nut and right nut combined," I grumbled.

He hadn't lied when he'd told me we were in the middle of nowhere. There was literally nothing around. The cabin was completely secluded. No other cabins, no other buildings, no sign of other people. Not even a vehicle. Nothing. It was just desert and more desert as far as the eye could see. It was as if my stalker had plucked me up and dropped me on a foreign planet.

But I knew that wasn't the case. A familiar tree jutted up from the ground straight ahead of me—a kind I knew well. If there were Joshua trees in this desert, then we couldn't be too far from Las Vegas. They typically only grew in the Mojave. If I walked long enough, I'd likely run into someone.

At least, that's what I hoped.

Doing one last check to make sure my stalker hadn't magically reappeared in his stalkerish way, I made my best attempt at a run in the oversized boots, leaving the small cabin behind—hopefully for good.

THE THING about deserts was that—contrary to popular belief—they weren't always hot. Quite the opposite, in fact. When the sun went down, the blistering heat retreated with it, leaving frigid temperatures in its wake.

And while I could handle temperatures that rivaled that of the surface of the sun, I didn't do so well with the cold.

I wrapped my arms around myself, my teeth chattering as I shivered in the thin robe. I was pretty sure I was becoming a human popsicle.

Again, I found myself thinking that I should have taken my chances with sword boy.

I'd been walking through the desert for hours—stumbling was more like it. The monstrous boots had only slowed me down on my trek. At one point, I'd considered taking them off but ended up thinking better of it. At least they were keeping my feet warm. And by warm, I mean warmer than the rest of my body. My toes still felt like they were about to break off. Though I imagine that without the boots they already would have. Like my fingers were threatening to do.

I hadn't found a single person on my journey. Animals, yes, but no people. I'd started to think that maybe he *had* dropped me onto an alien planet. But each time I'd seen a Joshua tree, hope had blossomed within me.

But hope could only get a girl so far in the middle of the desert. Especially without water. I'd polished off both of the bottles I'd taken from the cabin, sweating them back out almost immediately. And now that layer of sweat seemed to be frozen to my skin.

"Escaped a madman just to freeze to death," I mumbled through numb lips. "Awesome."

My bad luck strikes again.

I tucked my hands under my arms, trying whatever I could to warm them. I should have checked the bag of clothes for a jacket. What I wouldn't give for a scalding-hot shower right about now. I'd even tell my stalker I was a demon if it meant he'd let me stand under boiling hot water for five full minutes before he killed me.

Hell was actually sounding pretty damn good right about now.

Pausing in my aimless wandering, I scanned the blackness around me for the millionth time. I wasn't sure why I even bothered—I couldn't see my own hand in front of my face. Not even the billions of glistening stars overhead could illuminate the darkness surrounding me.

A howl traveled through the night and I groaned, wishing it was something simple—like coyotes. I shuddered against the icy wind as it slammed into me, cutting straight to the bone. The wind had been picking up over the last hour or so. Now it was an almost constant presence, making the already freezing temperatures that much worse and stealing what little body heat I had left.

I just needed to curl up and sleep until morning. If I could just sleep for a while, it would all be better.

Without another thought, I dropped to my knees, hardly noticing the sharp bite of the rocky sand. I curled into a ball on the desert floor, pulling my knees into my chest. Almost immediately, I noticed my shivering had eased. Yes, this was what I needed. I'd sleep for a few hours and the morning light would warm me right back up.

Everything would be okay.

My eyes drifted shut and a strange warmth settled into me as the sounds around me faded away. All of them except the sound of beating wings.

The vultures were swooping in.

LUCAS

Her body was solid ice when I scooped her into my arms. I shuddered, the cold seeping into my own skin.

"Foolish woman," I hissed, holding her tightly to me. She was too still—I hardly felt the rise and fall of her chest against mine. I needed to get her back to the cabin before it was too late.

I'd been searching for her ever since I'd returned to the cabin to find she'd escaped. I'd scoured the desert, but she was nowhere to be found. I knew she couldn't survive through the night, not in what she was wearing—even if she had stolen my boots.

I should have just let her die. It was my job to kill her, after all. But I couldn't seem to get myself to let her freeze to death.

She whimpered as I took to the skies. I glanced down

at her to see her lips were blue in the moonlight. I shifted the way I held her, trying to block out as much of the cold air as possible from kissing her bare skin. I could have walked back, but it would have taken far too long, and I knew she didn't have that kind of time.

Again, I should have just let the desert finish her off. I should have dropped her and let her fall back to earth like a fallen angel. But as the thought crossed my mind, my arms tightened around her.

Landing in front of the cabin, I tucked my wings behind me as I barged through the door. I laid her on the bed, not liking the blue hue of her skin, or the way she wasn't shivering. I might not have been truly human, but I understood the human body. Not shivering was a bad sign —her body was shutting down. And just like I understood that, I also knew I couldn't set her into the shower and turn on the hot water. Her body needed to come back naturally.

I knew what I had to do if I wanted to save her. I just didn't know *why* I wanted to save her.

But there wasn't time to overthink it.

Leaving her on the bed, I started tearing into the cabinets in search of blankets. A growl slipped past my lips when I only found one—an old comforter that had seen better days but appeared to be clean. It would have to do.

I tugged the boots from her feet and tossed them across the room. Pulling on the sheets, I covered her with them before tossing the heavy comforter onto the bed, hoping to God it would be enough on its own without having to do what I feared I must. She groaned, her eyelids fluttering but not opening. If anything, the blue of her lips had deepened.

"Curse this wretched woman." I should have let her die a hundred times already.

I kicked off my boots and reached for the top of my jeans, fingers lingering on the button before I finally popped it open.

"What are you doing?" a weak voice rasped as I dropped my pants to the floor.

My eyes shot up to see her staring at me from where she lay in the bed. She still wasn't shivering. She looked like she was a breath away from death.

"God help me, I'm saving you. Again," I bit out, yanking off my shirt.

The way her half-lidded eyes immediately dropped to my bare flesh had my dick twitching within my underwear. Knowing she was practically naked beneath the covers that I was about to crawl into with her didn't help matters.

But I had to do this if I wanted to save her life. So that I could kill her myself.

It was *my* job to end her life and send her back to Hell, not this blasted desert.

I could do this. I was stronger than the desires of the flesh. I was no weak human.

"I am going to use my body heat to warm you back up safely," I told her as I pulled up the covers and slipped into the bed with her. "You will not look at me. You will face away from me. Do you understand, demon?"

"Just let me sleep," she mumbled, her words slurring

together. Her glassy amber eyes met mine, the fire that once burned brightly in them all but gone out. She was slipping away. "I'm not even cold anymore."

I forced myself to scoot closer to her until I was mere inches away. I felt the icy chill radiating from her body before we even touched; it was such a sharp contrast to the heat she normally put off. Reaching out, I grabbed her shoulder and flipped her away from me. Inch by painful inch, I closed what little space there was between our two bodies until my front was flush with her back.

A shudder ripped through me as my body connected with hers, one I told myself had everything to do with how cold she was. Only, after a few seconds, I didn't feel the cold anymore.

My arm wrapped around her small frame, pulling her snugly against me, and almost immediately she started to shiver. I sent a silent thank you to the Almighty and nearly cursed myself for being grateful for her survival. This went against everything I knew—all I'd been trained for my entire existence. We didn't save demons. We *killed* them. They were the ruination of this world and they needed to be eradicated. It's what I'd done with her for centuries.

What was wrong with me?

A sigh slipped past her lips and my breath caught in my throat. Her body still shivered as she nestled deeper into my arms, tugging the comforter up under her chin.

Why did she have to seem so helpless—so fragile and innocent? This wasn't the creature I'd chased down for hundreds of years. That woman had been openly hostile.

She thrived on chaos. She would have run me through with a blade just for the fun of it, even if she knew it couldn't kill me.

Was I being tested? If I was, I was likely failing. But even hunters felt remorse when they came across a wounded animal—no matter how sharp the claws. The difference was that hunters put those animals out of their misery and I was cuddling up behind mine.

Slowly, her shivering eased, the pink hue of her skin returning. Like a tidal wave, her natural heat returned, washing over my skin in a way that felt all too good.

As if she could read my darkest thoughts, she whispered, "Why do you feel so good?"

I should have moved away from her. She was out of danger, she didn't need me holding her anymore. I should have let her go and gotten off the bed. But I didn't.

My arm tightened around her middle of its own accord.

"I don't know," I finally responded. "Stop talking and go to sleep, demon."

She mumbled something incoherent as sleep took her. Almost immediately, her breaths evened and her body relaxed against mine.

But even in her sleep, she was dangerous.

She shifted, nestling closer into me and stealing every shred of my heat and sanity. Her perfectly rounded backside was pressed into my crotch, driving me crazy. I was just grateful she was no longer shivering because I wasn't sure I could handle that kind of constant movement. Even still, the slightest shift set my body on fire like only she was able to do. And she was right, it felt amazing. Far better than it should.

I fisted my hands in the sheets, refusing to fall victim to her wicked temptations.

She arched into me and I sucked in a breath, feeling myself lengthen against her back. Hundreds of years of living and she was the only creature who could make me hard, and I hated her for it.

Angels didn't feel lust. We were above the temptations of the flesh. Why couldn't I have been assigned a male demon? After I took care of her, perhaps I would talk to the Arches about a change.

It wasn't unheard of for my kind to occasionally request new assignments. The change in scenery—so to speak—was necessary from time to time. It didn't happen often, though. The longer we hunted our targets, the better we knew them and the easier it was to track them down and kill them. Still, it happened. The Arches would likely approve the request if I asked.

Though I wasn't sure I could let another angel hunt her down and kill her. I just didn't know why.

I hadn't realized the growl slipped out of my throat until her hips rocked into mine once more, a small moan on her lips. My hand landed on her hip to find her robe had hiked up around her waist, and I again wished I had just let her freeze to death. Fingers digging into her naked skin, I held her hips still against mine until she settled, trying to calm my breathing.

Before I knew what I was doing, my hand was trailing upward, skimming over her hip and across her narrow waist where her robe had gathered. Why did a demon have to have such soft skin? It was like satin under my fingertips. Goose bumps exploded across her flesh and she shuddered against me, heat radiating from her body and consuming me.

And, Lord above, it felt divine.

I yanked my arm away and scrambled to get out of the bed and put as much distance between her and me as possible. She whimpered in her sleep, stirring before settling back down.

With a groan, I adjusted myself. I was painfully hard.

And she was the cause. She did this to me. Even now, standing across the room from her, I could feel the flames of her touch on my skin. It had me wanting to crawl back into that bed.

Storming across the small room, I burst into the even smaller bathroom and turned on the shower, cranking the old dial to cold—as cold as it could possibly go. Without wasting another second, I dropped my underwear and stepped into the weak stream of water, tucking my wings tightly to my back to fit into the shower stall.

A hiss escaped through my clenched teeth as the icy liquid cascaded around my overheated body. But even the cold couldn't chase away the burn her touch had left deep within me. Quite the opposite; it seemed to only amplify it.

I growled, turning to face the showerhead, letting the water splash down my front. Men claimed cold showers could help, but apparently not against succubus charms. Bringing my hands up, I scrubbed them down my face and chest, trying to wash away the feel of her body pressed against mine. Only the more I tried to rid my mind of her, the more I saw her lying there in my arms, her backside nestled in my lap. The way she rolled her hips into me. The little sounds she made when I growled into her ear.

I sucked in a breath as I pumped a hand up and down my hard length, trying to ease the mounting pressure she'd created. It felt good—too good. My head fell back as I stroked myself again, a moan falling from my lips.

"No," I bit out, releasing myself, much to my own traitorous body's dismay. "No!"

My knuckles connected with the shower wall, tiles shattering upon impact. I pulled my hand free, savoring the brief moment of pain while it lasted.

"No," I told myself again, chest heaving with each breath. I would not be pulled into her darkness.

She would not ruin me.

GISELLE

I groaned when the sun illuminated my face.

"Five more minutes," I mumbled, pulling the sheets over my head.

"Get up," a deep voice rumbled, and suddenly I was wide awake.

I peeked out from under the covers to see my stalker looming over the bed, arms crossed and signature scowl firmly in place.

Did this guy constantly live with a stick wedged firmly up his perfectly sculpted ass?

"We really need to stop meeting like this," I told him before drawing the sheet back over my face.

The covers were ripped off me and I shrieked, the air in the cabin still cold from the night. I'd had about enough of all things cold for the rest of my life. Room temperature or higher, thank you very much.

"Why are you such an ass?"

"Why are you so foolish?" he shot back. "Did you really think you could escape me, demon?"

I rolled my eyes, enjoying how much the simple action seemed to piss him off. "It was worth a shot, jackass. Freezing to death out there in the desert was worlds better than having to spend another second with you in this cabin."

Okay, so that last part wasn't entirely truthful. I quite enjoyed his big body pressed against mine last night—way more than I ever should have. I found it calmed the restlessness I always felt deep within me. I'd never had anyone hold me like that before, had never been anyone's little spoon. Hell, I'd never been anyone's any type of spoon. I was a party of me, myself, and I. There'd never been anyone who wanted to take care of me. Mark was the closest I'd gotten to that, and my stalker had ruined it.

"Hopefully you learned your lesson," he bit out. "You nearly got yourself killed out there."

"So?" I snapped, leaping from the bed and meeting his hard gaze. "You want me dead anyway, so what does it matter if I do the deed myself? Don't start pretending you care about me. Why did you even save me?"

He barely hid the surprise on his grumpy face as I jabbed a finger into his chest, the electric sensation of his touch spiraling up my arm. I ignored it.

"You keep telling me you want me to die so I can go back to Hell and you can go about your happy, delusional life. So why the fuck did you save me? You should have just let me die!"

His scruffy jaw ticked, those stormy eyes narrowing on my face. "Watch your language," he growled and I clamped my thighs together.

"They're just words!" I shouted, throwing my arms up in frustration. "Fuck, ass, bitch, shit. *Words!*"

His eyes darted downward before immediately flicking back to my face. A glance down told me my robe—in its usual fashion—had pulled open, putting my breasts on full display.

"Cover yourself, woman," he said, hands fisting at his sides. Was he resisting the urge to touch me or to re-dress me? I was *not* okay with how much I hoped it was the former. "Do you have no shame?"

"Oh, get over yourself, Holy Boy," I shot back, resisting the natural urge to do exactly as he'd said. "They're tits. Women have them. Your mother had them."

"I have no mother."

My eyes were going to get a serious workout from the number of times I rolled them being around this loon. A few more times and they'd roll right out of my head.

"I forgot," I said, forcing myself to take a step closer to him, "you're a precious little cherub created by the big man and sent here to murder vile, dirty women. Well, you know what, Mr. I Think I Have Wings, I don't think I will cover up. This robe has been quite stifling, really."

I let the robe slip down my shoulders and pool at my feet.

I took another step toward him, smirking when he scrambled back another foot. Weapons of perky proportions.

"What's wrong?" I sneered. "Does the angel not like the body God gave me?"

I ran my hands down my breasts, his heated eyes tracking the movement as he continued to back away from me.

"You were made by the Devil himself," he hissed. I wouldn't have been surprised if he whipped out a crucifix and started praying my nudity away. It gave me great satisfaction. I found I liked ruffling this man's feathers.

A lot.

Ignoring him, I stopped my pursuit and smirked again. "Or maybe you like my body a little *too* much. Not very holy of you to be lusting after a woman. Especially one you claim is a demon."

His nostrils flared and I knew I'd struck a chord. One I just couldn't seem to leave alone. Everything about this conversation felt familiar—it felt *right*.

I sauntered forward, swaying my naked hips with each step. "*Can* angels even lust?" I said, backing him into the small dining table. My eyes flicked to his jeans. "Angels are probably built like Ken dolls below the belt. That must be so frustrating for you."

The low growl was my only warning.

He lunged for me, wrapping one large hand around my neck and pushing me across the room until my back slammed into the wall beside the bathroom door. He easily grabbed both of my wrists in one hand, pinning them above my head.

"Do I feel like a Ken doll to you, demon?" he snarled,

pressing his muscular body against mine and eliciting a gasp from me.

"Holy Hell balls," I breathed, feeling his very hard —*very* large—cock pressed into my stomach. My jaw dropped. The guy made Mark seem small. I thought I'd imagined it last night as he'd wrapped himself around me while I was on my deathbed.

A growly man with a six-pack *and* a dick the size of my forearm, and the dude thought he was an angel sent by God to kill me. Just my goddamned luck!

His breaths came hard and fast, his chest brushing against my bare nipples, sending bolts of electricity straight to my pussy. I found myself arching into him, grinding my hips into that rock-hard bulge, savoring the delicious friction it created. Instead of letting me go, he kept me pinned to the wall, his eyes dilating as he watched me.

I hated myself for being so turned on—I wasn't sure I'd ever been so wet in my whole life. I shouldn't have been feeling like this. This was the man who had tormented me and stalked me. Who took me from my life and was holding me captive in the middle of the desert. He was threatening to *kill* me.

What the hell was wrong with me?

We both panted, our breaths mingling. I was sure that any moment we would fog up the whole damn cabin.

I had a feeling we would have some amazing rage sex.

Again, the number of things clearly wrong with me could fill a damn dictionary.

Suddenly, he released me and stepped back. I barely

managed to stay upright, my legs wobbling beneath me. I braced myself against the wall, grateful for its presence. I swallowed hard.

"Am I allowed to take a shower?" I asked, happy that I was able to find my voice. Even if it did come out all breathy and wanton.

He turned his back to me, gripping the edge of the dining table with white knuckles. The thick cords of muscles under his tight shirt tensed and I resisted reaching out and running my hands down his back.

"Yes," he finally said, his deep voice strained. "But I will be right outside the door, so do not try anything stupid, demon."

"You know, I have a name," I snapped. I was getting pretty sick of being called a demon. The accusatory name had my skin crawling. "It's Giselle."

He made a noncommittal noise and I rolled my eyes. He still wouldn't turn around and look at me.

"Do you have a name?" I continued, tapping my bare foot on the floor and crossing my arms over my chest.

"A name?"

"Oh, for fuck's sake," I mumbled. "Yes, a name." It would be nice not to keep referring to him as my stalker. Or crazy asshat. Or sexy psychopath. Or any of the other things I found myself calling him as I cursed his very existence in my head.

He was silent for a long minute. "Lucas," he finally said. "My name is Lucas."

I was glad he didn't say some stereotypical angel name, like Gabriel or Michael—that was about the extent of my angel knowledge. But I was pretty sure Lucas wasn't some famous angel.

"Well, *Lucas,* feel free to join me," I said, mostly teasing and fully playing with fire. "I can help you with that little situation you've got going on over there."

It was anything but little.

He did look at me then. And look he did. I felt his eyes rake down my body like a physical touch and a shiver rushed through me, heat pooling between my legs.

"Your succubus lineage is the worst part of you," he bit out and I couldn't help but laugh.

I opened the bathroom door and stepped into the doorway.

"Just because I have a healthy sex drive does not mean I'm a demon, buddy." Okay, maybe *healthy* was a bit of a stretch. I'd always been above average in that department. It still didn't make me a damn demon or succubus, or whatever he thought I was. Not my fault he was a prude.

I gave him a little wave and slammed the bathroom door, sad to see there wasn't a lock.

Turning to the shower, I flicked the water on and could have cried when I saw the dial had a hot setting. I cranked it all the way up as high as it would go and waited to see if the water would actually heat up. When steam filled the room, I knew there most certainly was a God. Just hopefully not one that sent angels to kill mostly-innocent women.

I stepped into the shower and sighed as the scalding water cascaded over my body. It seared my skin, chasing away any lingering chill from the night before. But even as hot as it was, it couldn't compete with the fire I felt burning deep inside.

The same fire that had my core throbbing.

I scanned the shower until I found a small bottle that looked like soap. I picked it up and popped the top, sniffing it to make sure I wasn't about to wash my body off with something putrid. The sweet scent of mangos filled my nostrils and I poured a hefty amount of it into my hands, working it into a nice lather before scrubbing it over my body. Washing away my desert adventure and his touch at the same time.

Only his touch wasn't as easy to remove as the sand.

A soapy hand slid between my breasts and down my belly, moving lower still until my fingers were dancing between my legs. I bit back a moan as my thumb brushed against my clit, my head rocking back against the tile wall.

I tried to think about Mark, the way his body had felt pressed against me, his hot mouth over mine. But my stupid brain kept wandering back to *him*.

Lucas.

I knew I shouldn't have been fantasizing about him. There was nothing morally gray about the man. He was dangerous, and he clearly had a few screws loose. But no matter how much I tried, I couldn't get his face out of my head, or forget the way his body felt pressed against mine. I shuddered, working my body higher and higher, wishing it were his fingers in me instead of my own.

Something about Lucas was familiar. I felt drawn to him—connected somehow. How Mark said he felt a connection with me, that was how I felt about the man who had kidnapped me. It was like we were tied together in a way I couldn't put words to.

Fate.

His intense gray eyes flashed through my mind and I bit my lip in an attempt to contain my cries as the orgasm crashed into me. Blood coated my tongue as I rode the blissful waves of pleasure as his face faded from my mind.

Exhaling a shaky breath, I slid down the tiled wall until I was sitting in the shower basin. The water, already growing cold, continued to rain down around me as my body came back to earth.

Lucas had called me a temptress, but who was really tempting who?

17

LUCAS

I thought I'd break the wooden table with how hard I was gripping it.

Her cries of pleasure had carried through the thin bathroom door and filled the cabin. Even long after they were gone, they were all I heard echoing in my mind and wreaking havoc on my slipping sanity.

I sucked in a deep breath, hoping the oxygen would somehow clear my head. Even though that hadn't worked the last fifty times I'd tried it. At this rate, I was going to be perpetually hard. This wretched creature was plaguing my every thought. She was going to be my undoing—my absolute ruination. I needed her to remember what she was so I could end her life and wash my hands of her for good. Or at least for a couple of decades until she returned for another round.

Though I wasn't sure I could handle any more. After I

killed her, I knew I had to ask the Arches for reassignment.

I just needed to get myself to complete my task this one last time.

But as she stepped out of the bathroom in nothing more than a towel, her amber eyes bright as they met mine, all thoughts of running her through with my blade vanished. Instead, those thoughts were quickly replaced by the memory of her lips against mine those many years ago. The urge to slam her into the wall just to feel that body pressed against mine once more hit me hard and I held onto the dining table for dear life, rooting myself in place.

Maybe I needed to swallow my pride and allow Zain to finish her off for me as he'd offered. But the mere thought of Zain touching her, whether with his blade or otherwise, had my grip on the edge of the table tightening until it snapped off in my hand with a loud crack.

The demon—I refused to refer to her by her name—jumped back, her eyes growing wider as they fell to the piece of splintered wood in my hand. Fear bled into her normally fiery gaze. Fear caused by me. I wasn't sure how I felt about that.

Tossing the wood aside, I reached into the bag sitting on the table and pulled out the pair of leggings and sweater I had picked up for her the day before. It was what I'd been doing while she was out in the middle of the desert trying to get herself killed.

"I got you clothes," I said, shoving them into her arms, careful not to brush my fingers against her skin. I wasn't sure I could handle the effect her touch had on me in that moment. Not while so much of her flesh was showing.

She stared at the clothes before her eyes flicked to her bare feet. I'd gotten her shoes as well, but there was no way I'd be giving them to her after her little escape attempt. I'd also hidden my extra pair of boots.

She wasn't leaving this cabin again. Not alive at least.

Finally, she looked up from the clothes, meeting my gaze. I didn't like the mischievous gleam suddenly dancing in her eyes. "Maybe I don't want to wear them."

"Put them on," I said, fingers clenching into fists at my sides. "Now."

She shrugged. "I don't think so. Not really my style."

I shouldn't have been surprised by how easy the lie rolled off her tongue. I'd watched her for over a month, I knew exactly what she wore when she wasn't working.

"Demon," I growled in warning and her eyes dilated, her pink tongue darting out to lick her lips.

Flashing me a devilish grin, she whipped off the towel and tossed it and the clothes at my head. I snatched them out of the air, trying to keep my eyes on her face and failing miserably as she strolled to the bed.

She sat on the edge and leaned back on her hands, not bothering to hide her nudity in the slightest. The woman had not a shred of shame. Not that she had anything to be ashamed of. She was perfect—for a demon. I suppose that was the point. Easier to lure people to their doom that way. She was a natural beauty with those succubus genes of hers. I'd heard her mother was also a sight to behold. This wicked apple didn't fall far from the tree.

But her beauty be damned, I refused to be her next victim. My control was already slipping. I couldn't take much more of her body on display.

Forcing myself closer, I dropped the clothes on the bed next to her before flinging the towel over her naked form.

"I won't tell you again," I said through clenched teeth.

Her laughter seemed strained, not quite reaching her eyes as she sat up, letting the towel pool in her lap. "What's wrong?" she asked. "I thought you enjoyed watching me. It's all you've been doing for a month. Besides, that giant ass bulge in your pants says you very much like this."

"Get dressed, demon."

She was on her feet in a single rapid beat of my heart, the fire in her eyes burning straight through me. She closed the distance between us, my shirt doing nothing to shield me from her erect nipples as they grazed my chest. "I'm not a goddamned demon!" she shouted in my face, and I tried not to shrink away from her. Even her breath was tempting, like sunshine in spring. "Stop fucking calling me that, asshole."

My hands shook at my sides, breaths coming faster as her fire once again seeped under my skin, making me see red. "Careful..."

Defiance shone in her eyes. "Or what?" she snapped. "Are you going to kill me? Get a new threat, asshole. That one's growing old."

In a fraction of a second, the tip of my sword hovered an inch away from her throat, cutting off whatever vile words she was preparing to spew next. The fear was back in her wide eyes as they locked onto the weapon that threatened to end her very existence. Her entire body started to tremble and I didn't think it had anything to do with the cold.

"I told you to get dressed," I said slowly, voice thick with my anger and something else that I didn't want to put a name to. "I will not ask you again, *demon*."

She pursed her lips at the title but didn't open her mouth to argue, for which I was grateful. I was even more grateful when she took a shaky step back, her eyes never leaving the blade as she grabbed the clothes from where I'd left them on the bed. Tossing me one last glare, she stormed back into the bathroom with the clothes in hand, slamming the wooden door behind her so hard I thought it might break off the hinges.

Blowing out a breath, I sheathed the sword before I did something I'd regret. Then again, *not* killing her was something I should have regretted.

And yet I found I didn't.

Five minutes later, she stomped out of the bathroom wearing the black leggings and sweater. They weren't much better on my sanity. The leggings fit her like a second skin, the sweater hanging off one shoulder, the flash of peachy skin taunting me.

But it was still better than her gallivanting around in the nude.

"Happy now, asshole?" she sneered.

Rather than answer her, I mentally and spiritually prepared for what I needed to do next. I strode across the room, bending next to the bed and pulling out the thick rope

I'd tied to the heavy metal framework while she was in the shower. I wasn't taking any chances of her escaping again.

Her eyes zeroed in on the rope. "What are you doing?" she asked slowly, retreating a step.

I held my hand out to her. "Give me your wrists."

"I won't go anywhere," she argued, taking another small step away from me. The fire in her eyes said otherwise.

"No," I said, "you won't. Now give me your wrists."

Why I thought she'd obey was beyond me. But I wasn't entirely stupid. I was prepared for what came next.

She bolted for the door and I dove for her, blocking her path. I grabbed her arm and pulled her back to the bed, throwing her onto it. Straddling her hips, I easily restrained her, ignoring the shrieks and curses falling from her wicked lips. Her body thrashing beneath mine wasn't quite as easy to ignore, however, and I felt myself starting to lengthen all over again.

With a growl, I grabbed her wrist as her hand came sailing toward my face, catching it before she landed the blow. I quickly snatched up her other arm in the same hand, pinning her two slender wrists together.

She screamed, her body bucking wildly beneath mine until I nearly forgot what I was doing. Forcing myself to focus, I carefully wrapped the rope around her wrists, looping it together and tying it off in a couple different spots until I was sure it was secure. The only way she was breaking free of those bindings was to chew her way out.

I leaped clear of her kicking feet, shoving away from

the bed and putting space between us. I'd only left her enough rope to move around the perimeter of the bed. She couldn't even get to the bathroom.

"You sick, delusional, fucking psychopath," she spat, her eyes wide with rage as she sat up, tugging at the rope. "Let me go!"

"So that you can walk out that door and nearly kill yourself again?" I asked. "I don't think so. Be glad I gave you such a long leash."

"Leash?" she all but screamed. "You're insane! Untie me, you crazy fucking—"

Diving forward, I shoved the fabric I was holding into her mouth, muffling her angry words. If looks could kill—well, it was a good thing I couldn't die. At least, not by her.

A vibration in my back pocket drew my attention away from her. I pulled out my phone and checked the caller ID, not at all surprised to see Zain's name flashing across the screen.

"Behave," I growled and she narrowed her eyes at me, nostrils flaring. I was pretty sure I knew what two foul words she was trying to form around the gag.

I put the phone to my ear as I moved to the front door, away from her muffled screams. I didn't need Zain hearing her in the background. "What?" I snapped, stepping out onto the cabin's miniscule porch.

"I am officially your superior," he said. "Show some respect when you answer my calls."

"What are you—"

"The notice should be coming through right about...*now.*"

With perfect timing, my phone buzzed and I yanked it away from my ear to look at my screen, glaring at the offending message coming across my screen.

The message announcing Zain's promotion.

He'd been given the archangel position that I'd been pining after for nearly two hundred years. I'd been passed up and now it would be another half a millennium before another opportunity arose.

My breaths grew more ragged as the anger swelled within me. I gripped the phone so hard, I thought I might snap it in half.

"Did you call to gloat?" I asked when I finally brought the device back to my ear. Knowing Zain, he'd probably spend the next five hundred years writing me up. I waited for him to do just that.

"I know you wanted this position," he said instead. His voice didn't hold its normal cockiness, but I wasn't about to let my guard down with him. Not anymore. "It was a close race between the two of us, brother. My track record has been better recently, add in my ideas to change how we hunt... Well, the choice was easy."

"*My* idea," I bit out. "I was the one who told you my thoughts on having more than one high-powered target for each of us. You presented it as your own to get the position and you know it."

Zain chuckled. "Your memory is slipping as much as your ability to finish a job, it seems. There will be more promotions, don't worry. I'm sure if you work hard—and learn to respect your superiors—you'll have a good chance of making the next archangel position. I'll even put in a good word for you."

Right, like he'd done this time around. He'd likely do everything he could to make sure I remained beneath him for eternity.

"What do you want, Archangel Zain?" I asked again, swallowing down the bile that threatened to surface at using his new title. The title that should have been mine.

"That's better," he said, the smirk evident in his voice. "I am just calling to check in on the status of your mark."

"She will be taken care of soon," I replied coolly, eyes darting back to the still-closed front door. "Very soon."

Any ideas I'd had of swallowing my pride and asking Zain to finish her off for me disappeared like my chances of becoming an archangel. I wasn't letting him anywhere near her now. He'd use the opportunity to further slander my name among our kind.

"That is very disappointing to hear," he said. "It should have already been taken care of by now. Where is she?"

As if she could hear us, her screams came blaring out from inside the cabin, no longer muffled by the strip of cloth I'd gagged her with.

"Help!" she screamed. "Help me, someone! Please help! He's holding me hostage! You have to help me!"

If ever there was a time for cursing…

"You have her with you?" Zain hissed into the phone.

"You don't understand," I mumbled, putting more distance between the cabin and me, but her voice seemed to be filling the entire desert.

"What don't I understand?" he shot back, his deep voice getting louder. "What reason would you have to hold her without killing her? Finish the job, warrior."

"She doesn't remember what she is," I blurted out, running a hand through my hair. "She doesn't know she's a demon. I don't know how, but she doesn't."

"And you actually believe her?" Zain all but yelled. "You really have lost your edge. She's lying to you—that is what they do. You know this. She is playing you for a fool. She needs to die."

"And she will," I growled. "I *will* kill her."

"No," he snapped. "The time for that has passed. You clearly cannot be trusted to finish this task. I have no choice but to intervene now. Once she is killed, you will be reassigned. I cannot believe you of all our kind would allow yourself to be so foolish as to trust the word of a demon."

Asking for reassignment was one thing. Being forced to change targets was different. It was a demotion, and I knew it. I'd be lucky if I was given a lower-level demon to track and hunt. I'd never make archangel now.

I never should have let her live so long. She was ruining my entire existence.

"Where are you?" he asked.

"I told you I'll handle it," I said through clenched teeth.

"Tell me where you are, Lucas," he said, his voice turning menacing. "That is a direct order from a superior. I will not ask again."

My jaw ticked, hand fisting at my side. I turned around, glancing at the rickety old cabin. "I have her on a rooftop tower in the city," I told him, the lie slipping right off my tongue. "I don't know the name of the hotel. It's tall."

"Very well. Stay put and keep her there. I'm on my way. I will finish this—" Zain's angry voice was cut off as the phone snapped clean in half in my hand.

I dropped the crumpled remains into the sand and charged toward the cabin.

GISELLE

"Help!" I screamed, my voice echoing throughout the small cabin.

I'd been calling for help since Mr. Stalker-Turned-Kidnapper stepped out of the cabin to take his call. I knew there was a chance that the person on the other end of the phone was just as deranged as Lucas, but I had to try. If there was even the smallest chance whoever called would get me help, then I had to take it. I had to get away from him.

Even if the feel of his body pressed against mine did feel right in so many ways. Clearly, Stockholm syndrome was hitting me hard. All the more reason to get the hell out of here, and soon.

I continued to scream until the cabin door flew open, crashing into the wall and splitting the door in two. The second I saw his face, my big mouth clamped shut.

He was pissed with a capital P. And all that rage was directed at me.

His chest heaved with each rapid breath he took, his fingers clenching and unclenching at his side. Those stormy gray eyes, full of murder, locked onto me and I struggled to swallow, tempted to pull the gag back up.

Oh shit.

With terrifying speed, he reached for his sword, yanking it free with a sickening metallic sound that had my heart pounding against my chest.

"I-I'm sorry," I rushed to say as he stormed toward me with a deadly purpose. I scrambled off the bed as best I could with my bound hands, trying to escape his fury. The rope attached to my wrists pulled taut as I pressed my body into the wall, cowering away from him. "I'm sorry. I won't do it again!"

The sun caught the edge of his blade as he lifted it, the light gleaming in my eyes. I could practically taste his rage —it filled the entire cabin, suffocating me. This was different than before. I could see it in his eyes—he meant business.

I'd finally pushed him too far.

"Please, no," I cried out, holding my bound hands up to block the impending blow. "I'm sorry, I won't do it again. Please don't kill me."

Tears streamed down my face, my voice shaking nearly as much as my body. I didn't care about putting on a brave front anymore. I just wanted to live.

"Please, Lucas."

His name on my lips had him stopping dead in his

tracks, his hard eyes landing on my tear-streaked face. He furrowed his brows, conflict flickering in his angry eyes.

"Do you have any idea what you have done?" he seethed. My eyes darted to where his fingers flexed on the hilt of his weapon.

"I'm sorry," I said again. "I'm so sorry, Lucas. I promise to behave. I'll do whatever you want. Just don't kill me. I-I'm not ready to die." My voice cracked on the last word as a sob ripped through me.

And that was the truth: I didn't want to die. My life hadn't been the greatest, but I wasn't ready for it to end yet. There was so much I still hadn't done—so many dreams unfulfilled. I'd like to think there was still time to turn it around. I wanted the chance, at least.

Lucas stood over me, his breaths coming hard and fast, much like my own. He stared at me for a full minute—the longest damn minute of my entire life—his eyes tracking the tears streaming down my face. He seemed offended by the salty moisture. Well, I was offended by him trying to *kill me*. Not that I was about to tell him that while staring down the sharp edge of his sword.

I forced myself to meet his eyes. "I'll do anything you want," I told him. "*Anything.*"

Something flashed across those intense eyes and then the sword was moving.

"No!" I screamed. But yelling wasn't going to stop the blade as it came barreling toward me. I scrunched my eyes and pressed myself into the wall, hoping to hell there was something for me in the afterlife other than what he said there was.

Only death didn't come for me.

I gasped as the tip of his sword kissed my skin through the thin sweater, hovering directly over my heart without drawing blood. I held my breath, afraid that the slightest movement of my chest would have the blade slicing through my skin.

"You will not try to escape again," he said in that deep voice of his that sent unwanted shivers down my spine.

I nodded so fast I thought my head might bob right off my shoulders. "Of course," I rushed to say. "I won't try running again. I'll stay here. You can even untie me."

His eyes narrowed and I snapped my stupid mouth shut. I'd figure out another way to escape if I had to. I'd gotten out of the cuffs. I could find a way out of these bindings as well. And then I just had to figure out where the hell in the desert we were.

Because that had worked out so well for me the last time.

"And you will stay fully clothed from now on," he added, his eyes trailing down my body before flicking back up to my face.

I bit my tongue to stop myself from making a snide comment about how he could just *not* constantly check out the goods. It wasn't my fault he couldn't control himself. And he had another think coming if he thought I was going to shower fully clothed.

I gave him a jerky nod. "No nudity."

One point for me for not saying anything stupid. I would have patted myself on the back if not for the giant ass sword still dancing over my heart.

"And no more vile language," he continued.

Yeah, there was no stopping the eye roll on that one, impending death be damned.

Good luck with that one, asshole.

Another point for keeping my thoughts *inside* my head where they belonged. I was on a roll. Maybe I'd survive this yet.

"I'll try my best," I forced out.

The sword left my chest but before I could relax, it moved to my neck. I was getting really sick of staring down his blade.

He used the flat side of it to force my chin up, making me meet his eyes. Eyes narrowing on me, he cocked his head to the side, studying me like I was some strange creature he'd never seen before. Like maybe *I* was the crazy one in this situation.

Yeah, fucking right.

I started to taste blood from how hard I was biting my tongue.

"You've changed since New York," he finally said, retracting his blade and sheathing it at his hip.

Only when the sword was out of sight did I blow out the shaky breath I'd been holding. My knees buckled before completely giving out, and I slid down the wall until I was sitting in a heap on the floor, looking up at his hard eyes.

New York?

His words didn't make any sense to me. Then again, nothing he was doing made much sense. It was hard to explain crazy and he was some serious next-level shit.

"I've never been to New York," I told him, voice still trembling. "I'm not the person you think I am. There's been a mistake."

"Liar," he growled and my traitorous body came flaring to life despite the fear racing through my veins.

"I'm not lying," I insisted, biting back my urge to curse at him. I didn't need him bringing out that damn sword again. "I haven't even left Nevada before."

And that was the truth. I didn't have the money to travel anywhere else. I rarely even left the city.

"You were there," he shouted, and I flinched away from him, curling into myself on the floor. More tears replacing the ones that had dried on my cheeks.

Stop pissing off the raging lunatic, Elle.

I needed to learn some self-preservation skills, clearly. Preferably before the next time I pissed Mr. Anti-Nudity off. Which, knowing me, was guaranteed to happen sometime soon.

"I know you were there," he said again, only slightly more calmly this time. "I saw you there. I watched you destroy countless lives. You spread your chaos throughout that city every single day until the day I killed you in that dark subway tunnel."

A sharp pang shot straight through my chest and I sucked in a breath, grabbing it with my bound hands until the ache faded as quickly as it came.

"I've never been on a subway before," I whispered, shaking my head. But even as the words left my mouth, they felt like a lie. My lips tingled and I reached up, pressing my fingers to them to try to remove the sensation.

What the...

"And then there's the boy," he said, ignoring me as he sat on the side of the bed, pinning me with a glare. I was starting to think he didn't have any other expression. "Even after all these years, I can't figure out why you spared him."

"What are you talking—"

My words turned into a cry as a searing pain shot through my skull. I tried to grab my head, a bright light flashing in my eyes. My eyelids slammed shut, face scrunching as I shook my head, trying to rid myself of the blinding pain. What was happening to me?

A shrill metallic sound filled my ears, like brakes squealing, and I groaned, rocking my head back into the wall. I was pretty sure I was experiencing a brain aneurysm, or maybe a stroke. Maybe God really *did* want me dead.

As quickly as the sensation came upon me, it was gone, leaving me gasping for air on the cabin floor. When I opened my eyes, Lucas's gray eyes came into focus mere inches from mine, his big body kneeling in front of me. Concern was etched into his stupidly handsome face, contradicting the fact that he'd just tried to kill me. I wasn't sure how he could want to protect me and kill me in the same breath.

"I don't know what you're talking about," I said once I found my voice. "What boy?"

"The one you saved."

"Saved?" I echoed. What was he talking about? "You think I saved some kid?"

"I don't think," he shot back, "I know. I watched you risk your own life to do it."

He seemed upset about that little tidbit. Like the idea of me doing something good and noble was so impossible to comprehend.

I cocked an eyebrow at him. "That doesn't sound like something a demon would do," I said, unable to control the sass that bubbled out of me. "Sounds more like I'm the hero in your little delusional world, not the villain."

He stood once more, reclaiming his spot on the bed. "One heroic act does not make up for the countless atrocities you've committed during the centuries you've plagued this world, demon."

I wasn't sure how to respond to that. Not in a way that wouldn't have him drawing his sword on me all over again. I just needed to keep my big mouth shut. Of course, that wasn't what I did. Some people never learned. Namely me. I was *some people.*

"If you're supposed to be the angel, then why didn't you save him—the kid?"

His jaw ticked and I reminded myself to tread carefully, swallowing the urge to tell him he was a shit angel.

"You were closer," he finally said. "He fell on the tracks because of you. Because you ran from me."

"Maybe you shouldn't have been chasing imaginary me and that wouldn't have happened," I said under my breath.

"It is my job to chase you down and kill you," he shot back like that was explanation enough.

"Well, you have a pretty shitty job."

I regretted the words the second they were out of my mouth. Lucas was on his feet and towering over me, his hand hovering above the hilt of his sword.

"Do you realize what you've done?" he asked me for the second time. "You have destroyed my life."

The snort was out before I could stop it. "*I* ruined *your* life? Are you serious, dude?"

I gasped as his big hand wrapped around my neck, lifting me to my feet. He backed me into the wall, standing so close that I could feel the heat radiating off his body, his muscular frame a mere breath away from mine. The primal urge to arch into him was strong but I fought it. I hated how much I wanted him to touch me, to feel the electric sensation of his skin against mine.

I held his stare, a strange sense of calm settling over me. His hand tightened around my throat until I struggled to pull in air, but I didn't fight him. He pointed a big finger at my face. "You took everything from me, demon."

When I didn't respond, he shoved me into the wall, taking a step back.

"Everything," he repeated.

"I guess we can call it even then, Holy Boy," I rasped, stumbling to the bed. "Because you ruined my life too. Which is saying a lot with how shitty it's been. You ripped me from my home, probably lost me my job, and took me away from the first truly good man I've ever met."

He bristled at the mention of Mark. "I saved him from you," he bit out.

"While also threatening to kill him," I replied. "Just like you're threatening to kill me now. Face it, buddy. You should have just left me alone. Maybe then we both would've been better off."

His stormy eyes stayed on my face and then he turned on his heels and headed for the door. He paused in the doorway.

"No one is better off while you still draw breath," he whispered, keeping his back to me. "Stay put. I have to go fix yet another problem your existence has created."

And with that, he was gone.

19

LUCAS

I swooped onto the roof of the same hotel where I'd first taken my demon from. The second my feet touched down on the concrete, I was filled with the memory of her standing in that blasted robe, her wide eyes pleading for me to save her from the drunk.

Right then and there, I should have run her through with my sword. Maybe then I wouldn't have been in this position. Letting her live was the biggest mistake of my long life. And yet, I still couldn't get myself to finish the job. I wasn't even sure when I'd started referring to her as "my demon." The term should have bothered me a lot more than it did.

But in many ways, she *was* mine. After all, she was my mark, no one else's. For a bit longer, at least. Soon, there would be another angel assigned to her; Zain was making sure of that. The next time she stepped foot on this Earth, she'd be someone else's problem. Another of my kind would be hunting her down, watching her every move, and driving their blade through her blackened heart.

She would plague their every waking thought instead of mine.

Fury rose within me. The thought of someone else looking at her—touching her—had me nearly as angry as it did to know that Zain planned to kill her. That he was on his way here right now with the intention of ending her life.

But he wouldn't find her here. He wouldn't find her anywhere. I'd make sure of it. If anyone was going to kill her, it was going to be me.

This was my job to finish.

"Mine."

The word was out of my mouth before I could stop it. Only I wasn't sure if it was directed at the job…or her.

I groaned, pressing my forehead into the ledge of the hotel tower.

Why couldn't she have just stayed in Hell like I'd told her to? Why did she have to go and save that boy? Even if she hadn't ever directly harmed a child in her many lifetimes, she'd also never gone out of her way to protect one. She was a demon. Her kind were selfish and rotten to the core; they craved chaos and bloodshed and misery.

And yet she'd been willing to sacrifice herself to save his life. No one else on that subway platform had been willing to do that.

My life would have been easier if she had just let him die. And if she'd kept her sinful mouth to herself…

I'd spent nearly three decades dwelling on both acts. They had completely consumed me. Each time I closed my eyes, I either saw her leaping in front of that train to save the boy's life, or I felt the press of her lips against mine. It was those thoughts that kept me from killing her when I'd finally found her, living out her life as normally as a high-powered demon could.

And the more I was around her, the more I believed she was telling the truth when she said she didn't remember. I just didn't understand why.

None of it made sense.

The beating of wings drew my attention upward and I scanned the mid-afternoon sky, locking onto an approaching figure. Zain's large frame landed gracefully on the roof twenty feet away from me. He immediately pulled his sword.

"Where is she?" he said, wasting no time.

I shoved away from the ledge, facing him head-on. "She escaped while you had me distracted on the phone," I told him. "I don't know where she went."

For the second time in one day, lies fell from my lips with ease. And the worst part was that I was lying for the creature I was supposed to kill. I should have let Zain go to the cabin and finish her off when he'd called me. But my pride wouldn't let me do it. At least, I told myself it was my pride, and not the fact that him killing her made me want to run *him* through with my blade.

What wicked magic was she weaving over me? No angel would ever choose a demon over their own kind.

Even if their own kind was taking everything they'd worked so hard for.

"You let her get away?" Zain raged, closing the distance between us, his sword still in hand.

"I didn't let her do anything," I bit out, holding my ground. I wasn't about to let Zain intimidate me. I didn't care what title he now held, I was still the better fighter between the two of us. I always had been. Besides, I knew he hadn't been given permission to kill me. Not for something like this. Killing another angel required the approval of numerous archangels and was for serious transgressions. It had only happened a handful of times in my lifetime.

No, Zain was just trying to throw his weight around. The power was already going to his head.

"She escaped," I said simply.

I drew my sword just in time to meet his as it came sailing toward me. The clashing of metal echoed in my ears along with Zain's laughter.

"At least you still have your reflexes, even if you have completely lost your senses," he sneered.

I leaned forward, pressing my blade harder into his until I saw his muscles start to strain, the thinnest bead of sweat forming along his brow. Archangel or not, I was stronger than him. And he knew it.

I blinked and his sword was gone, his body twirling away from me. The blade came back again, and I once more blocked the blow.

"We used to spar like this daily," Zain said through heavy breaths, a grin dancing on his face. "Do you remember, brother? Those many days of training. We've come a long way since then. Well, one of us has."

I felt the jab all the way down in my eternal soul.

Yanking my blade away, I immediately swung it toward his head. He brought his own sword up just in time, the smug smile on his lips slipping as he stumbled back a step.

But Zain wasn't one to show weakness, especially not in front of someone who was supposed to be his subordinate.

"Don't worry," he said through clenched teeth, with-drawing his sword and strategically moving away from me. It was brave of him to show me his back, walking to the edge of the building. But Zain wasn't stupid in the slightest. He knew I couldn't touch him, especially not after his promotion. If I killed him—or even attempted to do so—my life would be forfeit. Just as his would be if he tried to kill me without prior approval.

He sheathed his weapon and ran a hand through his golden curls before his blue eyes met mine. "You have many years ahead of you to fix what you've done here, Lucas. I'm sure in a couple thousand years you'll be able to move past this failure and regain your position."

He turned and leaned over the side of the rooftop, scrunching his nose at the city far beneath him. I shared his disgust. The nickname this city held was an under-statement. It was filled with vile humans doing unthink-able things. There wasn't anything good in this wretched place.

My demon didn't fit here. Not this time.

"Where is she?" Zain said, facing me.

"I told you, she got away."

"Where has she been staying?" he asked, taking a no-nonsense tone. I was dealing with Archangel Zain now. "What do you know? You've been hunting her for a couple of months. Fill me in so we can end this quickly."

By *we,* he meant *him.*

"I believe you told me I was off the case," I said through clenched teeth. Petty wasn't the best look for someone of my kind. I knew that, but I couldn't seem to help myself. The man standing in front of me, holding the title I'd worked so hard for, had taken everything I wanted in the span of a week. And now he wanted me to help him continue to make me look bad.

"Lucas," he snarled. "You will tell me, your direct superior, what you know about this demon."

My jaw ticked. "I don't know," I lied. "She was kicked out of her previous residence."

That was closer to the truth. Lying didn't come naturally to our kind and Zain was already suspicious. I had to tread carefully.

"She works at that casino over there," I told him, pointing down the busy street. "Though I doubt she'll go back after being caught. She'll likely go into hiding."

"If you had killed her like you were supposed to, then we wouldn't have to worry about that, would we?" Zain asked, disappointment on his face. "I can't believe you would believe her lies like that, Lucas. How long have you been hunting her?"

Too long, I wanted to tell him but thought better of it.

"I am bringing in a group to hunt her down," he continued, once again giving me his back to scan the cityscape below. "We cannot risk her going into hiding or moving to a new city. She grows in power with each new day she wakes on this Earth. We need to end this quickly."

"I will help," I told him.

Why I offered, I wasn't sure. I had no intention of leading Zain—or anyone else—to my demon. But if there was even a chance that I could make Zain look bad on his first big mission as an archangel, then I had to take it.

In the meantime, maybe I'd be able to get her to remember what she was. Then I could end her myself and deliver her to the Arches and salvage what was left of my reputation as a demon hunter.

"No," he snapped. "You have failed at your task. You will return to headquarters for reassignment."

I met Zain's hard eyes. "Please," I forced myself to say with as little contempt as possible. "Give me a chance to help correct my mistake. Let me help with the hunt, Archangel Zain. And then you can reassign me."

He stared at me for a long minute and just when I thought he'd say no, he nodded. "Fine."

I opened my mouth to speak but he held up a hand.

"One week," he said. "You have one week to help with the search, whether we find her in that time or not. When the week is up, you *will* return to headquarters for your reassignment, do you understand me?"

Not trusting myself to speak, I nodded.

"It is bad enough that others are being brought in to clean up your mess," he continued, taking a step toward me until we were only a couple feet apart. "Do not disappoint me again, Lucas. And I want you checking in with me daily. You will not ignore my calls anymore."

"My phone was crushed when she escaped."

More lies.

With a glare, he extended his empty hand toward me and I stiffened as a cell phone manifested out of thin air. He'd been given the archangel power of creation. I shouldn't have been nearly as surprised—or hurt—as I was.

"One week," he repeated, slapping the phone into my hand.

His wings extended, blocking out the sun as he took to the skies.

20

GISELLE

I groaned, flopping back on the bed and staring up at the ceiling, counting the knots in the wood for the millionth time.

If the way the sunlight shined through the window was any indication, Mr. Tall, Dark, and Crazy had been gone for nearly three hours. Maybe longer.

After an hour straight trying to saw through my bindings by scraping the rope against the dull metal edge of the bedframe with no success, I'd given up. Which left me with literally nothing to do except lie here in the scorching heat. The midday sun had turned the small cabin into an oven, coating my skin in a thin layer of sweat.

The sweater he'd forced me to wear hadn't helped matters. I'd tried to get it off a couple of times—threat of murder be damned. But I'd only ended up getting myself even more tied up. On the third attempt, I'd finally succeeded, leaving me with a ball of fabric coiled around my bound wrists and putting my breasts on full display.

Which completely went against his whole "thou shalt not take your clothes off" rule.

As hard as it was to get the sweater off with my hands tied in front of me, it was impossible to get it back on. But I didn't really want to put it on again.

The moment the fresh air hit my skin had felt divine, erasing all worries of my stalker's temper and phobia of female nudity. I was sure the fear would return when he came storming back in with his permanent scowl and that stupid sword of his in hand, yelling about shame and sin and demon titties.

But who knew when that'd be.

Another groan slipped past my lips. I was so bored. At least when I was holed up in the hotel room Mark had gotten for me, I had a TV and even a few magazines to flip through. Even better, I'd had my Kindle. Not to mention, when I was there, I wasn't tied up like a prisoner.

I had nothing here.

It was either count the knots in the wooden ceiling or sleep. But each time my eyes drifted shut, Lucas's ridiculously handsome face was right there waiting for me. Those stormy gray eyes, his strong jaw with its thin dusting of hair, that body that I was sure had been carved from granite. And that *package*.

I was positive at this point that he'd clawed his way out of one of my dark romance novels.

He had me so frustrated. In more ways than one.

My bound hands drifted down my stomach, pausing at the top of my leggings. I tried not to think about how he'd known my exact size. Or the many other crazy aspects of him.

Like how he thought he was an angel sent here to kill me.

Instead, as my fingers slipped between my legs, my mind drifted once more to the way his body felt pressed against mine. His large hand trapping my wrists above my head, his even larger cock digging into my lower stomach as he pinned me to the cabin wall. I'd been so turned on, I'd nearly asked him to take me right then and there. I wanted to feel those big hands on my naked flesh. I ached for it.

My thumb brushed over my legging-clad clit and a shudder ripped through me.

A low growl filled the room and I froze. My eyes flew open to find Lucas standing at the foot of the bed with a bag of food in his clenched fist. His gaze was locked on my hands before climbing higher, glaring at my naked flesh.

Shit.

I sat up, scrambling to cover my breasts with the crumpled mess of fabric hanging from my arms.

"I'm sorry," I blurted, eyes darting to where his sword was still strapped to his hip. "It was so hot and I was cooking in the sweater. You weren't even here so I didn't think it would be a big deal. But then I couldn't get it back—"

"You will not touch yourself," he ordered and my body shivered again, my nipples hardening as his low voice washed over me.

And then his words broke through my lust-filled haze.

"Excuse me?" I shot back. My anger should have extinguished the fire burning deep within me, but it seemed to only fan the flames, making them burn that much brighter. Heat pooled between my legs as he stared at me. Something sparked in his eyes and I wasn't sure what it was until it was too late.

Lucas dropped the bag and shot forward, grabbing hold of my ankle. I gasped as he jerked me across the bed until I was flat on my back in the middle of the mattress. Before I could push myself back up, he climbed on top of me, grabbing my bound hands and yanking them over my head, the air once again caressing my naked breasts.

His breaths came hard and fast as he leaned his face closer to mine, stopping only when his lips were no more than an inch away from my own. I swallowed hard, meeting his gaze.

"I said, you are not allowed to touch yourself anymore," he ground out. "You will not pleasure yourself in my presence."

"You technically weren't here when I started," I breathed, voice trembling with need. I'd barely just begun when he'd shown up, but his presence seemed to have my engines running at full power in a matter of seconds.

"I won't allow you to sin," he growled and my legs clamped together, a whimper leaving my parted lips.

"Then you should probably leave," I managed to say, my body rocking into the growing bulge in his jeans, earning me another rumble that sent vibrations straight to my pussy. "Because this is basically your fault. You're a walking orgasm, especially when you do the whole growly man thing."

He was silent for a long minute and I almost cried when he shifted his glorious weight off me. Only he didn't release my hands like I thought he might.

Instead, he reached down with his other hand and unclasped his scabbard from his belt, setting the sheathed blade behind him. Once it was out of the way, he stretched his big body out beside mine, making me feel so small and oddly safe.

I shouldn't feel safe with the man who was regularly threatening to kill me, even if he had saved me a time or two.

His hand hesitated as it moved toward me, hovering over my bare stomach. His eyebrows pulled together, conflict etched into his beautiful face.

"Do it," I whispered. "Touch me."

Was I really begging the man who'd captured me to put his hands on my body?

Yes. Yes, I was.

I'd find a good therapist for it later. Right now, I just needed to feel something other than fear and frustration. I needed to feel something good. And if he wasn't going to let me seek that on my own…

"Please," I added, trying to arch into his touch. I wasn't above begging.

He released a shaky breath and then his hand connected with my skin.

I moaned as that electric sensation pulsed over me until my eyes were rolling back in my head. Why did his touch feel so incredible? It was like my entire body was on fire each time his skin connected with mine, burning me in the best way possible. He was driving me crazy, and he was only touching my stomach.

What would his hands feel like in other places? Or his mouth?

His hand slipped lower down my stomach and I bit my lip when it stilled at the top of my leggings. It lingered a moment too long and just when I thought he was going to pull away, his fingers slid under the black fabric.

And then those fingers found my core and a gasp filled the room. But it wasn't mine.

My eyes snapped open to find him watching me with fascination as his hand stroked through my wet folds, his eyes dilated. Normally being stared at so intently would have made me feel uncomfortable, but I found it only turned me on that much more when he did it.

A moan rose in my throat as the tip of one big finger dipped inside of me. I couldn't help the cry of frustration that left me when it almost immediately retreated. Lucas's eyes narrowed on my face as he repeated the motion, his nostrils flaring as a different sort of sound slipped past my lips. He did it again. And again, and again until I was panting beside him.

He was driving me wild with his little game of just the tip. It wasn't even the tip I really wanted.

"More..." I pleaded. I needed so much more. I needed everything he could give me.

War waged on his perfect face before he slipped his long finger the rest of the way into me.

My head rocked back into the mattress because, holy hell, it felt fucking fantastic. I'd been with men over the years whose dicks couldn't even compete with the size of this man's one finger. Not that size necessarily mattered, but it sure as shit helped. A lot. And my body seemed to agree with me.

His eyes widened in what looked like surprise as my body clenched around his singular digit. I didn't have time to overthink the strange expression before he oh-so-slowly pulled his finger out only to drive it right back into me, studying my face as he did so. It was almost as if he was trying to read me, to figure out exactly what I liked. And what he determined I liked, he repeated over and over until he had me writhing on the bed.

Fuck.

Built like a Greek God *and* attentive in bed? Not to mention hung like a damn horse. Yeah, I could forget all about the fact that he was insane. For a little while, at least. A girl had needs.

"Another," I rasped, panting through the mounting pleasure as my hips bucked into his hand.

Confusion clouded his stormy eyes at my command but quickly cleared. Thank fuck he was a fast learner. He retracted his finger and a second finger joined the first, pushing right back into me without missing a beat.

I cried out at the sensation of two of his massive digits

stretching and filling me, exploring my throbbing core. Even as big as they were, they didn't hold a candle to his rock-hard cock that was pressed firmly against my trembling thigh. It was a good thing my hands were tied or else I might have reached for it.

Lucas shuddered against me, his breath hot on my face. There was a wild hunger in his eyes as he watched me inch closer to my release, pumping those fingers into me hard enough to be just this side of painful. Just as I was about to suggest he untie me for some mutual fun, he brushed the heel of his palm over my throbbing clit.

I practically levitated off the bed as the orgasm ripped through me. I wasn't sure if I'd ever come so hard in my entire existence, which was suddenly feeling incredibly long. I threw my head back, screaming my release to the heavens as wave upon wave of pleasure crashed violently into me.

And yet his fingers didn't stop their wicked assault on my pussy. If anything, they pounded into me harder, making me climb right back up to the top of that glorious cliff so fast that I was afraid to fall over its edge a second time.

His mouth moved closer to my face and my breath hitched in my chest as his lips brushed against my cheek. "Again," he growled, and my pussy clenched around his still moving fingers even as I shook my head back and forth.

His fingers curled within me, brushing against my sweet spot and I didn't just see stars—I saw the whole fucking galaxy as my second release took hold of me.

And I'd thought the first orgasm had been world shattering. I was pretty sure my soul left my damn body.

My screams echoed off the cabin walls, my sweat-slicked body heaving with each ragged breath I pulled in. His face came into focus as I drifted back down to earth, his hand still gently stroking my pulsing core, wringing every ounce of pleasure from my shaking body before he slid his hand from my leggings.

The second his hand left me, the room felt immensely colder. His other hand released my wrists, and he all but leaped from the bed, snatching up his sword in the process and rushing to get to the other side of the small cabin. Even from across the room, I could see the rapid rise and fall of his muscular chest, and the way his white knuckles clutched his weapon. His heated eyes were glued to my disheveled clothes.

"There," he said, voice thick with unfulfilled need. "You got what you wanted, demon. Now behave for a while."

My eyes dropped to where his cock strained in his jeans and I felt moisture flood between my legs all over again. He clearly hadn't gotten what he wanted. I should have let him suffer, but I found I couldn't do that.

With every bit of strength I had left in my thoroughly spent body, I sat up and reached out for him with my bound hands.

"I can help you with that," I whispered, biting my bottom lip. His eyes tracked the movement and for a second, I thought he might accept my offer.

I didn't like how much that thought excited me.

"No," he forced out, taking another step away from me and reattaching his sword to his hip. His fingers, still glistening with my moisture, didn't stray too far from the hilt of his blade.

I rolled my eyes. "You can't just pray *that* away," I said as he turned his back on me, leaning over the broken dining table. "Don't want it to get infected and fall off."

His head whipped around, actual fear flickering in his eyes.

"Whoa," I started, holding up my hands. "I'm just kidding. Wait, have you never…"

Nope. No way. I wasn't going to go there. I was not having any sort of sex talk with the psychotic, hot guy who'd turned my life upside down. Even if he did give remarkable orgasms. If he didn't know what blue balls were, I wasn't about to try to teach him. He could just suffer through the pain and discomfort if he didn't want to take care of it.

With a growl, he shoved away from the table, turning that fierce gaze back on me. He stormed over to the bed and my stupid heart started racing as he reached for my hips. His hands gripped my leggings, tugging them back in place and making me gasp as the seam rubbed along my sensitive flesh. With shaking hands, he moved to my sweater, struggling to get it yanked back over my head until my flesh was once again covered. Just the way he claimed to prefer it.

Liar, liar, tented pants on fire.

Lucas pulled away from me again, this time with far more effort. He moved to the foot of the bed and scooped up the discarded bag of food. Just seeing the grease soaking through the paper had my stomach growling. He tossed the bag at me. "I got you food," he said, not meeting my eyes as he moved toward the cracked front door. He swung it open and then paused in the doorway, one hand gripping either side of the frame. I wasn't sure if he was trying to keep himself from leaving…or staying.

"You're leaving again?"

"I won't be gone long this time," he said, the dying light of day shimmering through the door. It outlined his powerful body like a strange halo, making him look almost…angelic. "Try to get some rest."

With that, he forced himself out of the cabin, closing the broken door behind him. And just like before, I never heard the sound of a vehicle starting up, just a gust of desert wind beating against the cabin walls.

Tucking my legs into my chest, I hooked my bound arms over them, resting my chin on my knees as a chill raced down my spine. The entire cabin seemed to drop in temperature and I didn't think it had anything to do with the setting sun.

And then I saw it, out of the corner of my eye. The flash of blinding white at the foot of the bed, so bright it seemed to be glowing as night began swallowing the room.

Setting the bag of food aside, I crawled to the edge of the bed, panic clawing at my heart as I stared at the large feather—just like the one I'd found outside my old place that morning.

"How…"

Reaching out with trembling fingers, I picked up the silky soft feather, and tingles raced up my arm. I gasped, dropping the feather to the ground and staring in disbelief as it slipped underneath the bed.

It felt just like Lucas's touch.

LUCAS

I was an idiot.

My feet stumbled in the desert sand as I paced through the darkness for the millionth time. Not even the moon would shine its light on me after what I'd done.

I groaned, running my hands over my face before yanking them away. My fingers still smelled of her sweet essence. It wasn't right for a demon to smell so heavenly. But perhaps that was the point. She was absolutely intoxicating—*addictive.* She was consuming my every thought. Even miles from the cabin, I could hear her cries in my head.

Cries I'd coaxed out of her.

They haunted me, reminding me of how utterly stupid I'd been.

I never should have stepped foot inside that cabin knowing what she was doing to herself. But I was weak. Worse yet, I was thinking with my cock like a foolish *mortal.* I was no better than the vile, sinful men who fell victim to her succubus charms. I'd allowed her to tempt me, and I couldn't even hate her for it.

After all, she was created to lure men to their doom. I was the angel. *I* was the one who should have been stronger.

When I'd returned to the cabin after meeting with Zain, I'd passed by the window and saw her on the bed as she'd started touching herself. Unlike the first time—when I'd watched her through the window of her old place—I knew what she was doing this time. And I knew I shouldn't have gone in. I should have gone far from that place.

But my body wasn't listening.

Even as the thought to stay out had passed through my head, my feet were already walking me through the front door.

I'd planned to stop her. At least, that's what I'd told myself. I wasn't going to allow her to sin on my watch. It went against everything in my nature. How I'd gone from stopping her to being the reason she was writhing on the bed, I wasn't sure. One moment, she was blaming me for tempting her, and the next I was convincing myself that if I touched her instead, it was somehow less sinful. I was starting to understand why humans made excuses to justify their bad decisions.

But the second my skin had connected with hers, I'd forgotten all about bad decisions. She was all I saw. All I wanted.

I nearly came undone the first time she'd cried out in release, her body clamping down on my fingers as she arched up to the heavens. I'd never seen anything like it. She was in pure rapture—and I'd been the one who'd caused it. I should have ended it right then, but I'd needed more. I had to see her fall apart around me all over again.

But when she'd thrown her head back the second time and screamed my name, I knew I had to get out. I wasn't even sure she knew she'd said it, but my body was painfully aware. Hearing my name fall from her full lips while I brought her pleasure… I'd barely been able to escape before doing far more than putting my hands on her.

And God help me, I'd *wanted* to do more. So much more.

Each second I spent with her was taking me one step closer to my ruination. She was going to destroy me.

And yet, I found I didn't want to leave her for long either. I told myself it was because I knew Zain had a task force out looking to kill her. But I knew it was more than that. One small taste and I was hooked. Even now, knowing what a mistake it had been to allow myself to touch her, I ached for more. Or at least my body did.

I wasn't sure how I could ever be around her again and *not* touch her. Bringing her pleasure felt as natural as breathing—more so than centuries of killing her ever had.

I could spend the rest of eternity watching her body come alive like that. It was literally all I could think about as I aimlessly roamed the desert. The smallest part of me wished I'd taken her up on her offer to reciprocate…

"No," I growled. "I will not allow her to lead me into temptation."

But I was already walking through the valley of the shadow of death. And she was my guide.

My phone—the one Zain had manifested with his new abilities that should have been mine—rang in my back pocket and I swallowed my growl as I pulled it out. I didn't recognize the number on the screen but I knew there'd only be one person calling me.

"Yes," I said upon answering. That was as close to respect as I was going to get.

"Where are you?" Zain's deep voice rumbled.

"In the city," I replied curtly. "I have been watching her old place of residence to see if she returns. It seemed like she knew the owner when she was last here. I thought there was a chance she might come back."

It terrified me how easily the lies were coming now.

There was a pause on the other end of the phone. "Good," he finally said.

I waited for him to say more and was shocked when he didn't. He'd proven how much he enjoyed giving orders, especially to me. I knew he was going to spend centuries holding this new position over me.

"There was a woman at the casino where she worked," I said when the silence stretched on between us. "A server.

She seemed to be friends with the demon. She might prove useful if you want to have someone check it out."

I needed Zain and the others to keep sniffing around the city until I figured out what I was going to do. Zain had only given me a week, but I knew he would never stop hunting Giselle.

My feet faltered in the sand, wings twitching at my back.

Giselle.

I'd never once referred to her by name. I'd never in my long life referred to *any* demon by name. Ever. They weren't worthy of names. They were monsters, nothing more.

But if she was a monster, why had she been willing to give her life for the boy's?

"Not necessary," Zain bit out, bringing my focus back to the conversation.

"Have you or the others had any luck then?" I couldn't help but ask. I didn't like how tight-lipped Zain was being. He really didn't want my help in this.

Not that I actually planned to help him at all.

Another long pause—long enough that I pulled the phone from my ear to make sure the call was still connected.

"We have a promising lead," he replied. "It won't be long now."

"Good," I forced myself to say. "What's the lead? I can meet you and help you end this."

"Don't worry about it," he shot back, and I swallowed

the growl that threatened to erupt from my throat. "I will see you soon, brother."

The audible click on the other end of the line was the only sign I'd had that he hung up. I stared at the phone for a long minute, contemplating chucking it across the desert. Instead, I made myself tuck it back into my pocket after powering it off. I had to be prepared if he called again.

Enemies closer and all.

Only I wasn't sure who was the enemy in this situation: Zain or *her*.

Almost immediately, Giselle's face flashed through my mind. Those burning amber eyes like molten lava, the halo of fire that was her hair, and her silky skin that felt like fire against my own. She was a raging inferno that was consuming my very being. She had me feeling alive for the first time in my life.

I had to get back to her.

My wings extended behind me and I froze, my breath catching in my chest.

I will see you soon, brother.

A chill raced down my spine that had nothing to do with the icy bite of the evening air.

It won't be long now.

"No," I hissed.

It couldn't be. There was no way they'd figured out she was with me. Our kind didn't use modern tracking devices. It wasn't possible...

Right?

With a single flap of my powerful wings, I was

shooting through the air, racing through the darkness in the direction of the cabin.

THE ONLY THING that kept me from flying right past the small cabin was the miniscule porch light flickering like a beacon in the night, guiding me back to her. It made me that much more grateful for the obnoxiously-loud generator.

The cabin appeared undisturbed from where I was in the sky, but that wasn't enough to ease my racing heart. I had to see her. I needed to know she was okay.

The second my feet touched down, I was sprinting toward the still-closed front door. All I could see in my mind was her lifeless body sprawled on the floor, Zain's blade protruding from her heart.

I flung open the door and stumbled inside, my wings catching on the splintered frame, trying to hold me back. My gaze landed on the bed where her motionless form was curled into a ball, blanketed in shadows.

Why was she so still?

The floor creaked as I rushed to the bed, heart pounding violently against my ribcage with each step I took until I was hovering over her.

I blew out a shaky breath when I saw the rise and fall of her chest. She was alive.

That shouldn't have brought me so much relief.

Before I could overthink the comfort I felt in her still drawing breath, she mumbled something in her sleep, her face scrunching up as if she were in pain. Was she having another nightmare?

Pressing one knee into the side of the bed, I reached out for her.

"How could you?" a deep voice rumbled from behind me and my hand stopped short, my entire world shattering with those three little words.

I spun around, meeting Zain's hard gaze.

He rose from the dining chair with his sword in hand. How long had he been sitting there? How had he found me?

"You've had her this entire time?" he said slowly, taking a step toward the bed.

My fingers danced over the hilt of my weapon. "This is not what it looks like."

"Really?" Zain snapped. "Because it *looks* like you're hiding the demon you swore an oath to kill, instead of fulfilling your duties."

"I'm keeping her prisoner," I shot back.

"In your bed?" he snarled, disgust-filled eyes narrowing on me.

If ever there were a moment in my long life to curse.

I shook my head. "No," I said even as my brain shouted yes. "That's not it."

"Enough!" he barked. "I had a feeling I should follow you when we last parted, but I had truly hoped my intuition was wrong. I never would have thought you would fall so far as to protect one of these vile creatures. She really got into your head, didn't she?"

He took another step toward the bed until he was

standing at the foot of it, hard gaze shifting to her sleeping form.

"Worry not, brother," he whispered and my heart stopped as he raised his sword. "I will end this, and you will be dealt with accordingly."

"No!"

My sword met his with a loud clank that reverberated up my arm and into my soul.

"Giselle, run!"

22

GISELLE

The light was closing in, barreling toward me in the pitch darkness like a demon in the night.

Light was supposed to be a good thing—a sign of peace and salvation. It was meant to chase away the dark, to rid us of our monsters. But this blinding light was coming for my very soul. It was going to destroy me, I could feel it.

And no matter what I did—no matter how hard I tried —I couldn't seem to outrun it.

Flames shot up out of the ground, coiling around my legs like fiery serpents, holding me in place. Loud shrieks of metal grinding against metal filled the blackness, drowning out my screams.

"Giselle, run!"

"I can't," I cried out, struggling against the fire's burning hold. The more I fought to escape, the more entangled I became. A blaring horn sounded and the light drew closer until it was all I saw. I threw my hands up in front of me and braced for the end.

"Giselle!" a deep voice called out to me again.

Lucas?

I stirred on something soft, trying to reach out to him in the darkness.

"You dare defy me?" a voice that wasn't Lucas's snarled and any remaining grogginess instantly cleared.

I sat bolt upright in the middle of the bed, sweat dripping down my spine despite the cold chill hanging in the evening air. I blinked away the nightmare only to wake in an entirely different one. My heart hammered within my chest as the small cabin came into focus—along with the two large men standing at the foot of the bed with swords locked.

What the...

I had to still be dreaming. Shit like this didn't happen in the real world. Not that anything with Lucas thus far had been normal. I mean, dude thought he had wings and was destined to kill me.

The image of the pure white feather flashed through my head and I pushed it to the back of my mind with the remnants of the nightmare. Now wasn't the time to be thinking about such insane things. Not when there were men five feet away from me with fucking *swords*.

"She must be taken care of," the man fighting Lucas growled. That sound leaving his lips had the complete opposite effect of when Lucas went all growly man on me. Where Lucas had me clamping my legs together, this man's growl made me feel like my soul was about to be ripped out of my damn body.

The man's harsh blue eyes met mine over Lucas's shoulder and I gulped. Despite his soft curls and the dimple in his left cheek, there was a hunger in his eyes. And I knew it wasn't the same hunger I saw when I looked into Lucas's.

This man was out for my blood.

Great, another asshole that wants me dead.

Withdrawing his sword, he reared back before planting a booted foot into the center of Lucas's chest. I screamed as Lucas sailed across the room, crashing through the one window in the cabin. His body disappeared into the dead of night, leaving me alone with Mr. I Have a Big Sword 2.0.

Sword man shifted his focus back on me.

Shit.

I scrambled off the bed, only to have my arms nearly yanked out of their sockets as the ropes that bound me tugged me back. I pulled the bindings taut, crying out in frustration as the man closed in on me.

"Please," I breathed, tears spilling over my cheeks. I wasn't normally a crier, but there were only so many death threats a girl could take in the span of a week. "I didn't do anything wrong. I'm not who or what Lucas thinks I am. He's holding me against my will."

"I won't believe your lies like he did, *demon*," the man snarled. "He should have killed you from the start. But where he failed, I will not. By my hand, you will return to Hell tonight."

My eyes darted to the window. Where the hell was Lucas? Was he seriously just going to let this guy kill me? I guess I shouldn't have been surprised. How many times had he told me he wanted me dead? Maybe this was his out—letting another psycho do the deed for him.

Why did that thought hurt as much as it did?

"I'm not a demon," I shouted, but—much like Lucas—this guy wasn't listening.

He lunged for me, sword raised. I dove back onto the bed, rolling to the other side, but the man was already moving. He grabbed onto the rope tethering me to the bed and wrapped it around his hand, pulling me toward him like a dog on a leash.

"Lucas!"

A flash of white shot through the window and Lucas barreled into the man, tackling him off the bed and onto the ground.

"Run!" Lucas's deep voice bit out and I wanted to wave my bound hands in his face and scream at him that I couldn't thanks to him. He had a serious kink with tying women up. Or at least, me. It better have just been me.

The bindings in question bit into my wrists, ripping and tearing my skin as I fought them. I glared at the offending ropes, wishing to hell they were gone. I had to get out of here. I didn't want to die like this. I wasn't ready to die at all.

Metal on metal echoed in my ears, both men grunting as they grappled on the cabin floor. I glanced up to see Lucas trying to pry the other man's sword from his big hand. Lucas's own sword was on the ground under the dining table, just out of his reach. There was fresh blood on his arm but I didn't know who it belonged to. The man was inching his blade closer to Lucas's throat.

It was utter and complete chaos.

And that felt oddly…right.

A whiff of smoke pulled me from my trance. I glanced back at my bindings and gasped when I saw the flames dancing along the rope, racing toward my hands.

I should have screamed, but I didn't. I was mesmerized by the tiny inferno, watching as it ate away at the rope thread by thread like a long-lost friend coming to rescue me.

Waiting another moment, I tugged on the rope and it snapped apart, sending me stumbling back onto my ass.

"Oh shit," I mumbled when I saw what happened next.

The fire flashed up the end of the rope that was still connected to the underside of the bed, slamming into the mattress. In a matter of seconds, the entire bed was engulfed in flames. They stretched up toward the dry wooden ceiling like angry tendrils ready to destroy everything in their path. In a matter of minutes, the entire cabin would be on fire.

I scrambled to my feet, hands still bound in front of me. I sprinted to the front door only to stop short at the threshold, glancing back into the burning cabin. Lucas was beneath the other man, struggling to break free. The man raised his sword in one hand, his other pinning Lucas to the floor.

He couldn't die, right? I'd watched him get shot and the bullet had literally *popped* out of him.

How many times had he saved me, despite his many threats on my life? I had to do something.

My eyes darted to the blaze consuming the cabin. Almost immediately—as if it understood what I needed—a burst of fire jumped across the room. It slammed into the man, coiling around him until he was screaming, dropping his weapon to the ground. Lucas took his opening, rearing back and punching the man in the face.

I didn't wait to see more.

Barefooted, I stumbled out of the cabin, coughing the thick smoke from my lungs. I took one last look at the raging inferno at my back and then took off into the darkness without looking back.

I RAN and ran without stopping, not even feeling the rocks that sliced at the soles of my naked feet. I had to get as far from that cabin as humanly possible. I wasn't sure where I was going, but I knew I needed to keep moving. It would have been a hell of a lot easier with a pair of shoes and my hands free.

"Damn you, Lucas."

His name falling from my lips had my feet slowing. I glanced over my shoulder. Far off in the distance, there was a faint glow in the utter blackness, a thin trail of gray smoke reaching up to the heavens.

Had he gotten out? Did the other man survive too? Would they come for me?

The thought of one of them coming for me didn't worry me nearly as much as the other did.

Turning, I forced myself to keep going. Already I was feeling the rush of adrenaline sputtering out. Sharp pains shot up through my feet with each hurried step, taking my attention off of the raw skin around my wrists.

"Don't stop, Elle," I told myself. My feet would heal, a sword wound…not so much. Especially if that other man plunged it through my damn heart.

The air shifted around me and I found myself picking up speed, sprinting blindly through the desert.

"Giselle!"

Lucas's voice had me stopping dead in my tracks, heart pounding in my chest as a sliver of moonlight broke through the thick clouds overhead.

Heavy footfalls approached me from behind and I spun around. I hated how relieved I was to see him standing in the darkness. There was no sign of the other man and I blew out a breath.

"Are you okay?" he surprised me by asking.

I swallowed hard, nodding. I wasn't sure if I really was okay, but I was alive. And that was something.

"You saved me." It looked like it hurt him to say that.

"I didn't do anything," I whispered. Even as I said the words, they felt like a lie. But I hadn't done anything. Right?

The fire flashed through my mind and I quickly blinked the image away. There was no way. Freak coincidence. I probably created enough friction trying to pull away from the bed and the rope ignited. Sure, that's exactly what happened.

He took a step closer to me, his eyes falling to my bound wrists. "You did," he said.

I pursed my lips, meeting his stormy gaze. "Then I guess we can call it even," I told him.

He reached out for me and I withdrew, stumbling back a step and wincing as my frozen and bleeding feet connected with a rock. He rolled his eyes and lunged forward, grabbing my arm and pulling me to him. Without releasing me, he drew his massive sword and I gasped, struggling against him.

"Trust me," he growled, giving me a hard shake. "If I wanted you dead, you'd already be dead."

"But you *do* want me dead," I said, my voice small but not without my usual sass. I should have just kept my stupid mouth shut. But then I wouldn't be me. "You've said it repeatedly since you took me."

Lucas was silent for a long moment, and then placed the sharp edge of his blade to my wrists and sliced away the remaining ropes. But he didn't release me. Instead, he pulled one of my hands up, looking at the rope burn in the dim moonlight. His eyebrows pulled together as his thumb brushed gently over the wound.

"I don't know what I want anymore." His words were so quiet, I wasn't sure if he'd actually said them or if I'd imagined it.

He dropped my hand and sheathed his sword before stepping back.

"Who was he?" I couldn't help but ask as I massaged

my aching wrists. I wanted to know the name of the man who wanted to kill me. Well, the second man who wanted it. I was quite the popular lady with the crazy men.

"Another of my kind," he said, running a hand through his disheveled hair. He winced, looking down at his arm. There was a lot of blood. Too much.

Before I knew what I was doing, I was standing directly beside him, grabbing his forearm. Immediately, my skin started to tingle in that way that only his touch could do. My thoughts drifted back to his fingers dancing between my legs.

Not the time for that, dumbass.

Shaking away my lustful thoughts, I turned him to better see the cut along his bicep. I sucked in a breath when I realized how deep it was. I was pretty sure I was seeing bone.

"You're hurt," I stated the obvious like an idiot. "But the bullet. You healed."

Now I was starting to feel like the crazy person, but I knew what I'd seen when Mark had shot him.

He pulled away from me, brushing a hand over his forearm like he could wipe away my touch. Did I affect him in the same way he did me? For some reason, that only made me want to touch him all the more.

"We can only be injured by our own kind," he finally said.

"Is he..."

"Dead?" Lucas finished for me. "No. Fire cannot kill him. He will heal."

What sort of *Twilight Zone* was I living in that I actually *believed* what he was saying.

"We need to leave," Lucas continued, reaching out to grab me once more. I skirted out of his reach, heart pounding in my chest all over again.

"*We?*" I snapped.

"You need to come with me if you want to live."

"Seriously?" I shrieked. "You think you can go all *Terminator* on me and I'll just go along with you? Up until now, *you've* been threatening to kill me. Why in the world would I trust you now? What's to stop you from suddenly deciding you want to put your stupid sword through my heart?"

Conflict flickered across his handsome face, his hands clenching and unclenching at his sides. "Because, whether you believe me or not," he ground out, "I'm your only hope."

I hesitated a moment too long and he closed the distance between us until his chest bumped up against mine.

"You can go off on your own," he went on to say, inching his face closer to mine. "I give you my word I won't try to stop you. But you should know that Zain will never stop hunting for you. *Never.* He has an entire team out looking for you. And, unlike me, they will not for a second stop to think before killing you. If you choose to go alone, you will be dead in a matter of days."

"Fan-fucking-tastic," I mumbled, ignoring the way his nostrils flared at my choice of words. "Damned if I do, damned if I don't."

"You were born damned," he said and his hot breath fanned across my face, making me shiver.

I tipped my chin up, locking eyes with him. "Why?"

"Why what?"

"Why don't you want to kill me now?" I asked. "Why are you suddenly wanting to protect me?"

I held my ground as he reached for my face.

His fingertips grazed my cheek, slipping down along my jaw and setting fire to my body. "I don't know," he said, and I heard the honesty in his voice. "But for the first time in my long life, I'd rather see you breathing."

His fingers slid down my neck before falling away from me. He watched me expectantly. Fucker knew I couldn't turn down his offer, not if I wanted to live. I wasn't sure if the other man was really alive or not, but I didn't want to stick around in the middle of the desert to find out.

"I can't keep walking," I finally said, looking down at my feet. I was glad for the darkness. I didn't want to see what they looked like after running barefoot through the rocky terrain. I winced as I shifted my weight, bringing my gaze back up to his.

He cocked an eyebrow at me and I could have sworn there was a hint of a smirk tugging at the corner of his lips.

"You won't have to walk with me."

"And no more calling me a demon," I growled, and this time I was sure he was fighting a smile. "I have a name and I expect you to use it."

"You aren't really in a position to be negotiating."

I turned away from him and started to hobble away. "Fine, I'll take my chances with your psychotic friend. He's hotter anyway."

Wrong thing to say.

Lucas's hand whipped out, coiling around my arm and yanking me back to him. He wrapped an arm around me, ignoring my protests as he tugged me into his hard chest. His other arm coiled around my waist, holding me firmly to him. His heart pounded wildly in his chest and mine echoed the sentiment.

His nostrils flared, jealousy flashing in his eyes at my blatant lie. My lady parts all but purred at his response.

"I will use your name," he finally ground out, releasing me and taking a small step back.

"And no more threatening to kill me," I added.

"Don't push your luck, de—*Giselle*," he growled, and my eyelids fluttered shut as the sound washed over me. Yep, clearly only growly Lucas brought me a breath away from orgasm. For a moment, I considered adding nightly pleasure sessions to my list of demands. I knew without a shadow of a doubt that would most definitely be pushing my luck.

He held his hand out toward me. I was going to thoroughly regret this decision. There was no reason I should ever trust this man—not after all he'd done to me.

I blew out a breath, setting my hand in his and shuddering as the electric sensation between us pulsed stronger.

I was an idiot.

23

GISELLE

Lucas tugged on my hand, pulling me back into him until my body was flush with his. He wrapped those muscular arms around me and held me tightly to him.

I tilted my head back to look at him through the darkness, furrowing my brows. Was he hugging me?

He bent his head down so his lips grazed my ear and a chill raced down my spine that had nothing to do with the cold desert air. "Hold on tightly."

I didn't have time to question him as he crouched down and rocketed us into the sky. Like, all the way into the fucking sky.

Screams poured out of me, my body instinctively flailing against him. Lucas's arms cinched down, holding me that much tighter.

"Stop squirming," he bit out. "Unless you want to die, woman."

"What the fuck?" I shrieked. I wrapped my arms around his neck, clawing into him and hanging on for dear life.

I looked down and the screaming started up all over again as I watched the desert go by in a blur far below us. As in hundreds of feet far. Mid-scream, Lucas's hand snaked up my body to clamp over my mouth, silencing me.

"Enough," he rumbled, giving my jaw a small shake. "Do you want to lead him right to us?"

At this point, I didn't give a flying fuck about the other crazy person who wanted to kill me. I was literally *flying* through the night sky in Lucas's arms. The guy who told me he was a goddamned *angel*.

I glanced over his shoulders, seeing a shimmer of something white in the pitch-black sky. I blinked through the lack of oxygen and whatever I saw was gone.

"What the fuck is happening?" I whispered between panted breaths. I was hyperventilating, the world tilting around me.

"Breathe," Lucas ordered, and I shook my head, slamming my eyes shut. The world was definitely spinning.

This had to be a dream. A horrible, twisted dream that went on and on for days. What other explanation was there for *anything* that had happened to me lately? Maybe I was already dead and this was my version of Hell.

Did one get orgasms in Hell?

"I've got you," he said softly. "I didn't drop you the last two times. I'm not going to drop you now."

"Two?" I squeaked.

He'd done this with me before? The balcony of the hotel room he'd taken me from flashed through my mind and my stomach rolled.

"I'm going to be sick," I muttered.

Lucas shifted me in his arms as if I weighed nothing, turning me so he was holding me bridal style.

"Open your eyes." His breath was warm on my face. I shook my head, scrunching my eyes shut even tighter. If I didn't see it, then it wasn't real. "Look at me, Giselle."

Hearing my name on his lips had my racing heart slowing until I didn't feel like I was actively going into cardiac arrest. My eyelids fluttered open to look into his eyes, silvery like the moonlight reflecting in them. Something about those eyes grounded me.

"I've got you," he said again. "Take a deep breath."

I forced air into my lungs, holding onto it before letting it slide back out in a shaky breath.

"Good girl," Lucas mumbled, and a whole different sensation overtook my stupid body at his praise. This was no time to be wanting to join the Mile-High Club. Especially when we were soaring through the air with no damn *airplane*.

"I changed my mind," I choked out. "I think I could manage to walk."

I'd gladly walk barefoot through glass if it meant being back on solid ground. My vision went in and out of focus. Something didn't feel right.

Lucas's chest rumbled with a laugh. It sent vibrations shooting throughout my entire body, which definitely didn't help my raging libido or my desire to climb him like a tree. Had I ever heard him laugh before? I hadn't thought his grumpy ass was capable.

"Not possible," he finally said. "We have too far to go to walk if we want to put enough distance between us and Zain."

I tucked my face into his chest, breathing in his masculine scent tinged with smoke. It calmed me the smallest bit.

"Where are we going?" I asked, not taking my face out of the crook of his neck. I didn't want to see the world rushing by around me. I already felt like I was tumbling in a washing machine—or maybe a tornado. I was getting dizzier by the minute.

"California."

"What?" I practically screamed, jerking in his arms.

"Stay still," he growled, his fingers digging into the flesh of my ass as he held me tighter. Could someone have an orgasm while also having a heart attack?

"You need to put me down," I rushed to say. "I can't go to California."

He tossed me a look before his eyes focused back on the horizon—eyes on the skies as if he were driving a car instead of *flying through the freaking air*.

"We don't have a choice," he told me sternly like his word was law. "We have to get as far from Las Vegas as possible. If we stay, you die."

I shook my head, struggling to breathe. Black crept in

around my vision, my chest constricting. I wasn't sure if passing out while being carried hundreds of feet in the air was a good thing or bad. At least I wouldn't be freaking out. "No, no, you don't understand," I started. "I can't leave Vegas. It's my home. It's where I belong. I have to be there."

"You just feel that way because it's the city you have been assigned to."

"It's where I was born," I said with a groan, my head falling into his chest once more. I really didn't feel good.

"You'll be okay," he assured me. "No demon has ever died leaving their assigned territory."

I didn't like the uncertainty in this voice, but I couldn't seem to form the words to tell him that. My tongue felt like lead in my mouth. My body shook in his arms, my head splitting the farther we got from the city I had always called home. I felt like I was being torn apart.

I'd felt off when he'd had me in the cabin, but I figured it was the stress of being kidnapped and threatened at sword point—repeatedly. As far out in the desert as he had me, we must not have been all that far from the heart of Vegas.

"Lucas," I whimpered.

"You will be all right," he said again, one big hand squeezing my shoulder. "Stay with me."

Only no matter how much I tried, I couldn't stay with him. I couldn't. The darkness wouldn't allow it.

The blackness closed in around me, taking me under in one painful gulp.

I WOKE with a splitting head and an aching body. I was thoroughly spent. It felt like I'd just run twelve miles. Uphill. Both ways.

Lucas's arms were still coiled around me, holding me tightly against him.

I groaned into his chest and he startled, pulling me away enough to see my face. Concern creased between his brows.

"You're back," he said, exhaling. "You wouldn't wake up."

I wished I wasn't awake.

"I don't feel right," I said, my voice weak. I reached up and clutched a hand in his shirt, his muscles flexing under my fingertips. "Something's wrong."

"I think your body is adjusting to being outside of the place you were physically tied to," he explained.

But I wasn't a demon. I wasn't. He had to be wrong.

It was just a panic attack. It had to be. I mean, the dude was flying hundreds of feet in the air with me in his arms. He thought he was an angel. He claimed I was a demon. Supposedly an army of holy men were on their way to hunt me down and kill me because it was their stupid job.

Yeah, it definitely could have been a panic attack. Which would explain why I felt so physically drained now. But even as the thought passed through my head, I knew it was more than that. I felt...*homesick*.

All I wanted to do was curl up in a ball and cry.

I didn't even really have a home anymore, not after

that asshole Chad had kicked me out. But I missed my city. As shitty and depressing as it could be, I longed to be back in it. It felt wrong to be away.

As if sensing my distress, Lucas's arms tensed around me. That was when I realized we were no longer moving. And, better yet, we were back on solid ground, the first rays of light dancing around us. That one thing brought me so much joy that I nearly crawled out of his arms to kiss the sand we were standing in.

My feet touched the ground and I breathed a sigh of relief before sucking in a sharp breath at the pain that shot up through them. Lucas quickly lifted me back into his arms with a growl.

"I should have given you shoes," he grumbled.

I didn't bother to agree—even though it was true. No use making him feel worse. Because, surprisingly, he did seem to feel bad about it if the way he looked at my feet was any indication. He apparently didn't like to see me hurt, as much as he was the root cause of most of my pain.

A foreign sound caught my ears and I forgot all about the pain in my feet. My heart started to race for an entirely different reason, pushing away my longing to get back to Vegas, if only for a few minutes.

"Where are we?" I forced out, half expecting him to say we'd left the country with how my heart was constricting in my chest.

One of these things just doesn't belong.

Me. I was the thing.

"Monterey," Lucas answered.

My mouth popped open and I nearly crawled out of

Lucas's arms to run to the water, bleeding feet be damned. I'd never seen the ocean before. Not in person.

"Can we go to the ocean?" I asked, needing to see the waves crashing onto the sand with my own eyes. I'd fantasized all my life about reading a book in a lounge chair on the beach with a tropical drink in my hand. But that's all it had been, a fantasy. I never thought I'd actually get the chance to take a vacation like that, and I certainly didn't have the funds.

Except this wasn't a vacation. I was on the run with the man who'd originally kidnapped me to kill me. And now we were hiding from more crazy people who also wanted me dead.

"Maybe later," Lucas finally said, surprising me. "Right now, we need to check in so I can take a better look at your feet."

"Wouldn't that be an anticlimactic ending?" I said with a snort, trying to ignore the ache still throbbing in my chest. "Man takes woman to kill her. Man decides not to kill woman. Man helps woman escape other crazy men who want her dead. Woman dies of infection from a cut."

"Do not speak like that," Mr. Bossy Pants snapped.

The eye roll felt natural even if where we were didn't. "Don't worry, you're stuck with me a bit longer."

Lucas plopped me down on an Adirondack chair in front of one of the many seaside bungalows and pinned me with one of his signature grumpy glares.

"Stay."

I resisted the urge to salute him, instead offering him another eye roll and waved him off. He watched me for a moment longer before ducking into what I assumed was the resort lobby.

I leaned back in the wooden chair and rested my eyes. Wrapping my arms around my middle, I shivered against the cool ocean breeze. Even this early in the morning, it was still warmer than the desert had been in the middle of the night. The salty air was a nice touch; it was a soothing sort of scent. Which was exactly what I needed while my world crumbled around me.

"Let's go," Lucas said, appearing beside me and making me jump.

Without thinking, I stood, crying as the pain in my feet once again took hold of me. Lucas swooped in and lifted me into his arms as if I weighed no more than a feather. A feather... Just like the one I'd found outside my old room, and in the bed of the cabin. Pure white, soft, almost magical.

Nope, still wasn't going there.

He carried me to one of the adorable oceanfront rooms. Anyone who saw us would likely think we were newlyweds on our honeymoon. Talk about farthest from the damn truth.

Lucas opened the door and carried me across the threshold, kicking the door closed behind him. He strolled across the room with purpose and set me on a small sofa in front of an electric fireplace already putting out glorious heat.

When Lucas kneeled in front of me, my brows pulled together.

"What are you doing?" I asked as he picked up each of my feet one at a time, grimacing at whatever he saw.

Without answering me, he headed into the bathroom and I heard him start the sink. A few minutes later, he was back with a washcloth and an ice bucket filled with water that I hoped to hell was hot.

He resumed his position in front of me, dipping the washcloth in the water before picking up my right foot and lightly pressing the cloth to it.

I hissed as the hot water hit my broken flesh and I thought I heard him mutter an apology. He continued washing my feet, carefully and gently—almost reverently. After a few minutes, he stood and headed back into the bathroom only to return a minute later with a fresh tub of water and a clean towel. He started the process all over again and this time I sighed as he did, savoring the heat as it caressed my damaged feet.

Tears pricked at my eyes and I tried to blink them away, my heart squeezing in my chest.

When had anyone in my life ever taken this kind of care of me? The guy was literally washing my feet. And was that lavender I smelled in the water this time? It wafted up, filling the room.

When he was satisfied, he lifted me into his arms once more and carried me to the one large bed in the middle of the room. He laid me out on top of it, checking my feet once more before stepping away.

"I need to take a shower," I told him around a yawn. The bed was so incredibly comfortable. Just like the hotel

Mark had gotten for me, I wasn't used to such fineries—like a bed that hugged my body like a cloud.

"Rest," he said firmly. "You can clean up when you wake."

I didn't want to satisfy him by obeying his command, but the next thing I knew, I was drifting off into the darkness once more.

24

LUCAS

I was going to be the first angel to go to Hell.

I chose a demon over my own kind. That decision would haunt me for the rest of my life, which might not be all that long after Zain got his hands on me next.

The look he'd given me when I'd left him in that cabin to burn…

I wasn't sure how I was going to talk my way out of this one with the Arches. There was no way to explain protecting a demon.

A groan slipped out of me as I scrubbed a hand over my face. I flopped back on the bed, wings stretched out to either side of me as I listened to the sound of the shower running. It took everything in me to keep myself out of that bathroom, knowing she was naked. The water caressing her bare flesh. When she'd woken from her nap and insisted on taking a shower, I'd nearly offered to join her to help her stand.

I felt myself lengthen in my jeans and cursed my traitorous body. I was supposed to be stronger than the sins of the flesh, but I wasn't. Not when it came to her. I physically ached for her. The earlier discomfort had steadily increased and now felt more like a throbbing, heavy pain. For a moment, I worried she wasn't kidding about things...*falling off*.

Listening closely, I waited for the muffled cries of pleasure that never came. Maybe she was going to behave for once and do as I'd said. I'd told her I didn't want her touching herself anymore. I didn't say it was because I wanted to be the only one touching her. And after watching her come undone on my hand—*twice*—I wanted to be the only one to ever make those sounds leave her lips.

I was definitely going to Hell.

I sat up as the bathroom door creaked open, my eyes dancing over her bare flesh as she padded out of the shower in nothing more than a towel. And suddenly I was rock hard. My eyes fell to where the short towel brushed along her upper thighs and her legs clamped tightly together.

"Down, boy," she mumbled.

Looking up, I met her dilated eyes. I hadn't even realized the growl had slipped past my lips.

"The clothes you got me smelled like smoke," she said with a shrug, but there was a nervousness about her. She was still afraid of me. In her defense, I had threatened to kill her if she didn't stay fully dressed.

But I'd meant what I'd said to her in the cover of darkness: I didn't know what I wanted anymore, but it wasn't to kill her. Not after seeing Zain barreling toward her with his sword drawn. And not after hearing her call out my name to save her. To think, if I'd gotten through that window a minute later, it would have been all over. I would have lost her. Possibly forever.

I wasn't sure what happened to her after she saved that little boy, or why I'd ended up saving her from the same fate. I often told myself it was because it was my job to kill her, but I knew now that was a lie. Had that one act somehow redeemed her blackened soul? Was that why she no longer remembered what she was? These were all questions I'd ask the Creator—if I was ever allowed to stand in His presence again after what I'd done. I had a feeling Giselle wasn't the only one my kind would be hunting now.

I'd attacked one of my own to protect the life of a demon. Zain knew that and I was sure by now everyone else did as well. My name was probably on the list of the Fallen. And the Fallen were listed as *kill on sight*, their souls eternally damned.

I wasn't sure there was any coming back from that.

What I did know was that Giselle wasn't the same creature I'd spent centuries hunting. And this new version of her had me desperately wanting to be near her—to protect her.

Standing, I walked past her to the sliding closet along

the wall. I pushed the door open and reached up to grab a spare blanket and tossed it to her, not looking away as she fumbled to catch it and keep her towel up at the same time. She wrapped the large blanket over her shoulders and let the towel fall to her feet.

"I'll get you more clothes," I said, hating how gravelly my voice had become.

"Thanks," she mumbled, picking the towel up and stepping back into the bathroom to hang it up. When she came back out, I was sitting on the foot of the bed again.

"Who was that guy?" she asked. I held my breath as she sat on the other side of the bed, her clean scent intoxicating. Were all succubi like this or was it just how she was? I had a feeling it was the latter.

"Why?" I shot back, automatically going on the defensive. "You have made it clear that you believe me to be crazy."

She rolled her eyes and I swallowed the growl that threatened to come up at her defiance. "You flew us here," she said. "Fucking *flew us*—through the goddamned sky!"

This time the growl did slip out of me. She rolled her eyes again before flopping forward on the bed to lie on her stomach. She propped her chin in her hands, bare feet dancing in the air behind her.

"After that, I'm willing to at least hear you out. So," she drawled, "who was he? A friend of yours?"

A humorless chuckle rumbled in my throat. "Zain is no friend of mine," I told her, staring at the black screen of the television across from me. "He's my brother."

"Brother?" she squeaked.

I stood, shaking my head. "Not in the human sense. My brother in arms. We have fought alongside one another for centuries. He is the one who took everything from me."

"I thought you said I took everything from you?" Her voice was small but still held her normal attitude.

I shot her a warning look which didn't have the intended effect.

"Both of you," I amended, and she nibbled on her bottom lip, those amber eyes glued to me.

And then the humor in her fiery gaze vanished. "And he wants to kill me too? Because he thinks I'm some sort of demon?"

Before I realized what I was doing, I kneeled in front of the bed, tucking a lock of her flaming hair behind her ear.

"We know you are," I whispered, hating the flicker of anger that burned in her eyes at my words. It didn't matter whether or not she remembered what she was, she was still a demon. One good deed and a lost memory couldn't change that fact. She was still considered the enemy.

"And Zain isn't the only one who wants you dead," I continued. "He will have hundreds hunting you. You're considered high-powered for your kind. They won't let you live. Zain will devote every waking moment to chasing you down and ending you. This is personal for him now."

She reached out and clutched my hand in hers. It was getting easier and easier to resist pulling away from her, especially when she looked at me with those wide eyes, glassy with unspent tears. I didn't want to scare her, but she deserved to know the truth.

"I'm not a demon, Lucas," she said, squeezing my hand and my heart at the same time. She'd said that to me a number of times and each time I wished I could believe her more and more. "This is me. I'm just a normal person trying to survive like everyone else. I'm not perfect—not by a long shot—but I'm not a bad person. You have to believe me."

"But you were," I found myself saying, watching her face crumple as I withdrew my hand. "You were a very bad person for a very long time."

I was surprised when she didn't argue with me. "You told me I saved some kid's life."

"And stole countless others." I didn't mean for it to come out as harsh as it did. She flinched away from me as if I'd physically struck her. She pushed up to sit, clutching the blanket tightly around herself as she scooted away from me, pressing her back against the headboard.

"I'm not a bad person," she repeated as a single tear slipped down her cheek.

The sight of it broke something inside of me.

"I don't believe you are this time," I said, and was surprised that I meant it. "But the rest of my kind will never believe it. In our experience, demons don't change; they only get worse. Their powers grow and their destruction increases until irreparable damage is done."

"I don't have any powers," she shot back. "If I did, I

sure as hell would have used them to get away from all this long ago."

I was glad she didn't say to get away from *me*, even though I knew it was what she meant. Escaping this situation also meant escaping me. I wasn't sure I could blame her for it, even if it did tear me up inside.

I reclaimed my spot at the foot of the bed and pinned her with a look. "Didn't you use them to get away, though? And again to save me?"

The last part was what really got to me. Seeing her wield her power over fire again wasn't all that surprising. But when she'd used it to stop Zain from running me through with his blade—that had shocked me. She'd saved me. Zain would have been totally justified in killing me after what he'd found, and even more so after I'd attacked him when he'd tried to kill her. If she hadn't struck him with her fire, he likely would have succeeded.

"What are you—" She clamped her jaw shut when the realization hit. "I didn't do that!"

I raised an eyebrow and her face paled.

"You have always had the power to create chaos. A single look at a vehicle and it would careen off the road or burst into flames. It's probably why you are so accident prone now—you've been suppressing your power for so long that it's leaking out and creating its own chaos. Haven't you ever wondered why no one ever wins at your table? Why bad things tend to happen around you? It's what you are."

"I've just got shitty luck," she mumbled, tucking her face into the blanket.

From what I'd seen of her life the past couple of months, that was an understatement. But the more I was around her, the more it made sense. Her innate need to wreak havoc wasn't being satisfied and it was backfiring on her.

"So, how do we get them *not* to kill me?"

It was the same question I'd been asking myself. The answer wasn't one she'd want to hear any more than I wanted to say it out loud. "We don't. They won't stop until you are dead and back in Hell."

The air left her lungs in one breath and I reached out for her, resting my hand on her leg.

"I proved it to you that I don't remember," she rushed to say. "Maybe I can show this Zain guy somehow. Maybe I can prove I'm not this monster he thinks me to be."

I was shaking my head before she even finished. "Zain won't stop to ask questions. He'll just take your head. Like I said, demons don't change in our world. You are an anomaly, Giselle. I don't know if it was what you did for that boy or something else. But it doesn't matter—my people will kill you on sight. Your life is forfeit if you go out there on your own."

She was shaking now and I had to resist the desperate need to crawl over to her and pull her into my arms.

"And what about you?" she said with a sniff that twisted my insides.

"What about me?"

"What will happen to you now? Won't you get in trouble for what you did? For what you're still doing to protect me?"

I met her eyes. She looked genuinely concerned. First, she saved me, and now she was worried about my safety? When had anyone in my life cared about what happened to me? I was raised to be a warrior, trained to kill for the good of mankind.

And now I had this demon reaching out to me in the darkness.

A tightness took hold of my chest until it was hard to draw breath. I rose from the bed, running a hand through my hair and down my neck, keeping my back to her.

"I don't know," I lied.

I knew damn well my life was as forfeit as hers was if they found us. Not unless I found a way to spin it and beg for mercy. Even that might not work.

Without looking at her, I headed toward the bathroom.

"I'm going to take a shower and then I'll get us some new clothes," I said, pausing at the threshold. "Please don't try to run off. I can't protect you if you do."

I didn't wait for her answer, heading into the bathroom and closing the door behind me.

GISELLE

Cinching the blanket around myself, I scooted off the bed and plopped down in front of the electric fireplace, staring into the fake flames.

I struggled to draw breath as reality tried to suffocate me.

People were coming to kill me. They wouldn't stop until I was dead. And, despite his horrible attempt at lying, Lucas was clearly in as much hot water as I was for choosing to protect me.

Speaking of hot water.

I glanced at the closed bathroom door as the shower sputtered to life, pulling my mind from the dark thoughts that consumed me. In a matter of seconds, I was thinking instead of a wet and naked Lucas, my entire body flaring to life. I'd seen him shirtless, and that sight alone was enough to make any woman spontaneously orgasm. I licked my lips, thinking about what he would look like completely naked, the water dripping from his corded muscles.

I wanted to find a way to thank him. He was risking everything for me—even if this entire situation did start because of him. If what he was telling me was true, he had attacked one of his own to save me. I had a feeling I wasn't going to be the only one being hunted down now. And that was because of me.

Before I realized what I was doing, I was standing, heading in the direction of the bathroom door. I paused outside of it, hand lingering over the knob.

Blowing out a shaky breath, I cracked open the door and stepped into the room. I was surprised at the lack of steam. But it didn't matter; if I got my way, I was going to create some steam of my own.

The door clicked shut behind me and my eyes landed on the shower, Lucas's massive silhouette shifting behind the crisp white curtain. I let the blanket slip from my shoulders and pool at my feet before inching toward the shower, my still-aching heart pounding in my chest so loudly, I thought he might hear it over the water.

Reaching out, I grabbed hold of the curtain and drew it back until all I saw was Lucas.

Completely, gloriously, fantastically naked Lucas.

"Holy Hell balls," I blurted out.

Lucas whipped his head up and I scrambled to scrape my jaw off the floor. Dude put every book boyfriend to shame. He was almost too hot for a book cover. I was pretty sure his chest would cause the book to burst into flames.

And that *package*. Yeah, that wasn't going to fit anywhere I wanted it.

Forcing my eyes back to his face, I waited for him to say something—anything. He just stared at me, frozen in place outside of his heaving chest. His stormy eyes raked down my body and I swear I could feel them like a physical touch.

When he didn't say anything, I took a deep breath and stepped into the shower with him.

"Holy shit!" I shrieked as the water splashed against my back. "Why is it so cold? What kind of monster showers in ice?"

I spun around and cranked the knob all the way up, grateful that we were in a fancy resort where the change was almost instantaneous.

"Not all of us bathe in the flames of Hell." His voice was gravelly, husky with desire. I almost completely forgot about the icicles I'd been assaulted with. Almost. "And you leave me no choice," he added, his eyes once more trailing down the length of my body as steam billowed into the air around us, trapped within the curtain.

Of course, he'd blame me for having to take a cold shower. In my defense, I'd offered to reciprocate the last time and he'd refused. Not my fault.

"Maybe you should let me help you," I offered again, my own voice dropping with my desire. Heat rushed between my legs, far exceeding the temperature of the water. I reached a hand out to him, keeping my eyes glued to his face as if he were a wild animal that might attack at any moment.

My fingers connected with his chest, splaying out over the wet skin and sending bolts of electricity up my arm, throughout my body, and straight to my throbbing pussy. His muscles jumped under my touch, but he didn't move.

I moved closer, keeping my hand on him. His intense gaze never left mine, his heart pounding beneath my fingers and his breaths coming faster. The tip of his stupidly impressive erection brushed against my lower stomach and his eyes dilated, a growl reverberating in his chest, making my eyes flutter closed.

I wanted him—I wanted this. More than I could express. The physical attraction was beyond comprehension. But it was more than that. There was a deeper connection between us. It was the same powerful force that had goose bumps racing across my skin and a burning energy pulsing through my veins. The same one that had me inching toward him even though I knew he would likely destroy me in the end.

This was right in all the wrong ways.

Tentatively, I slid my fingers down his body, taking his massive cock in my hand, coiling my fingers around as much of his thick shaft as I could. I gave him an encouraging squeeze, my core clenching as a hiss slipped between his teeth.

When he didn't push me away—or pull a sword out of thin air to kill me—I stepped even closer.

"What are you doing?" he ground out.

"I'm thanking you for saving me," I whispered. I leaned forward until my lips brushed along the underside of his jaw, my nipples grazing his chiseled chest. He shuddered against me, his dick jerking in my hand. I gave him a long stroke, my lips trailing down his chest and over his rock-hard abs.

I wasn't sure I'd ever been so turned on by a man before in my life, and he wasn't even touching me. But I wished he was. It wouldn't take me much to fall over the edge at this point.

I gave his hard length another slow stroke, crouching in front of him as I placed a trail of wet kisses down that insanely sexy V. The fingers of my free hand slid down my own body heading for my molten core.

My mouth hovered over the tip of his dick and suddenly his hands were around my arms, yanking me back to my feet.

"No," he growled.

I tried to shake off his death grip, reaching out once more for his bobbing erection. I knew he wanted this.

Lucas shook his head, scrunching his eyes shut. He released me as if I'd burned him, backing away as much as he could in the tight confines of the shower.

"I can't."

The words were full of pain that wasn't entirely physical.

"Of course you can," I told him, closing the distance between us once more and reaching out for him.

He held a hand out, stopping me in my tracks. "No," he

said again, finally meeting my eyes. "I *can't*, Giselle. I can't do this with you."

"Can't do it, or can't do it with *me*?" I regretted the question the second I asked.

When he didn't answer, I blinked away the moisture building in my eyes.

"This was clearly a mistake," I muttered. I never should have even come into the bathroom. I was a fool. Heat tinged my cheeks as I spun on my heels to leave.

Note to self: smooth surfaces are slippery when wet.

I lost my traction and slipped across the tub. If it weren't for the fistful of curtain I'd managed to grab, I would have fallen on my face. Not that this situation could get much worse. I'd literally offered myself up to him and he'd shot me down. I shouldn't have been so surprised. God forbid Mr. Holy Man get his dick wet with a filthy, murderous "demon."

Regaining my footing, I stepped out of the tub without looking back at him, flicking the curtain closed behind me with more force than was needed. I quickly padded back to the blanket I'd discarded and wrapped it around my wet shoulders before fleeing the bathroom, slamming the door shut behind me.

"No," I hissed as the tears threatened to spill. I refused to let Lucas affect me like this. I wasn't going to let him get me down. If he didn't want me, then so be it. I didn't need to please him and I sure as hell didn't need help getting my own pleasure. I'd been taking care of myself for years.

I plopped down on the side of the bed with purpose.

Kicking my feet out in front of me, I listened to make sure the water was still running. I let the blanket fall open, sighing as one hand came up to cup a breast, my thumb brushing over my erect nipple. I was already so close. I slipped my fingers down my stomach until they were nestled between my legs, feeling the moisture Lucas had put there.

I hated how hot and bothered he'd gotten me without even laying a single finger on me. Those growls. That heated stare. The way his hands fisted at his sides, his muscles trembling as I touched him. I was starting to wonder if he really hadn't ever...

The bathroom door flew open, crashing into the wall and making me jolt on the bed. I yanked my fingers away from my core as he stormed into the room, still fan-fucking-tastically naked. The way his hungry eyes locked onto me, fury dancing within them, I knew he saw.

Oh shit. Was he going to decide he wanted me dead all over again?

Lucas lunged across the foot of the bed and grabbed hold of my ankle, giving it a hard tug until I was flat on my back in front of him with my legs dangling over the edge. He stepped between my parted thighs, his gray eyes raking my naked flesh before locking onto my face. I shuddered under his intense stare, feeling my insides quiver.

"I told you not to touch yourself anymore," he said slowly.

"You won't do it," I shot back with a shrug, hating how breathy it came out. Dammit, I couldn't even be properly mad at him right now. Not the way he was looking at me like he was a man starved and I was a seven-course gourmet feast being served on a silver platter just for him.

"You won't pleasure yourself," he growled, and a whimper slipped from my parted lips, my usual need to argue with him vanishing into thin air like my sanity. "Your pleasure is mine and mine alone."

I gulped. *Holy hellfire. Is this really happening?*

"Do you understand me, Giselle?" he asked, bending so he was looming over me. My heart beat wildly, chest rising toward him with each panted breath. One more growl and I was sure I'd burst into flames. "I am the only one who will give you this."

As if proving his point, his eyes darted to my exposed core.

I wasn't normally a shy person when it came to sex or my body, but having Lucas staring at my lady bits as I was spread wide in front of him had me torn between squirming under his scrutiny and slamming my thighs together and hiding under the covers. He was driving me crazy.

His hand landed on my knee and bolts of electricity shot straight to my core, eliciting a gasp. From touching my *knee*. My hips bucked off the bed, trying to get his hand where I desperately needed it. Tearing his eyes from my aching center, they feasted once more on my body. Those stormy grays raked over every bare inch of skin, his fingers sliding up until they reached my thigh, kneading the goose-pimpled flesh.

His eyebrows pulled together. "You're perfect." He didn't sound happy about it.

I swallowed my apology. It wasn't my fault he liked what he saw.

Fire pooled between my legs as his fingers inched higher and higher until they stopped a breath away from my aching center.

"Please, Lucas," I panted. How I'd gone from wanting to thank him for saving me to writhing beneath him, I wasn't sure. But I wasn't about to complain.

"Please what?" he growled, the tip of one finger brushing lightly against my clit. "What do you need, temptress?"

I was pretty sure *temptress* wasn't all that much better than *demon*, but I was too far gone to care at the moment. He could call me whatever he wanted as long as he put his hands where I wanted them.

I gasped as his wicked digit grazed my sensitive bud a second time. "You," I cried out. "I need you to touch me. Please."

And I did need him. I needed this—I needed something good. Something that only he could give me. I needed what he'd given me back at the cabin, and so much more. Because he was right, he was the only one who could give me this sort of pleasure. Never in my life had a man done to me what he had. And we hadn't even had sex yet.

His fingers slipped between my legs, sliding through the moisture he'd created. His other hand landed on the bed beside my hip, supporting his weight as he leaned that muscular body over me, careful not to let his skin touch mine. His breath fanned out over my stomach and a shiver ripped through me. The tip of one finger dipped inside of me, moving in and out to the first knuckle, torturing me.

Before I could beg him for more, he plunged that big finger all the way into me, grinding the heel of his hand into my sensitive bud. I cried out at the sensation, arching off the bed into his hand. He pulled it back out and lined up a second finger, pushing right back into me almost immediately. Just like the last time, it was too much—and not enough.

Lucas pumped those fingers into me, his hooded eyes dancing back and forth between my face and my sopping core. He looked like a man possessed, and yet utterly fascinated. His thumb brushed against my clit and it was all over. I screamed out my release as my legs came up to clamp around his middle.

And just like before, he didn't stop.

Those fingers continued to drive into me, curling to rub against that glorious spot that had me already climbing back to the tip-top again.

I shook my head back and forth even as the *yes* left my lips. It was too much. Too good.

"Lucas." His name came out as a strangled prayer.

"More," he growled and my core clenched down around his still moving digits. Apparently, my body liked to take orders even if I didn't.

Lucas pulled away from me just enough to kneel at the foot of the bed, his fingers never stopping their torturous rhythm between my legs. His face moved forward until it was nestled between my thighs, his breath fanning out over my sensitive flesh. And then that mouth was on me, replacing his thumb, and I was sure I'd died and somehow managed to make it through those pearly gates.

I wasn't sure what was hotter, the liquid fire of his mouth on my clit or the way his eyes locked onto mine from over the flat plane of my stomach.

He watched me intently as his tongue flicked out over my sensitive flesh and I came off the bed, throwing my head back at the intense sensation. He repeated the move, circling the bundle of nerves before sucking it into his mouth, drawing a second orgasm out of me with a desperate cry that echoed against the room walls.

Lucas eased his fingers out of me but instead of stopping, he grabbed hold of my hips with both hands, tugging me closer to his face.

"Lucas," I whimpered, "I can't."

He ignored me, his mouth descending on me once more, licking up and down and lapping up my essence like a man starved. For someone who seemed terrified of the naked female body, he was the world's fastest learner. I wasn't sure I'd ever had a man so attuned to what I wanted. Each cry and moan he elicited from me had him repeating exactly what my body needed until I was dancing on the verge of yet another orgasm, white taking over my vision.

I cried out his name as I came again, sure that my soul had left my body and floated to the heavens.

Yet still he didn't let up. He was trying to kill me—there was no other explanation for it.

And, oh, what a hell of a way to die.

Lucas once more sucked my hyper-sensitive bud into his mouth, his fingers finding my entrance once more and pushing deep inside of me, zeroing in on my G-spot. His other hand gripped my ass, kneading the flesh roughly. He pumped his fingers into me in long, hard strokes, matching the rhythm of his tongue as he rocketed me right back up to the edge.

"No more, Lucas," I whimpered. "I can't, it's too much!"

"Again," he growled, his wicked tongue wreaking havoc on my sensitive flesh until I was throwing back my head and screaming out his creator's name. My body exploded for the fourth time, sending me into oblivion. I was fairly certain I'd died.

He pumped those delicious digits into me a few more times, drawing out every last bit of pleasure from my body before slowly sliding them out of me.

My chest heaved, my sweat-slickened body trembling from exhaustion. The world teetered around me, the room coming in and out of focus. I was vaguely aware I reached out for him. Not that I could handle anything more. Though the idea of his hard cock pounding into me, stretching and filling me completely, had my core throbbing all over again.

I shook my head. *Down, girl.*

Lucas stumbled away from me, his own chiseled-from-granite muscles glistening with sweat. Was it horrible that I wanted to lick him? His large member bobbed in front of him with need and I genuinely wondered if it would fit.

If he ever let me have it, that was.

"Come here," I breathed.

Lucas ran a hand through his disheveled brown hair, pacing the room. The sight of his perfect, naked form walking back and forth at the foot of the bed was enough to make the nicest, most proper girl sit up and beg.

"This is all I can offer you," he finally said. "My kind… we can't. I can't do more. I can't lie with you."

His hard cock said otherwise. It was very clear that he *could*. But he wouldn't.

"Just like you can't save demons and protect them from being killed?" I asked, cocking a brow at him. I shouldn't have been so upset that he didn't want to fuck me. After all, I got mine—multiple times. But I *was* upset. More than that, I was confused.

Had he really not been with a woman before? And why did that thought make me so incredibly happy?

Lucas froze where he stood, his eyes glued to the floor. There was shame on his face that contradicted his raging hard-on. He wanted me, I knew it. I could tell he was aching for more—just like me.

"That's different," he finally said before stomping into the bathroom, probably to get his discarded clothes.

"Why?" I asked when he came back out. I was more than a little sad to see him fully dressed. "You can't pick and choose what sins you commit, Lucas. I'm no angel and even I know that."

"Enough," he snapped. "My kind don't have sex. But I

don't expect a vile, filthy demon like you to understand that."

Oh hell no.

My anger killed what was left of my post-orgasm bliss. I stood from the bed, wobbling for a moment on my jelly legs before I steadied myself.

"First of all, I am not a goddamned fucking demon. I told you to stop calling me that," I shouted, getting right in his face. It wasn't lost upon me that his eyes trailed down my still-naked body. Or that my scent lingered on his lips. "And secondly, what we just did is called oral *sex,* you naïve, pompous, asshole."

"Giselle," he growled in warning. I ignored it.

"No," I bit out, shoving a finger into his chest and poking the growly bear. "New rule. This is *my* body and I'll do whatever I fucking please with it. I don't need you to give me what I want, Holy Boy. I don't need you to take my sin for me or whatever it is you think you're doing. I don't need you."

Lies. So many lies.

Lucas's nostrils flared as if he could scent my deceit like some shifter stud from one of my books. His chest rose and fell with his mounting anger, his hard eyes boring into me, but I refused to back down. I would not cower to him, not anymore.

Mr. Holier Than Thou didn't want me to touch him, then fine. I wouldn't. And I wouldn't let him touch me either. This wasn't some twisted one-way street.

"I should have killed you when I had the chance," he

said through clenched teeth, and I felt his words slice into my soul.

"Maybe you should have," I bit out. "At least then I wouldn't have to deal with you anymore."

Fire raged in his eyes, jaw ticking. "I'm going for clothes and food," he all but snarled. "Don't leave."

I rolled my eyes, turning back to the bed and sitting, not bothering to cover myself. "Don't let the door hit you on the way out."

He opened his mouth to speak and then snapped it closed, his jaw ticking. He headed for the door, pausing halfway to look over his shoulder at me. "Promise me you will not leave."

"Yeah, yeah," I mumbled.

"I need to hear you say it, Giselle."

"Oh, so we're back to my name again?" I sneered.

"Giselle."

Another eye roll. "Fine, I promise I won't leave."

With that, he spun and headed out the door, slamming it behind him and making the walls shake with his fury.

Yeah, well he wasn't the only one who was pissed off. The asshole.

I flopped back on the bed with a groan, cursing Lucas's stupid name and his even more stupidly flawless body. That's when I saw them, fluttering through the air out of the corner of my eye.

Swallowing hard, I sat up just in time to watch the three white feathers kiss the floor. Feathers that looked like they belonged to a very large set of wings.

LUCAS

I wasn't gone more than twenty minutes but when I saw the door to our room, I nearly sprinted to it. I told myself my eagerness was just to make sure she was still there. She'd promised she wouldn't leave, but the word of a demon wasn't one I was quick to believe. Even if it was hers.

Her scent had followed me to the store and back, lingering on my fingers and lips and reminding me of her body writhing on the bed. I was starting to think she was going to have me eternally hard. If I hadn't gotten out of that room when I did, I would have taken her right then and there.

But I couldn't. It was bad enough that I'd done what I had.

I didn't know what had possessed me to put my mouth on her. But—Lord above, forgive me—it was *glorious*. She tasted like pure heaven. I could have spent eternity between those creamy thighs. I needed more.

But it couldn't happen again. I wasn't sure I could resist her again if the opportunity presented itself.

It was one of the reasons I'd called her a demon again. I needed her to stay mad at me. It would be better for both of us that way. I couldn't control myself around her, not when she all but threw her perfect body at me. Even her declaration that she didn't need me to get pleasure almost had me shoving her right back into the bed to prove her wrong.

She made me forget myself—forget what I was.

I opened the door to the room and stepped inside, not liking the silence that greeted me. I dropped the bags of clothes and food to the floor and rushed into the main part of the room, scanning it to see it was empty.

She'd taken off. I never should have believed a demon. What was I thinking? What had I been thinking this whole time?

And then a flash of red caught my eye through the sliding glass door.

I blew out the breath I'd been holding, making my way to the door. I slid it open and stepped out into the salty ocean air, eyes glued to her mop of flaming hair. She was sitting in one of the wooden beach chairs on the small enclosed porch, her bare feet propped up on the railing, blanket wrapped tightly around her sleeping frame.

Moving to the other chair, I sat down, watching the steady rise and fall of her chest. A red lock blew across her face and I reached over, carefully tucking it behind her ear. My fingers lingered, knuckles brushing against her flushed cheeks.

Demons shouldn't look so angelic.

"Don't touch me," she bit out, her burning amber eyes snapping open and glaring at me.

I retracted my hand, swallowing my growl and the need to prove to her that my touch was, in fact, everything she needed. This was what I'd wanted. For her to be mad enough to keep more distance between us. Still, I didn't like the anger and hurt in her eyes.

Which is probably why the next words fell from my mouth.

"Do you want to go down to the beach?"

It was a horrible idea. I knew that. While we were far from Las Vegas and Zain, that didn't mean we should be out in the open. There were others of my kind stationed all over the world. Surely her photo had circulated by now, her signature red hair a beacon to anyone looking for her. Not to mention my own face. It wasn't often a name was added to the list of Fallen. We should have been lying low.

It was too risky. But seeing her excitement win out over her anger was well worth it. Tomorrow wasn't a guarantee for either of us anymore. Or, at least, not for me. When she died, she would come back like she always did.

I was still holding out hope that I could find a way to get out of this, which was why I was trying so hard to keep myself away from her. But each hour that passed, that possibility seemed more and more impossible. Both getting out of this and staying away from her.

The way I saw it, there were two possible outcomes for me now. I would either be captured, executed, and forced to spend an eternity in Hell for failing at my duties and protecting a demon. Or, I would turn myself in and beg for mercy and *still* risk death and eternal damnation. They were called *deadly sins* for a reason.

There wasn't much leniency for Fallen angels, not after Lucifer.

Giselle sat up in the chair, hands clutching tightly to the blanket to keep it from falling.

"Really?" she asked, a smile tugging at her full lips that had my heart squeezing in my chest. I found I wanted to make her happy—my little Hellion—even if I couldn't make her scream my name anymore.

Not trusting myself to speak, I nodded.

"Yes! I've never seen the ocean."

Clearing my throat, I stood. "I got us new clothes and something to eat. Then we can head out. But you need to stay close to me. I mean it, Giselle," I said as she started to roll her eyes. "It isn't safe."

"Fine," she drawled and then sprang from the chair and bolted back into the room, the blanket trailing behind her like a cape. It took me a second to realize I was smiling, the tightness in my chest lifting.

I stepped into the room and closed the slider behind me. When I turned, she was already on the floor in front of one of the bags, pulling out articles of clothing and munching on one of the bags of chips I'd gotten for us.

Glancing up at me, she tossed me a bag and I snatched it out of the air. The downsides to being on Earth, I felt the human urges for food, drink, and sleep. I didn't need them to survive, but my body craved them. Apparently, my body was capable of yearning for other things too.

Like her.

My eyes danced over Giselle's body as the blanket slipped over one shoulder. She quickly adjusted it, sticking another chip into her hot mouth.

I stepped forward and grabbed one of the pairs of jeans and shirts I'd bought for myself and took them into the bathroom to quickly dress in something that didn't smell of smoke. Though I hardly noticed the smoke anymore—only the scent of her sweet nectar. It seemed to be permanently ingrained in my nostrils. I hoped it never faded.

By the time I got out of the bathroom, she was dressed in a pair of leggings and a too-tight long-sleeved shirt that I'd bought for her, flip-flops donned on each foot. I still blamed myself for the state of her feet. She was lucky she hadn't been bitten by something out there. I wouldn't have been able to forgive myself if that had happened.

"One more thing," I said, picking up the discarded bag and pulling out two ballcaps. I tossed the white one at her. "Tuck as much of your hair up as you can."

She looked like she wanted to argue but surprisingly didn't. Instead, she twisted her hair up into a tight knot and tossed the hat on top of it. A few fiery tendrils escaped, but it was better than nothing. It would help if anyone flew over the beach.

"Remember, you stay close to me at all times," I told her, annoyance flickering in her eyes. "And if your feet start to bother you, we come back."

"Yeah, yeah," she said, waving me off, though I noticed her eyes softened the slightest bit.

I slapped the black hat onto my head and nodded to her. "Let's go."

She practically bounced to the door, a few more locks of hair slipping free of the hat.

Yeah, I definitely could get used to seeing that sort of joy on her face. Too bad it could never last.

SEEING my demon run free on the beach as the sun sank into the horizon was more intoxicating than I could have imagined. I wasn't sure I'd ever seen her smile like that.

She stayed close for all of a few minutes once we reached the water's edge. She was so happy, I couldn't get myself to yell at her for it. Besides, we were the only ones on the beach.

I sat on one of the many sand dunes, watching as she splashed through the waves. I had worried the saltwater would sting her wounded feet, but she pushed right past it, her leggings cuffed up to her knees and sleeves rolled back. Most of her hair had fallen loose from the hat, the setting sun catching it and making it look like living flames pouring down her back. She was exquisite. All she was missing were the wings.

She truly was a sight to behold. And hear. Each time

the water splashed up her bare legs, she squealed, rushing away like it was the perfect game of cat and mouse.

The same game she and I used to play until she forgot what she was.

I didn't have the heart to tell her that she had seen the ocean before in her last life, and numerous ones before that. It was more fun to watch her experience it for the "first time" all over again with the sweet innocence of a human.

Even if she wasn't actually human.

"The water's great," my Hellion said breathlessly as she approached me for the tenth time. "Let's go for a swim!"

"It's freezing," I replied, unable to hide the humor in my voice. Even now she was shivering. "And you don't have a swimsuit."

She planted her hands on her slender hips. "Only because you didn't get me one. Come on, grump. Live a little." *While you still can.*

I was living on borrowed time. Pretty soon, redemption wouldn't be possible for me, no matter how much begging for mercy I did. I was slipping farther from grace with each second I spent with this creature. I hardly recognized myself.

And yet I still couldn't stop.

Giselle reached forward and grabbed my hand where it rested on my knee. She tugged on my arm, trying to lift me to my feet. I didn't budge.

Blowing out a frustrated breath, she released me. "Fine, suit yourself. Be a boring-ass, goody-two-shoes. I can have fun all on my own. I don't need you or a swimsuit."

Mischief flashed in her eyes before they darted up and down the beach. She smirked at me and my heart sank. This woman would be the death of me, in more ways than one.

"Don't even think about it."

"What are you going to do about it, Holy Boy?" she purred, backing away from me as she reached for the hem of her shirt.

Panic flared within me at the thought of someone laying eyes on her perfect body. *My* body. The thought alone made me want to kill every man within a ten-mile radius.

"Giselle," I growled.

She peeled the fabric off her flesh, her bare breasts on full display. Why hadn't I bought her undergarments?

I scrambled to my feet as she flung the shirt at my face. She danced away from me as I lunged for her, dropping her leggings and kicking them off in my direction as well before sprinting toward the water. The last rays of sunlight kissed her naked flesh as she waded out into the water's frigid depths.

I stopped short where the dry sand met the wet, glaring out at her. "Get back here," I shouted. I could practically hear her teeth chattering from where I stood on the shore. Could demons catch pneumonia?

She splashed in my direction, laughing. "Take that stick out of your ass and make me."

"Damned, wretched woman," I grumbled, kicking off

my shoes before unbuttoning my jeans. Looking around the beach one last time, I dropped my pants and ripped off my shirt before storming into the water.

Thankfully, the temperature of the water didn't affect me nearly as much as the heat of her touch did. As cold as it was, it still wasn't enough to neutralize the blood once again rushing to my manhood.

She squealed when I reached for her, trying to jump away from me even as the waves pushed her back toward my outstretched arms.

Finally, my arm snaked around her middle, pulling her flush against me until I was sure we were standing in a pool of boiling water and not the freezing Pacific Ocean. My painfully hard erection slipped between the apex of her thighs and all fight in her eyes left along with her laughter. She shuddered against me and my brain short circuited.

Almost instinctually, I coiled my other arm around her, pinning her to me. Her legs came up to wrap around my hips, her arms linking around my neck.

"So much for you not touching me," she breathed, more to herself than me. Her lips hovered an inch away from mine. I couldn't look away from them, a single drop of salty water dripping from the center of them as they parted. Would they be as soft as they'd been in that dark subway tunnel? I'd thought about that kiss for decades.

I had to resist.

And then she rocked her hips into mine and I was done for.

My lips crashed into hers and the world around us

stood still. The ocean stopped swaying, the wind died, and it was just her and me and nothing else. Electricity burst between us until all I could see was white. It was better than I remembered.

Giselle jerked against me and then her mouth went slack. I broke the kiss, meeting her wide eyes. Her breath caught in her chest and her eyes rolled up into the back of her head, her body collapsing against mine.

GISELLE

"Giselle!"

Lucas had been calling out to me, but I couldn't find him. Last thing I remembered, I was wrapped in his arms as the sun set around us, his lips inching toward mine. And then he was kissing me, stealing my breath and making my toes curl into the sand. I'd been dreaming of having those lips on mine—soft and familiar. Why were they so familiar?

Next thing I knew, I was here. Wherever *here* was.

I was sprinting down a street in the middle of the day, running for my life in the direction of Lucas's frantic cries.

I was in a city, a large one. Skyscrapers towered over me on either side, the sound of traffic blaring in my ears. Nothing was familiar and yet, at the same time, everything about it was. Which didn't make any sense, because I'd never been here before. No, that wasn't true, was it?

I just had to find Lucas. He'd save me. I knew he would. He'd done it many times before. I just wasn't sure what—or *who*—he was saving me from this time.

Or why the idea of him coming to my rescue in this foreign city seemed more like a memory than a hope.

"Face your fate."

I hit the brakes and whirled around, Lucas's voice suddenly coming from behind me. There was an anger to it I hadn't heard since he first took me captive. I scanned the busy street, looking for him before my eyes darted to the overcast sky.

"Lucas?" I called out, fear setting in. "Where are you?"

"You leave harm everywhere you go, demon."

"I'm not a demon," I breathed, chills racing up my spine. I stumbled back a step, a sharp pain stabbing my chest. I had to get out of here.

Turning away from Lucas's harsh words, I bolted down the sidewalk, darting around the many passersby that didn't even seem to notice me. With a blast of its horn, a bright yellow taxi careened off its course and crashed into the sidewalk directly behind me. With a scream, I kept running. I wasn't sure what was happening, but I knew if I stopped, I'd die.

"Giselle!" Lucas shouted again, once more out in front of me. "Come back to me!"

The beating of wings rose behind me and I picked up my pace. They'd found me. Lucas said they would and they did. That man—Zain—was going to kill me. I wasn't ready to go back yet. I didn't want to die. I didn't want to start all over again.

Start over?

A shriek of metal rang out as another car veered off course, slamming into oncoming traffic. Someone screamed. In the distance, an explosion went off, smoke billowing from the top of one of the buildings. More shouts and cries rose around me.

"Why don't you stay in Hell where you belong?" He was right behind me, closing the distance. But it wasn't Zain I heard on my heels.

It was Lucas.

Because it wasn't Zain—or any other angel, for that matter—who'd spent hundreds of years killing me. It was the man whose touch I craved on a cellular level. The one who made my heart race each time he looked at me with those stormy eyes. The same man who was assigned to make that heart stop beating.

Lucas had always been in my life, and he was always the one who ended it.

And I couldn't even blame him for it. I'd end me for all I'd done too.

I WOKE thrashing on something soft, two hands grabbing hold of me and holding me down on the bed.

Lucas's face came into view above me, concern

drawing his brows together. Seeing him calmed me for all of a second. Until I saw his fucking *wings* stretched out behind him. Wings I stupidly hadn't seen before.

How could I have been so blind? I'd been no better than a foolish human—seeing only what I'd wanted to see.

"The demon you saved," I whispered, blinking away the onslaught of memories—centuries' worth.

I threw him off me and leaped from the bed, racing across the room. I wasn't sure what I was doing or where I was going. I felt trapped, my heart hammering against my ribcage. I struggled to suck in air. The world felt like it was closing in around me.

Lucas easily caught up to me, wrapping an arm around my naked waist and pulling me back into his hard chest—also still bare from our swim in the ocean. I fought him and he snaked his other arm around me, pinning my arms to my sides.

"Hey, it's okay," he said softly, contradicting every word he'd ever spoken to me in the past. How many times had he told me he wanted me dead? How many times had he driven his blade through my heart? Hundreds, maybe more…

Moisture lined my eyes and I willed it not to spill over as he reached up to cup my cheek. "It's just me."

But that was the problem, wasn't it? It was him. The creature whose sole purpose in life was to exterminate my kind. *Demons.*

The tears did fall then.

"Why did you do this to me?" I said, burying my face into his solid chest, tears streaking down my face. "Why?"

He pulled away from me, one big hand landing on either shoulder as he held me at arm's length. When I refused to meet his eyes, he crouched, bringing his face in front of mine. But all I saw were the pure white wings at his back, a harsh reminder of what he was and what I was.

Enemies.

"Giselle, what's going on?" I flinched away as his fingers came up to wipe my tears. "Why did I do what?"

"Why couldn't you just let me live my shitty life in peace?" I snapped, anger bleeding into my voice. I welcomed it—anything was better than the pain. "My life wasn't perfect, but it was still mine. You took that from me!"

He gave me a hard shake. "I don't know what you're talking about. You aren't making any sense."

More tears raced down my cheeks. "I don't want to be this…this *monster*. You did this to me! Why couldn't you have just left me alone and let me live my life? I could have been happy for once. I had a chance at a real life and you took that from me. You ruined everything. I hate you!"

Lucas's hands fell away from me, his eyes growing two sizes bigger. Hurt flashed across them at my words. "You remember?" he said, so quietly that I almost didn't hear him.

Pursing my lips, I gave him a stiff nod.

His breaths came faster as he took another step away from me. The hurt on his face turned to panic and I wasn't sure why. He wasn't the one who'd just remembered she'd spent hundreds of years ruining and ending the lives of thousands of people. Many of them innocent.

And no, I didn't ever remember directly killing or harming a child, but how many had I orphaned over the years? How many families had I destroyed?

"I wasn't hurting anyone this time," I bit out. "But you couldn't help yourself, could you? You couldn't stand to see the vile demon happy for once. For the first time in my many lives, I had a chance at something normal—something good. Why couldn't you have just let me be? I could have had a decent life with Mark. He was a good man, and he liked me for *me*. He could have taken care of me—made me happy."

Even as I said the words, I knew they weren't entirely true. Mark was a great guy, but he wasn't for me. Lucas had ruined me for any other men. And I hated him for that. I hated how my heart beat for him.

His eyes narrowed and he was back in my face. "Do not speak his name in front of me. You do not belong to him, or anyone else."

"And who do I belong to, huh?" I shot back, jabbing his sternum with my finger.

Lucas glowered at me, his jaw ticking.

"That's what I thought," I hissed, pulling away from him. "You could never be with a filthy demon, right?"

He reached out for me. "I didn't mean that."

"Didn't you, though?" I snapped. "Who could ever care for someone like me?"

I paced the room as Lucas watched me with worried eyes. I was surprised he hadn't pulled his blade on me yet.

After all, he'd sworn he'd kill me when I finally remembered what I was.

And what I was, was a monster. He'd been right about me all along. Part of me—a large part—wished he'd just killed me from the start like he was supposed to.

I sank to the floor, sobs hiccupping out of me. "Just kill me," I whispered.

Lucas was kneeling in front of me in an instant. "Don't you say that," he growled. "Don't you ever say that."

"Please..." I said, unable to meet his eyes. "I can't live with myself knowing what I am—the things I've done."

"That wasn't you."

"Then who the fuck was it?" I bit out, glaring at him. "Who else did it but me?"

"You're different this time," he said, pulling me onto his lap with gentle hands—far gentler than I deserved. The tears fell harder as he started to rock me in his strong arms. One big hand landed on my back, stroking up and down my spine as he kissed my temple. "You said so yourself, you aren't a bad person."

"But I was," I countered, remembering his words. They coiled around my throat, suffocating me. "And I'm still a demon. Neither of us can ever change that, Lucas."

He was silent for a long moment, resting his chin on my head. His hold on me was tight as if he were afraid to let me go. But he had to. I was going to bring him down with me if he didn't. Now that I remembered what I was, I knew the ramifications for him.

I pushed away from him just enough to look at his beautiful face. "You need to do it," I told him, placing a hand on his scruffy cheek. "It's the only chance you have at redeeming yourself. You know they won't stop hunting me. Eventually one of them will send me back and then they will kill you for protecting me. If you kill me, you stand a chance of surviving. You can still beg for forgiveness. Just do it. You know I'm right, Lucas."

And I was right, but that didn't make the idea of Lucas killing me any less painful. I struggled to draw breath, lungs constricting within my chest.

His gray eyes stared at me long and hard. I waited for him to scoot me off his lap and unsheathe his sword.

"No," he growled. Instead of running me through with his blade, he fisted a hand in my long hair and tugged my face to his until his lips were claiming mine once more.

My eyes fluttered closed as I melted into his kiss, shifting on his lap so I was straddling his legs. I coiled my arms around his neck and pulled him impossibly closer. His lips moved over mine with a hunger that I desperately shared. Nothing in my life had ever felt so right—so pure.

But there was nothing right about this.

I jolted as feathers brushed across my bare shoulders, his large wings wrapping around me, cocooning me against him until it was just him and me. But no matter what we did, we couldn't block out our reality. It would always find us.

I snaked my hands up between us and pushed him away. "No," I breathed. "You can't. *We* can't. I've already ruined you enough. We've destroyed each other. We can't do this, Lucas."

Crawling off his lap, I stood and gave him one last look before heading for the bathroom.

"I'm going to wash off this saltwater, and then we can figure out what we're going to do," I said over my shoulder.

Too bad a lifetime of sin couldn't be washed away so easily.

28

GISELLE

I waited until steam billowed out of the top of the shower and filled the bathroom before stepping under the steady stream of water.

Now that I remembered what I was, the scalding shower water didn't seem all that hot—not compared to the fires of Hell. No wonder nothing ever burned me. For all the things I'd gone to the emergency room for over the past twenty-seven years, fire hadn't been one of them.

I let the water cascade around me, washing away the salt and tears that had dried to my skin. Even the ocean's nearness didn't bring me joy now. Not after realizing how often I'd seen it in my many lives. Hell, I'd lived alongside it at least five times—including in my last life.

The one where I'd saved that little green-eyed boy and kissed Lucas.

I glanced down and sighed, watching as the remaining

grains of sand spiraled and disappeared into the drain. If only everything was that simple to erase.

Like the hundreds of years' worth of memories that were spinning in my brain. And to think I used to enjoy the chaos I spread. I *thrived* on it. Now it only sickened me. It was no shock that Lucas didn't want to take things further with me. How often had I made his life hell over the centuries he'd chased me?

Not to mention he was a goddamned *angel.*

Groaning, I pressed my head against the tiled wall before the curtain flew open behind me. I looked over my shoulder, and there stood the angel that haunted both my nightmares and my dreams.

Lucas's shoulders heaved as he stared at me, his muscular body still gloriously naked. I couldn't help the way my gaze dropped to his massive cock, standing at full attention as he feasted his own eyes on me.

Fighting every succubus instinct running through me, I crossed my arms over my chest.

"Decided my fate?" I asked, the words coming out breathier than I intended. I wasn't sure if it was from the possibility of meeting my maker or the heat rushing to my core.

I had a feeling it was the latter.

Straightening my shoulders, I tilted my chin up and faced him head-on. If he was going to kill me, I would face it bravely. No more running. I knew now what was waiting for me on the other side. Fire and brimstone weren't so bad. And, for me, they were likely temporary. But knowing I'd never see Lucas again… That hurt more than any other fate I'd faced in my life. I wasn't ready to leave his side yet, and that was wrong on a multitude of levels.

We were enemies—fire and ice. We couldn't be anything else. Fate wouldn't allow it.

After a long moment, Lucas stepped into the shower, his stormy eyes boring into mine. He stalked toward me until I was pressed against the tile wall, his big wings—even tucked against his body—sheltering us from the spray of water. Placing a hand on either side of my head, he caged me in. I shuddered as his breath caressed my face, unable to tear my gaze away from his.

"What are you—"

His mouth crashed into mine, silencing me with a punishing kiss that had me seeing stars. I arched into him, his impressive erection pressing into my lower stomach and making my lady bits flare to life. My hands slipped over his powerful shoulders and around the back of his neck, fingers combing through his dark hair.

I tried to pull him closer and Lucas growled, nipping at my lip hard enough to elicit a cry from me. Despite my extensive experience and his lack of it, Mr. Bossy Pants clearly wanted to be in charge here. Fine by me. It was hotter than Hell—and I, of all people, knew just how hot that was.

One large hand plunged roughly into my hair, tilting my head back to give him a better angle. His tongue tentatively slipped between my parted lips, deepening the kiss until the entire bathroom was spinning wildly around me and I was clinging to him for dear life.

I'd kissed thousands of lips over my many lifetimes—I wasn't proud of that fact, it was an occupational hazard. But this...this was *real.* As Lucas's lips moved hungrily over mine, I realized I'd never truly been kissed before.

My legs trembled beneath me and I tightened my hold on him, fingernails digging into his shoulders until I was sure I was breaking skin. A muscular thigh came up between my legs, supporting my weight as his lips left mine. But as quickly as they'd left they were back, trailing wet kisses along my jaw and down my neck.

"We can't," I breathed even as I rocked over his thigh, tossing my head back to give him better access.

"We can," he said, pressing a kiss to the hollow of my throat. His mouth moved to my shoulder, his teeth scraping against my skin until I was whimpering.

I grinded down on his muscular thigh again, savoring the glorious friction it created. But still I needed more. As if he could sense it, Lucas's arm came around me, holding me up. His thigh dropped away, quickly replaced by his hand. His fingers slipped through my folds and I cried out as his thumb found my bundle of nerves, brushing over it in a lazy circle.

His mouth reclaimed mine once more as two fingers sank deep into my core. I couldn't take it—it was too much. The way his tongue teased mine, his fingers pumping into me, the languid strokes of his thumb over my clit. I felt my body tightening around him until I was heaven-bound, the galaxy lighting up behind my eyes as I screamed his name. I clung to him, spiraling out of control, the pleasure consuming me until I couldn't remember my own name, let alone my origins.

Lucas slowed his fingers before easing them out of me, his other arm holding me up as I floated back down to earth. Before I could find my voice, his hands moved to my backside, lifting my feet off the floor. My legs automatically wrapped around his waist, head falling to his shoulder.

Why did he have to feel so right? When he held me in his arms, the world felt *good* for the first time in forever. This was my Heaven, and I wasn't allowed to have it.

Lucas stepped out of the shower and carried me from the bathroom. Each step he took had the thick shaft of his massive member bumping against my already sensitive nub until I thought I'd come undone all over again.

Just as I was about to tell him to set me down, he tossed me onto the bed. He paced at the foot of it, his stormy eyes never leaving my face. His cock bobbed in front of him with desperate need, hands clenching and unclenching at his sides as he sucked in a breath. The sight of him struggling for control was sobering.

"Lucas, wait."

"No," he rumbled, hearing the protest in my wanton voice. Damn my mother's blood coursing through my veins.

"You know we can't do this," I told him, hating the words even as they left my lips. But I knew there was no coming back from this. Saving a demon was one thing, but sleeping with one? What would his kind do to him if they caught him?

"I'm a demon," I stated the obvious, needing him to remember through his lust-filled haze.

"I don't care what you are," he said firmly, his eyes pinning me in place on the bed as he stalked toward me. "Heaven and Hell be damned—you're *mine*."

The breath caught in my chest as he bent over me, one large hand wrapping around my throat but not squeezing.

"Do you hear me, Giselle?" he said, the words coming out dangerously low. "You. Are. Mine. And I will protect you with my dying breath. No one will ever touch you again. Only me. You belong to me and me alone, no matter what happens. In this life, the next—in a hundred lifetimes—you're mine. And I will never regret this. For the first time in my long life, I'm living. You have brought me to life."

Tears pushed at the backs of my eyes and I blinked them away, nodding.

Lucas crawled onto the bed, his wings spreading out on either side of him. Unable to resist, I reached up and ran my fingers over the silky feathers, loving the way that simple touch had his eyes rolling back in his head. He dipped toward me, his mouth dropping down to pull a hard nipple between his teeth. As his tongue flicked over it, I practically levitated off the bed, a moan slipping from my lips. For an angel, he had one wickedly talented tongue. Even getting my memories back, it still held true that no man had ever given me the sort of pleasure Lucas had.

It was like I was made for him…for more than just killing.

He moved to the other breast, paying it equal amounts of attention until I was writhing beneath him. I was already so close.

Lucas kissed his way down my stomach until his face was nestled between my thighs. As his tongue lapped into me, it was hard to believe this was the same man who was literally afraid to see my naked breasts a week ago. Now it seemed all he wanted to do was worship my body. Not that I was complaining.

But this wasn't just about me.

"Lucas," I breathed.

"Hmm," he mumbled, the vibrations nearly sending me over the edge.

I squirmed under him. "Let me touch you."

"No," he growled, nipping at the inside of my thigh before continuing his glorious assault, sucking my throbbing bundle of nerves into his mouth. He inserted a finger into my wet heat and I was done for.

My head rolled back into the pillow, crying out my release as the orgasm crashed into me, waves upon waves of pleasure washing over me.

"Hearing you scream my name is the most glorious sound to ever touch my ears," he said against my quivering core, his finger still pumping inside of me. "I will never tire of it."

"Please," I whimpered. "I want to touch you, Lucas."

While I was thoroughly enjoying what he was giving—what he'd been *continually* giving me the past few days—he hadn't allowed me to reciprocate. And I found I desperately wanted to see him come undone under me. I wanted to make him feel as incredible as he made me feel. Because Lord knew he lit my body on fire like no one else could.

Well, maybe not the Lord. That might be awkward in our situation.

Lucas's eyes found mine, his finger easing out of me and his tongue slowing. I could tell he was contemplating my words and, despite his proclamation, I worried he might deny me yet again. I couldn't handle another rejection. He was mine as much as I was his. It was my turn to stake my claim, if only for this one moment.

"Please," I said again, trying to push him away.

Lucas sat back on his heels, watching me cautiously as I sat up and scooted off the bed. I held out my hand to him and he tentatively took it, letting me pull him to the side of the bed. Giving him a little smile, I kneeled on the floor between his legs.

The air left his lungs in a hiss as I wrapped my fingers around his thick cock and gave it a single pump. I licked my lips and repeated the motion, his eyes rolling to the back of his head. The succubus in me purred at his reaction to my touch. The rest of me found immense satisfaction in bringing him pleasure. I'd never wanted to make someone feel good so much in my lifetimes.

His hooded eyes were fixed on me, his breaths coming faster. I looked up at him through my lashes as I took him in my mouth, his eyes growing wide as his own mouth popped open.

"Oh fuck," he groaned and I smiled around my mouthful.

Lucas shuddered as I took as much of him into my mouth as I could, wrapping my hand around what didn't fit, which was quite a lot. Mr. Holy Pants had a lot packed in those pants of his. I continued to bob over him, savoring each time his hips bucked up, fingers clenching in the sheets.

"Giselle, stop," he breathed, fingers tangling in my hair.

I ignored him, feeling him bump against the back of my throat as I took him deeper.

Lucas's hand fisted in my long locks, yanking me off him with an audible pop. "I said enough," he growled and heat pooled between my legs despite my fear that he'd changed his mind about tonight.

We'd come too far to stop now.

He grabbed my shoulders and lifted me to my feet before throwing me back onto the bed. His shoulders heaved as he stood beside the bed, his eyes feasting on my bare skin.

"Perfection," he whispered. I wasn't sure if I was meant to hear it or not but it affected me, nonetheless. It wasn't the first time a man had complimented my beauty over the centuries. It came with being a succubus. But when the word left Lucas's mouth, I truly believed it. Like he truly saw me—the real me.

Lucas crawled on top of me, trailing wet kisses up my body until his lips were once more capturing mine in a kiss that had my head spinning. I clung to him, fingers digging into his muscular back.

"Mine," he said against my lips, crushing his mouth into mine one last time before pulling away from me.

Sitting up on the mattress, Lucas kneeled between my legs, his stormy eyes locking onto my center. His eyebrows pulled together, apprehension flashing across his tortured face. My heart squeezed in my chest as all of his bravado fell away.

I pushed myself up, tucking my knees under me so that I was eye to eye with him.

"Are you sure?" I asked softly, praying to his creator and mine that he said yes.

Swallowing hard, he nodded. "I have never wanted anything more in my hundreds of years of living."

I put a hand on Lucas's chest, gently pushing him back into the stack of pillows along the headboard, his wings fanning out on either side of him. I wasn't sure he was breathing as he watched me straddle his waist.

Lifting myself to my knees, I took his throbbing erection in my hand, lining him up with my entrance. Exhaling, I started to slowly ease myself onto him, my body needing to adjust to his massive size.

The entire time I lowered myself onto him, I held his gaze, watching as his eyes grew increasingly wider. He most definitely was not breathing. I wasn't sure I was either. When I was finally seated all the way to his hips, I tossed my head back, savoring the fullness of him. He was stretching and filling me to a point that was just this side of painful. It was *divine*.

Lucas's fingers dug into my ass, holding me firmly in place.

"Need to move," I breathed, rocking my hips forward to grind my clit into the base of his cock. Already I was so close. Which was probably a good thing based on the look on his face and the way his body already trembled beneath mine.

His grip on me relaxed the slightest bit and I retreated off of him, sinking right back down. He was enthralled—his heated stare glued to mine as I rode him slowly. It only turned me on that much more.

"Never knew," Lucas mumbled, a shudder ripping through him and vibrating up into my body. "I never knew it could be like this."

Each sound that left his lips had me inching closer to my own orgasm. I splayed my hands on his chest, circling my hips and increasing my pace. Our breaths came faster, the bed rocking into the wall.

Now, *this* was a type of chaos I could get used to.

When panic filtered through Lucas's stormy eyes, I knew he was teetering on the edge. And I was right there with him, ready to fall.

Lucas came with a roar, hips bucking off the bed and pistoning into me until I was screaming my release right along with him.

He jerked into me a few more times before I collapsed onto his sweat-slickened chest, his heart racing in my ear. Or maybe that was my own heart. A big hand came up to cup the back of my head, stroking my long hair. Fighting back my uncharacteristic shyness, I rested my chin on his chest, surprised to see the heat still burning in his eyes. Heat and wonder.

"That was..."

"Spectacular?" I offered, worry gnawing at the back of

my mind. I didn't want him to regret his decision. To regret *me.*

"Heavenly," he breathed and the tightness in my chest lessened.

Already he was starting to lengthen all over again within me and it was time for my eyes to widen. He flashed me a wicked grin that could melt the panties off any woman—demon or otherwise—before flipping us so that he was on top of me.

I was right, he was definitely trying to kill me. Good thing I was great at dying over and over again.

29

LUCAS

I awoke in the large bed with fire nestled in my arms. Giselle's chest rose and fell with her even breaths, her red hair cascading over the arm she was using as a pillow. Her face was pressed against my chest, an arm draped around my middle, and fingers tangled in my wings. She looked so peaceful—*angelic*—with the dying moonlight haloing around her head.

None would've ever guessed she was born from the bowels of Hell.

I stroked her flushed cheek with my knuckles, feeling myself lengthen all over again. I'd been hard most of the night. Neither of us had gotten much sleep. I knew it was wrong, but for the first time in my long life, I didn't care.

I couldn't get enough of her.

The floodgates had been opened and there was no closing them now. I needed her like I needed the very air I breathed. She set my soul on fire, and I didn't think it had anything to do with the fact that she was a demon.

But that was exactly what she was.

It wasn't like I'd fallen for a mere human—not that I'd fallen for her. Throughout the history of my kind, a few angels had succumbed to the lure of love. They'd been forced to give up their divinity and immortality in order to be with their chosen mates. And they did. For "love."

Just the thought of losing my divinity was terrifying enough, but to *willingly* give it up? I shuddered. Our divinity was who we *were*. It was our entire being. To choose to have that torn away just to spend a few decades growing old with a human was baffling. Love was fleeting; we were eternal.

Which was why it had probably happened only a small number of times in thousands of years.

I glanced down at the demon in my arms and shook my head. I definitely wasn't falling for her. This wasn't love. This was just a craving of the flesh, nothing more. The only falling I'd done was falling victim to her wicked charms. Charms that had me never wanting to leave her bed.

Part of me—the rational part—knew I should be distancing myself from her. This could never last. It shouldn't have happened to begin with. She was my *enemy*. But I wasn't ready to let her go. Not yet. I'd worry about the ramifications of that later, after I found her somewhere safe to hide where Zain or the others would never find her. We could dye her hair and change her appearance. She could live the normal life she craved—

that she deserved. And once I knew she was safe, I'd worry about myself.

I was still hopeful that redemption was an option. After all, humans were constantly being forgiven for their many, *many* despicable sins. Though most humans weren't knowingly sleeping with a demon they were tasked with killing.

Leaning over my demon, I placed a kiss on her forehead, breathing her in to steady my mind. The thought of leaving her sent a pang shooting through my chest. Maybe I could keep her a couple more days. I just needed a little bit longer with her before I was forced to give her up. I had to work her out of my system.

"Again?" Giselle mumbled, stirring in my arms. Her lips found my chest, placing a kiss on my sternum as her hand snaked between us.

I sucked in a breath as her fingers closed around my manhood, pumping up and down my hard length, pulling a groan from deep in my throat.

She'd taught me all sorts of sinful positions throughout the night. I'd lost count of the number of times I'd been inside of her. I was honestly surprised she wasn't sore. My body healed and even I was feeling the effects of our repeated lovemaking.

But I wasn't sore enough to stop.

I rolled her gently onto her back, capturing her soft lips with my own and demanding her surrender. She kept her firm grip on me, her hand trapped between us as I blanketed her body with mine. I could hardly think straight with her fingers stroking me like they were. But her hand—even her mouth—was nothing compared to being buried deep inside of her. Nothing could ever compare to that. To feeling her heart beating against mine. One breath, one body, one soul.

Only demons weren't supposed to have souls. But when I held Giselle in my arms, I couldn't believe that. She was different.

She was mine.

I cupped one of her perfect breasts, thumb circling her already hard nipple, loving the way she arched into me. She was so responsive. I repeated the motion and she moaned into my mouth, my dick leaping in her hand. Giselle released her hold on me, rocking her hips up to meet mine. I wasn't the only one who desperately needed more.

"Please, Lucas," she whimpered against my lips. Her nails raked down my arms as I slid my shaft through her wet folds, the head of my dick bumping into her swollen nub. She was already so close and I wasn't even inside her. I wasn't a prideful being by nature, but it brought me great satisfaction knowing I had this sort of effect on her.

I'd meant what I'd told her. Her pleasure was mine, just as much as she was.

I pulled back far enough to watch her face before I rocked against her once more, rolling her nipple under my hand at the same time. She threw her head back as she cried out her release, her body coming up off the bed as the orgasm ripped through her.

"Magnificent," I mumbled, brushing a hand over her

disheveled hair as she struggled to catch her breath. I'd never tire of watching her come undone beneath me.

Before she could come back down, I lined myself up with her entrance, easing my hips forward inch by inch and sheathing myself deep inside her. With my hips seated against hers, I was finally home. I was right where I wanted to be. Even if it wasn't where I was supposed to be.

I could beg for forgiveness later.

Spurred on by her heels pressing into the backs of my thighs, I started to move. I groaned, her core clenching around me as I pumped slowly in and out of her molten heat. She was setting me on fire and I loved it.

If I wasn't careful, I'd spend an eternity burning with her…in Hell.

Giselle's heart raced against my chest, her breath mingling with mine as we moved together in perfect unison. Those fiery amber eyes found mine, moisture glistening in them.

My hips stilled against hers, fear gripping my heart. "I didn't hurt you, did I?"

She shook her head and a single tear slipped free. "Don't stop," she pleaded, trying to get me to move.

"Hey," I said softly, wiping away the offending droplet. "Talk to me."

She bit her lip before looking away. "I don't want this to end," she finally whispered, speaking my own fears out loud.

"We'll figure it out," I told her even though I didn't know how. Our situation was impossible and we both knew it. There was no happily ever after for us. But I could at least make sure she was happy for once.

I stroked her damp cheek, kissing her forehead. "I will make sure you get the life you deserve, Giselle. I promise. No one will ever hurt you again. You're mine."

"Lucas, I—"

I silenced her with a kiss, continuing my slow strokes in and out of her until her whimpers turned to moans once more. Giselle's fingers dug into my shoulders, clinging to me as I picked up the pace. Her body trembled beneath mine and I knew she was nearly there. The tingles racing down my own spine told me I wasn't far behind her.

I'd hoped to make this last longer, but I had no control when it came to Giselle.

Mewling sounds came from her lips each time the base of my shaft connected with her sensitive bud, lifting her higher and higher until she was tearing apart at the seams beneath me. Her throbbing center clamped down on me as she screamed my name to the heavens, pulling me right over that glorious cliff with her.

A growl tore out of me and I jerked into her, emptying myself deep inside her body.

My arms gave out on me and I collapsed onto the bed next to her, our panted breaths the only sound in the dimly lit room. Tugging her into my arms, I rested my chin on her head, holding her close as she burrowed into my chest. It wasn't long until her breaths evened and she drifted off to sleep.

There was something about the succubus struggling to keep up with the angel that had a grin tugging at my lips.

The sun started to rise, casting an orange glow across the ceiling. Giselle's stomach growled softly in her sleep and the desire to meet her needs overpowered my own need to hold her. Especially since I hadn't fed her last night—not food, at least.

As carefully as I could, I untangled myself from her arms.

"Lucas?" Giselle mumbled. Her eyes fluttered open as she reached out for me.

I leaned over her, pressing my lips to her forehead. "Get some more sleep," I told her, smoothing my hand over her hair. "I'll go get us breakfast."

My defiant little demon listened for once, almost immediately falling back to sleep. I smiled, brushing a hair from her face before scooting away from her.

That's when I felt it, the sharp bite of something digging into my leg. I shifted my body, searching for the violent offender and froze.

The entire bed was covered in feathers—*my* feathers. There were hundreds of them, illuminated by the new light of day. Even as I stared down at the bed, another feather floated to join the rest.

I shoved away from the bed, stumbling over numb feet, my heart hammering against my chest until I thought it might burst. My wings extended out on either side of me and I struggled to breathe, the room teetering around me. There were numerous bald spots where feathers should have been.

What was happening to me?

My eyes landed on the temptress sleeping soundly in the bed, looking far more innocent than she really was.

She'd done this to me. That's what demons did: they ruined everything they touched. And she was no different. Worst of all, I'd allowed her to do it. How could I have let myself fall so far from grace? And for what—a vile, despicable demon? No, this wasn't me. She was corrupting my mind—my *soul*.

And now she was trying to make me lose my divinity.

"No," I growled.

I snatched up my pants from the floor and pulled them on, keeping my eyes locked on the succubus who had tried to take everything from me.

Including my damned heart.

Pacing the room, I raked my hands through my hair.

I had to get out of there—I needed to get away from her and clear my head. Figure out what I was going to do next.

But I knew there was only one thing I could do.

I searched the room until I found the pants I'd been wearing when we'd escaped the cabin. Moving over to them, I yanked out the phone Zain had given me. I stared at the black screen, not recognizing myself in the reflection of its cracked surface. With a growl, I shoved the device into my back pocket and dropped the jeans before heading for the door.

Hand lingering over the knob, I paused, unable to stop myself from looking back into the room. Giselle stirred on the bed, blanketed more in my feathers than the actual covers. She mumbled my name and my heart squeezed.

She'd done this to herself—to both of us.

With that, I pulled open the door and forced my feet forward, stepping out of the room and shutting the door silently behind me.

I had to let her go. And I'd do so the only way I knew how.

30

GISELLE

Lucas had been gone for two whole days.

I paced the room, eyes flicking to the door as if the mere thought of him would finally bring him back to me. But it never opened. Not outside of the numerous times I'd flung it open when I'd thought I'd heard the beating of wings.

Panic seized my chest for the hundredth time in forty-eight hours. Something was wrong. I just wasn't sure what.

I hadn't seen Lucas since he'd woken me for yet another round of sex—he'd been insatiable the entire night. Not that I'd been complaining. The man was a fast learner. He'd had me screaming his name until I'd gone hoarse, my body aching in the best of ways. But when I'd finally gotten up late that next morning, I found myself in a bed of feathers, my grumpy angel nowhere to be found.

In my post-coital haze, I'd vaguely remembered him saying something about getting breakfast, but the feathers had put me on edge. There had been so many of them —*too* many. And then he'd never returned.

After a full day missing, I'd risked leaving the resort to look for him. I'd been careful about it, putting my hair up into a hat like he'd instructed me to do the day he took me to the beach. I knew he'd probably want me to stay put, but I couldn't do *nothing*. Not when there was a chance he was somewhere out there in trouble.

I'd combed the beach, the dunes, the surrounding grounds of the resort. Lucas was just…gone.

If it weren't for his clothes lying around the room, or the mound of feathers still blanketing the bed, I would have thought this was just some crazy dream.

The best damn dream of my entire existence.

I wasn't ready for it to end yet. I didn't know what I deserved in this life, not after all the horrible things I'd done. But I knew I wanted it to involve Lucas.

I had to find him.

No matter how much I tried to stay positive, I kept thinking of the worst. My mind flashed to Zain and a fierce anger swelled within me. If he'd killed Lucas—if he'd done *anything* to hurt him—there was no force on Heaven or Earth that could protect him from me. I'd hunt him down and find a way to end his eternal life. I'd make it my sole purpose in this world to make him pay for what he'd done.

"No," I snapped. I couldn't think like that—like Lucas was already gone. He was fine. He had to be. He was probably spotted by one of his holier-than-thou companions and had to lie low for a while. Right. That was it. He'd probably walk through that door any minute and tell me I was worrying for nothing.

But what if he didn't?

I glanced at the room phone sitting on the bedside table, wondering if I should call someone. But who would I call—the police?

Hi, yes, I can't find my hunky angel anywhere. I think another angel might have taken him for fucking a demon's brains out. Yes, I'm that demon, thanks for asking.

Yeah, that'd go over well.

"Shit," I grumbled, scrubbing a hand over my face as the room spun. I plopped down in the chair in front of the fireplace and groaned. I hadn't eaten anything for over two days. The muffin I'd gotten from the lobby this morning sat untouched on the glass coffee table, right next to the room service I'd ordered last night but never opened.

I was far too worried about Lucas to keep anything down.

When I'd gone into the lobby in the morning to see if any of the staff had seen him come through, the receptionist had shaken her head. She'd looked at me with sympathetic eyes, probably thinking I'd been dumped. She'd pointed me in the direction of the breakfast buffet and reminded me that the room was paid up for two more nights.

Which meant I was running out of time to find him.

I wasn't sure what I'd do after that. I had no purse. No

money. No identification. I didn't even have my cell phone. Moments I wished my powers did more than just cause chaos. At least they'd come in handy if any other angels came after me. Because I was sure those winged fuckers were still looking for me. They weren't going to let a demon get away.

But I wasn't worried about myself.

"Please, let him be okay," I whispered, not really sure who I was talking to. God, Satan, the damn Easter Bunny, I'd pray to whoever would listen to me at this point.

I knew I couldn't live with myself if something bad had happened to him because of me—the demon he'd saved. Protected. Fucked. All of which I was sure were punishable by death in his uptight world.

This was all my fault.

Guilt consumed me until I strained to pull in a breath, sinking lower in the chair.

Maybe he *had* left me. Maybe Lucas realized what trouble I was causing him and he decided to leave before things got any worse. But even as the thought crossed my mind, I knew it wasn't possible. Not after the things he'd told me. Not after all we'd been through together. I couldn't believe he'd just up and leave me like that.

Even if he probably should have.

"Please," I continued. "He can't die. Don't let him die because of me. This can't be over yet. I need him."

And it was the truth. For the first time in nearly a thousand years, I felt like I could be happy. With Lucas.

The door swung open and my heart leaped into my throat as I flew out of the chair, spinning to see Lucas step into the room. His stormy eyes locked onto mine and a sob bubbled out of me.

"Holy shit," I breathed, clamping a hand over my mouth as tears sprang to my eyes. I needed to do this praying thing more often.

I ran across the room and launched myself into his arms, arms that didn't quite come all the way around me. Lucas's chest rumbled as I snaked my hands up around his neck, holding him tightly to me if only to prove to myself that he was real.

He was *alive*.

When I finally pulled away, I reached up, cupping his face in my trembling fingers. His jaw ticked beneath my palms, his gray eyes clouded.

"I was so worried," I said, more tears replacing the ones that had soaked into his shirt. "I thought they'd killed you. Are you okay? Did they find us?"

Before he could answer, I withdrew my hands, whipping around him and darting to the still-open door. I poked my head out to make sure the coast was clear. When I didn't see anyone, I exhaled a shaky breath, shutting the door and turning back around to face him. Only then did I throw myself back into him. And, once again, his arms didn't come around me.

Why wasn't he touching me?

"Lucas?"

"I'm sorry," he said, pulling away from me.

"What are you—" The words died on my lips as I met his cold, emotionless eyes.

I furrowed my brows, taking a small step away from

him as fear took hold of me. "What's going on, Lucas?" I asked, even though I had a sickening feeling I already knew. "What did you do?"

"What I had to," he bit out, guilt flickering across his face. He quickly tucked it away until I was no longer looking at the man who'd made love to me all night—who'd told me I was his. No, this was the man who'd spent centuries hunting me down and killing me.

"No," I breathed, but it was too late.

The door behind me flew open. I spun around to see Zain standing in the doorway and my heart shattered within my chest.

Zain lunged forward and grabbed hold of me, yanking my arms behind my back as he kicked the door shut and shoved me farther into the room. I struggled against him, but it was no use.

"Lucas, help!" I shouted, but deep down I knew my angel wasn't going to be saving me. He wasn't going to save me ever again. Because he wasn't my angel.

He wasn't mine at all.

"Please," I whispered. "Don't do this."

Zain's other hand came up, cupping roughly over my mouth. "Silence, temptress," he hissed, giving me a rough shake.

He shifted his attention to Lucas, shoving me forward another step until I was standing directly in front of him. "Come back to us, brother," he told him. "End this vile creature once and for all and let's walk back into the light together. This is the only way."

Swallowing hard, Lucas turned those cold, angry eyes

back on me. What was left of my heart dropped when he unsheathed his sword.

His wings extended behind him, nearly half of his feathers missing. I couldn't look away from them, screaming into Zain's big hand.

This couldn't be happening.

"You did this to me, *demon*," Lucas spat, hatred lacing his words. "I will not allow you to destroy me."

Tears spilled over my eyes and Lucas's mask slipped, if only for a moment. In that split second, a thousand emotions flashed through his eyes—fear, guilt, pain, defeat…regret. And then his sword was sliding through my heart.

"Don't come back," he said, his voice wavering, breath hot on my face.

The world around me teetered on its axis, pain exploding throughout my body—pain that wasn't entirely physical. Lucas yanked his sword free and Zain released me, letting me collapse to the floor at their feet, blood quickly pooling around me. Just like so many times before, the world around me faded to black.

The last thing I saw of this life was Lucas following Zain out the patio door, leaving me alone to die like he'd done so many times before.

GISELLE

He'd killed me. He'd actually fucking done it.

I shouldn't have been nearly as surprised as I was. Or hurt. His betrayal had cut far deeper than his blade.

I stormed through the gates of Hell, the blessed flames kissing my skin and welcoming me home. Only this wasn't my home. Not for long at least. I was never here for more than a few weeks before I was sent out on my next assignment.

Only the next time I was sent back, Lucas wouldn't be waiting for me.

All eyes were on me as I headed for the temple. The other demons parted around me like the damn Red Sea, eyes awestruck and jaws dropping to the floor. Clearly, word had already gotten around of what had happened between Lucas and me.

Great...

A few lower levels reached out to brush their fingers across my skin in reverence and I had to resist the urge to pull away from them. I hated the way they looked at me like I was some sort of hero.

In a strange way, I was.

I was the demon who'd brought down an angel. I'd led him into temptation and delivered him to evil. It didn't matter to my kind that he'd killed me in the end. I'd done what had never been done before. Not even by my mother.

I'd made an angel sin. I'd damned the un-damnable.

The old me might have relished that fact, but not now. Not after living as a human. And definitely not after being with Lucas. He'd made me feel things I hadn't experienced before. And then he'd ruined me. *Betrayed* me.

Another stab of pain shot through me, stealing my breath.

"There's my beautiful girl," a sultry voice said.

A voluptuous woman glided through the growing crowd, hips swaying as she moved toward me. Those around her scrambled to get out of her way, bowing down to her. She didn't even spare them a passing glance. Her eyes, pools of fire just like mine, were glued to me. Her long fiery hair cascaded down her back, stretching down past her backside. A slip of clothing covered a small fraction of her naked flesh. Despite her true age, she didn't look much older than me. In fact, outside of her incredibly swollen stomach, we could have been twins.

My mother wrapped me in her arms, pulling me as close as she could.

"I am so proud of you," she whispered into my ear. "Not even I could tempt my own holy assailant, and not for lack of trying."

I bit the inside of my mouth to keep from crying. I couldn't look weak. Not out here in the open like this. Down here, I had a reputation to uphold. Instead, I nodded into her shoulder.

"You're pregnant again," I stated the obvious when she released me. I hadn't seen my mother since the last time Lucas had sent me back to Hell. That felt like a lifetime ago. Probably because it was.

My mother waved me off with a perfectly manicured hand. "Oh, sweetie, this is my twelfth since you've been gone. You know how Luci loves his powerful children."

Luci, as in Lucifer. The Devil. Satan. Lord of the Underworld. And my *boss*—among other things.

And it was true. My mother tended to produce powerful demons—I was a perfect example of that. I was the very reason "Luci" had retired her from her rampage on Earth. She'd lured him into her bed centuries ago and I was born. When dear old Dad saw the power I'd possessed in adolescence, he decided she was far more useful to him in the underworld. Being his breeder. She was one of the ten in his harem. His favorite, if you asked my mother.

I'd lost count of the number of siblings I had. My mother didn't seem to mind being Satan's prized possession. I was fairly certain she was in love with him. And as long as she was useful to him, he'd treat her like a queen. Like most men, he was just using her to get what he wanted.

Lucas was no different. He'd taken what he wanted from me and then killed me. Was that all I was to him, a body to use just like everyone else did? I'd thought he was different.

What a fool I'd been.

I was a succubus. All I would ever be good for was my appearance—my body. Looking at my mother, I wondered if that was my future. Being a breeder, whose sole purpose was to spread her legs and create more powerful Hellions to unleash on the world. I shuddered at the thought.

"What's wrong, my dear?" my mother asked, smoothing the line drawn between my eyebrows. It wasn't like I'd suddenly grow wrinkles—demons didn't age in Hell. Down here, I was as immortal as Lucas. "You don't seem like yourself."

I wasn't sure who *myself* was anymore. For the first time in hundreds of years, I felt like a stranger in my own skin.

My mother must have noticed the hurt flashing in my eyes. I might not have seen her often, but she was still my mother, and I was her very first child. I liked to think I held a special place in her wicked heart.

She wrapped an arm around my shoulder and ushered me into the temple, shooing away onlookers. "None here are worthy enough to look upon my daughter. Be gone with you!" she shouted and the crowd quickly dispersed. The Devil's concubine or not, my mother was a powerhouse in her own right, even while pregnant. There weren't many who would dare challenge her. Like, none.

I let my mother lead me down the obsidian walkway until we reached my old room. Only the most powerful demons were allowed to live in the temple. It was like a five-star resort for the underworld. Sure, it looked like one of those hotels built into a mountain face, but it was luxurious nonetheless—in a bowels-of-Hell sort of way.

I pressed my hand to a black keypad that blended into the wall. With an audible click, my door slid open and my mother and I stepped inside, the door automatically closing behind us. Only once we were alone did I let out the breath I'd been holding, bracing a hand on the stone wall before looking into the room.

My room hadn't changed at all, even if I had. My bed, draped in fresh linens, sat against the far wall where it had always been, black curtains hanging from each of its four posts. To the side was a cutout in the stone, leading to a pool of dark waters that was always near-boiling temperatures. The room was far superior to my rundown room back in Vegas, but I found the space didn't feel like mine anymore.

Nothing about any of this felt right. This wasn't me. I wasn't the same Hellion.

My mom took the burgundy chaise longue at the foot of my bed, sprawling out across it like a pinup model. A very pregnant one.

"What happened?" She looked at me expectantly,

fingertips trailing over her swollen stomach. "You have never come back looking so defeated."

I plopped down on the edge of the bed, sucking in a shaky breath.

"He killed me." The words came out in no more than a whisper. I still couldn't believe it.

"Of course he did," my mother said. "That is what those holy monstrosities do."

When I didn't reply, she pushed herself off the chaise and moved over to me with more grace than a woman so far along should have. She sat next to me, taking my hand in hers.

"Him killing you doesn't make you any less victorious, my child. You should be proud of yourself. You lured one of those winged fuckers to his doom. Even if he isn't killed for what he did, he will certainly be removed from his high-ranking position. You won."

Why didn't any of that make me feel better?

Oh, yeah. Because I'd allowed myself to catch feelings for that winged fucker. For the first time in my many lives, I'd trusted someone. I'd allowed myself to get close to him. And he'd killed me.

I tore my hand from my mother's and moved across the room, forcing myself to nod even as I struggled to breathe.

No one could ever know how I'd felt about Lucas—not even my mother. She was far too close to daddy dearest. Besides, she'd never understand. No one would. No, I could never tell anyone that I hadn't slept with him to destroy him. That I'd done it because I'd desperately wanted to. Because I'd wanted *him.* I might not have remembered what I was when I was reborn this last time, but I discovered what I wanted to be.

His.

Only he didn't want me. He'd made that perfectly clear when he ran me through with his blade and left me to die alone. Just like he'd done so many times before.

"You just need to get some rest," my mother said, heading to the door. "It has been a while, but I remember the toll it takes having your human life ended. You'll feel better tomorrow. And then we will celebrate your success. Luci wants to throw a grand feast. He can't wait to send you back."

I nodded again even as the Underworld began caving in around me. I braced myself on the window sill, looking over the river of lava passing by below. I didn't want to go back. I never wanted to set foot on Earth again. And yet, I didn't want to be here either.

The one thing I wanted, I couldn't have. Not anymore.

"See you tomorrow, darling," my mother called out, heading to the door. Only once I heard it click shut behind her did my legs buckle under me.

I collapsed to my knees, wrapping my arms around my middle as the first sob ripped through me. Tears streamed down my face as I curled in on myself, the weight of the pain too much. Each time I closed my eyes, I saw Lucas's angry eyes staring back at me, felt the kiss of his blade as he plunged it through my heart.

How could he do this to me? I'd trusted him. I'd

believed him when he'd said he would never let anyone hurt me. Apparently, he wasn't including himself in that.

He'd ripped my heart out and I wasn't sure I'd ever be the same again.

"No," I bit out, shoving myself off the floor.

I was not a fucking victim. I was the daughter of the most powerful succubus known to the Underworld—not to mention Satan himself. I was stronger than this. I refused to break because of Lucas. I would not wither under that holy fucker's betrayal. I was a demon—as Lucas so often loved to remind me. And demons didn't cry, we got even.

He didn't want me? Fine. But he would have my wrath.

He'd rue the day he decided to cross me. Hell had no fury like a succubus scorned. I'd make him pay for what he'd done to me.

Even if it was the last thing I did.

COMING SOON

Retaliation

Hellfire and Halos, Book 2

Coming Fall 2022

Preorder today!

ACKNOWLEDGMENTS

There are never enough words to thank my brilliant readers for all of their love and support. I love you all so damn much. I say it all the time, but I truly couldn't do any of this without you. You all have made my crazy little dream take flight.

I huge thank you to my amazing husband who has supported me completely from the very beginning (even if he does hate reading—I know, I know… I love him anyway). Thanks, babe, for always making sure I have time to write, even if it means you have to change more diapers. You're *literally* the best!

To my amazing editing team, Tina and Shannon, many thanks to you both! I appreciate all you brilliant ladies do to make sure I don't have giant, gaping holes in my stories. Both of you are a valuable part of this team!

A big thank you to my cover artist, Daqri, from Covers by Combs. This cover has definitely had many a wonderful readers fanning their faces. If only covers could growl, heh.

My brilliant alpha readers and my amazing ARC Crew, I will forever be grateful for you ladies and your opinions. You have all been the best cheerleaders. I don't know how I would do this without you all. I love each and every one of you!

Thank you all SO much! I can't wait to share more of this story with you!

MORE FROM J.N. BAKER

HELLFIRE AND HALOS

(Spicy paranormal romance)

Ruination

Retaliation (Coming soon)

Redemption (Coming soon)

UNTIL DAWN

(Slow-burn, post-apocalyptic urban fantasy)

Last Light

Night Falls

Into the Dark

Pitch Black

Dead of Night

TALES OF GRIMPORT

(Spicy, fairy-tale inspired paranormal romance)

Books and Burdens (Coming soon)

ABOUT THE AUTHOR

Teacher by day and writer by night, J.N. Baker has been telling stories since she was old enough to read them. With a passion for both paranormal romance and urban fantasy, J.N. Baker loves to write steamy stories with complicated, badass female leads with no filters. She believes the sign of a good book is the sudden urge to throw it across the room and run to pick it back up.

J.N. Baker lives with her husband and daughter on their farm in California. When she isn't writing, drinking the tears of her readers, or teaching, she enjoys curling up with a good book, a glass of wine, and one of her many furry critters.

For more shenanigans, follow J.N. Baker on Facebook and be sure to join her reader group, **Baker's Brilliant**

Bookworms, for release updates, cover reveals, sneak peeks, giveaways, and more!

The Official Site of Author J.N. Baker
http://authorjnbaker.com

facebook.com/AuthorJNBaker
instagram.com/AuthorJNBaker

Made in United States
Orlando, FL
01 August 2022